SMALL GAME

SMALL GAME

GAME

JOHN BLADES

HENRY HOLT AND COMPANY
NEW YORK

Copyright © 1992 by John Blades
All rights reserved, including the right to reproduce
this book or portions thereof in any form.
Published by Henry Holt and Company, Inc.,
115 West 18th Street, New York, New York 10011.
Published in Canada by Fitzhenry & Whiteside Limited,
91 Granton Drive, Richmond Hill, Ontario L4B 2N5.

Library of Congress Cataloging-in-Publication Data
Blades, John.
Small game / by John Blades.—1st ed.
p.   cm.
I. Title.
PR6052.L3425S6   1992   92-9790
823'.914—dc20   CIP
ISBN 0-8050-1789-5 (alk. paper)

Henry Holt books are available at special discounts
for bulk purchases for sales promotions, premiums,
fund-raising, or educational use. Special editions
or book excerpts can also be created to specification.
For details contact: Director, Special Markets.

First Edition—1992

DESIGNED BY LUCY ALBANESE

Printed in the United States of America
Recognizing the importance of preserving the written word,
Henry Holt and Company, Inc., by policy, prints all of its
first editions on acid-free paper. ∞
10 9 8 7 6 5 4 3 2 1

SMALL
GAME

As it was, I had just one sleepy eye half open, and it was through that that I saw the end of humanity. . . . It was really a very little episode, and if it hadn't been for the squirrel, I wouldn't have seen it at all.

—LOREN EISELEY,
The Fire Apes

Every spirit makes the house; but afterwards the house confines the spirit.

—RALPH WALDO EMERSON

1

I bought the gun on a Wednesday, that much I can be certain of. If I think back carefully, I can probably even narrow it down to an exact date. I know it was either two or three days before my second son's third birthday. That would put it toward the end of October, almost Halloween.

I was desperately working on the house then, painting, spackling, caulking, taping, stuffing cracks with oakum, wrapping pipes with insulation, trying to patch the holes in the eaves with sheet metal, sealing it up tight for winter. So even if it hadn't been my son's birthday, I knew it had to be late fall.

I've never been good on dates, especially birthdays. With three children to account for, along with my wife, my brother and sister, my parents, her parents, aunts, uncles, cousins, in-laws, and all the rest, I have trouble keeping birthdays straight. But I do remember distinctly what I got my son that year because I bought it the same night and the same place I got the gun. It was a Leonardo's Sewer Force Sword.

After picking it up in the toy section, I went straight over to sporting goods. From light weapons to heavy artillery, I thought, walking down the aisles of the discount store, listening to the frightening hum of the fluorescent lights, leaking and spreading their poisonous radiation. This Ninja Turtle, I resolved, was about to defend his shell, and not with any plastic sword.

So this was a Wednesday, I'm positive. I know because that's my regular tennis night, and on my way to the club I had stopped at the discount store to buy the birthday present, a reciprocating saw, and the gun. I had thought about shopping for the gun by catalog. I could dial an 800 number and order it by phone, just like I order vitamins and gift baskets of grapefruit and jelly. But this wasn't the type of package I especially wanted being delivered to our house in the mail.

Besides, I didn't know what kind of gun I needed, and the brief descriptions in the catalog weren't any help. A Marlin .22 semiautomatic with crossbolt safety, $4 \times$ 15-millimeter scope, and 15-shot clip? Or something that would do more damage: a Remington Auto Loader 30/60 with gas operation and a 22-inch barrel? Or a Winchester .12-gauge with Super X high-velocity shells?

Any one of them would probably get the job done, I figured, but I didn't want to be guilty of overkill. What I wanted was something neat, hygienic, and cost-effective.

Without any expertise on the subject, I couldn't make an intelligent or informed decision. I'm not usually an impulse buyer. I like to take my time, check out the available research in books, back issues of newspapers, consumer magazines, on microfilm and computer bulletin boards. But I didn't have much time. I had to strike swiftly and decisively. Winter was bearing down; we were under siege. In certain places, my house looked as if it had been shelled by a phantom enemy, so that I was worried about its structural stability.

I was glad for the excuse to leave home early that night so I could stop by Susan's on my way from the discount store to the tennis court. But I'd badly miscalculated how long it would take me to pick out the gun, all the complications that would result because I hadn't done my homework and was so poorly prepared. The salesman seemed suspicious, asking more questions than he needed to, and I was naturally reluctant to answer them. I'm afraid he could tell how strung out I was.

It wasn't just buying the gun that had me so anxious. I could see I wasn't going to make it to the club on time, much less to Susan's. I couldn't afford to be late again, even if I really had no business playing tennis. I belonged at home. Trying to fortify and defend the house. Trying to get some rest.

After all the replastering, the rewiring, the refinishing, I was ready for rehabbing myself. I felt as if I were spinning inside a carnival centrifuge, flattened against the barrel wall, terrified that it would come to a dead stop and send me flying out like a human cannonball.

I hadn't slept more than three hours a night all week. I hadn't slept at all the previous night. I had been too busy dealing with Susan, the neighborhood surveillance squad, and my terminal difficulties at the office, where I was afraid I was about to be permanently rebalanced—vocationally relocated. The shape I was in, I was certain I'd collapse on the court. The paramedics would take me off, the way they did Tom Fletcher last year. I wasn't going to be at the top of my game, that's for sure.

Carrying the rifle down the aisles of the discount store, with the lights pulsing and buzzing overhead, I had an urge to drop to my knees and hug the cold antiseptic tile floor, to crawl commando-style out the door to safety.

They locked the doors and turned out the lights as soon as I left. The parking lot was dark and nearly empty. A cold autumn wind was blowing dry leaves, sales fliers, and other debris across the asphalt. Walking through the shadows to my car, lugging the Ninja Turtle sword, the reciprocating saw, and the gun, I felt like a fugitive. I put the gun in the trunk, along with the toy, the saw, and two boxes of shells, and took out my tennis racquet.

Before closing the trunk I held the rifle next to the racquet, comparing them. I was relieved to see that they were roughly the same length. That would make it easy for me to smuggle the gun into the house and store it in the hall closet with the other racquets, the softball and Wiffle Ball bats, all the rest of the toys and sports equipment.

I had to keep the gun away from Kathy. She'd find out about it soon enough, but I didn't want her to know right now. She wouldn't approve, and that would mean even more un-pleasantness. She was already unhappy about me buying the saw. I was counting on her being asleep when I got home, so I probably didn't have to worry. But just in case, it was easy enough to conceal the gun under the tennis racquet, with its padded cover.

I was ten minutes late when I got to the club. The other players were warmed up and ready to go, annoyed that I was wasting their precious court time. Once I started playing, I knew I didn't belong on the court. I was tired. My timing was way off. My concentration was gone. I was double-faulting, slicing my backhand shots into the net, missing easy overheads. I was wiped out before the first set was finished.

I couldn't just quit. I had to start getting back into shape. I had committed myself to playing in the Turkey Open, which was, despite the name, a serious tournament played over the Thanksgiving weekend. But my tennis game had gone to hell. And the other players couldn't resist the sly remarks, the sarcastic comments, the rude jokes about why I'd missed so many Wednesday nights.

They weren't kidding, I was sure of that. They were suspicious, even envious. But it wasn't because they thought I had a woman on the side, as they liked to pretend. No, they'd always resented me because my game was on a higher level than theirs. Now that it had fallen off slightly, they couldn't wait to dump me, to find someone else to take my spot. But as long as they wanted me gone, I wasn't going to quit.

What worried me was that one of them—or their wives— would make some sneaky little comment to Kathy about my poor attendance record. All it would take was a word at a dinner party or a school potluck to set off an alarm. I could bluff my way out of it, I was sure, but I didn't need any more trouble.

And the more I thought about it, I had good reasons of my own to be suspicious about Kathy. What about the Tuesday nights she went to ceramics class? Or wherever it was she went to meet Mario? I didn't want to ask her those kind of questions any more than I wanted her asking them of me.

After the first set, my timing and my serve started to come back, but my backhand was still miserable, my feet were so heavy I felt as if I were wearing ski boots, and my concentration had almost totally evaporated. I must have had an attention span of about two milliseconds. As soon as the game was over, I rushed out, in too much of a hurry to shower or change. Going by Susan's, I could see that the lights were all out. That could be either a good or a bad sign.

I drove to the end of the block, turned around, and came back. I parked the car just down the street, where I could see both her windows and the front door. She lived in a building with three sets of apartments facing each other on four floors. They all used the same lobby, so it was impossible to tell who was coming or going from which place. But if the lights went on in Susan's bedroom and a man came out a few minutes later, I didn't need a detective's license to figure out that she wasn't being true-blue.

As I watched, her building started to tremble and shudder in the gusts of wind. It looked as if it were on the edge of collapse. It was a new building, made out of the cheapest, tackiest materials, contaminated bricks, diseased wood. An instant slum. The stairs were flimsy, the walls were as thin and insubstantial as cardboard.

Whenever I went to her apartment, the first thing I did was turn off most of the lights. Susan thought I was a compulsive romantic, but it was only because I couldn't stand the sight of the cracks and the peeling paint and wallpaper. I constantly felt a swaying and buckling. Once, while we were lying in bed, I told her the earth hadn't moved but I had felt the whole building shake.

I watched the dark windows for a sign of movement and listened to the car creak and rattle in the wind. After a while, I started to shiver. Then I noticed that the sweat was freezing on my body in the cold car, that I was covered by a thin coat of frost. I thought I'd better move around before I went to sleep and turned into an ice sculpture.

I got out of the car and shook myself so that the ice cracked and fell off my body, making a soft and delicate sound, almost like a crystal wind chime. I wished that my children could have been here, it seemed so comical and miraculous all at once.

I was bored as well as frozen. I went around and fumbled in the dark, trying to get the keys into the trunk lock. I opened the trunk and took out the rifle and a box of shells. In the murky yellow streetlights I was just able to see well enough to get the cartridges into the clip right side up.

I attached the infrared scope that I'd bought for night shots. I put on my camouflage vest and hat. I moved down the block toward Susan's building. Crouching in the shadows, I braced the barrel of the gun against a garbage can and aimed at her window. The scope worked. I could see two dark figures, embracing.

I heard a loud bang next to my head, then another. Somebody was knocking on the car window. I couldn't make out his face through the steamed window or hear what he was saying over the Leonard Cohen tape. He knocked again, harder, and shouted.

I couldn't be sure if he wanted to rob me or warn me about fumes from the idling motor. I wasn't going to stay around to find out. I shifted the car into drive and stepped on the gas pedal. The car lurched, nearly died, and took off. The man's face hung by the window for a moment, distorted in agony against the glass. Then I felt a thump and he vanished.

After a few blocks I was able to get control of myself. I let up on the gas pedal. I began to stop for red lights. I didn't want to get arrested for speeding or reckless driving. There was no reason for panic now. But I was shuddering because my tennis clothes were soaked with sweat.

When I slowed down, the car seemed to float along, as smoothly and quietly as a glider. On the tape deck, Leonard Cohen was agonizing over the whereabouts of his gypsy wife.

It had to be very late. There were no other cars on the streets. The glow from the streetlights was vague and feverish, as if they were operating on weak currents. As I drove past, the trees and houses and stores looked as flat as Masonite cutouts, blurred shadows. Then I realized that I was driving with only my parking lights on.

Two blocks from my house, at an intersection that makes a natural entrance to our neighborhood, I came to a police checkpoint. With a spotlight splintering through the windshield into my face, I was forced to stop. A policeman came up to the window, a flashlight in one hand, the other resting on the grip of his holstered pistol.

"Where you going?" he asked.

"Home," I said. "I live just a few blocks away."

I reached over to get my wallet. He tensed, his hand tightening on the gun. I quickly said: "I've got a driver's license. But it has my old address. I was waiting for it to expire before I got it changed." I offered him the wallet, but he ignored it.

"Do you have anything to declare?" he asked sternly.

"No," I said, "just this bag with my tennis stuff." I was afraid he was going to ask me to get out of the car and open the trunk, but he said, "Okay, move along. But don't look to the right or the left. Keep your eyes in front of you and go straight home."

He waved me around the barricade, and I drove to my house. I turned off the headlights, but I didn't pull into the driveway or shut off the engine. There were lights on downstairs and in our bedroom. Kathy was still awake, probably getting worried now.

Through the shutters and curtains I could see cracks on the ceilings and walls, holes that needed to be spackled and plastered. I could see the woodwork that had to be stripped, sanded, and varnished. Within the walls I could see the heating ducts, pipes, and wiring that needed to be replaced. I put the car in gear and drove off. I wasn't ready to go home yet.

2

We moved into the house on the same day that a six-year-old girl was murdered in another part of the city. The house had thirteen rooms. Each one was badly in need of renovation. It was the neighborhood spook house, vacant and neglected for more than a year while the dead owner's estate was settled. We got it at a closeout price, but it was no bargain.

From basement to attic, foot by foot, inch by inch, it had to be scraped, patched, and painted, gutted and rehabilitated. Walking through the derelict house made me anxious and dizzy, not just because of all the work that had to be done. The empty rooms seemed to lean at different angles and directions, so they were almost as steeply tilted as the rooms in a midway funhouse.

The outside was even sorrier. Loose shutters, a sagging front porch, warped siding, corroded gutters, crumbling mortar around the foundation. The wrought iron fence was rusting, the brick sidewalks had heaved and buckled, turning to rubble. The yard was a prairie, overgrown with violets and dandelions, junk trees and mutant shrubs.

From a distance the defects weren't so obvious. Late in the day, exhausted from working on the house, I would walk across the street and admire its graceful lines, the curve of the turret, the tall windows, the steep slope of the roof, all the odd corners and angles. With its harsh and glaring imperfections softened and distorted by shadows, the house had a twilight perfection.

But that was months later, when it was almost summer. We moved on a cold, damp day in early spring. We had rented a van to carry the small appliances, clothes, as many of the necessities as we could handle ourselves. Pulling up to the curb with the first load, I could see the neighbors spying on us from their windows, vague shapes behind thin curtains and blinds. We hadn't expected a welcome wagon, but they made us uncomfortable, watching us in hostile secrecy, as if we were invading their block.

The two older children were in school. We had to get the van unpacked quickly and pick up another load before the bus dropped them off at the corner in the afternoon. Kathy had put Peter in a playpen in an upstairs bedroom. He protested, screaming and shaking the sides of the pen. Then he began to play quietly.

We took turns looking in on him while we carried in boxes. After a couple of trips, I went up to find him asleep. I sat down on the bare wooden floor to rest myself. But the flaking paint on a window frame was like an irresistible scab, and I started to chip it away with my knife.

After a while, Kathy came into the room. "I thought maybe you'd crawled into the playpen with him," she said. "Don't start that now. You can worry about it next month. Next year. There's still a ton of stuff to bring in."

I put the scraper down reluctantly. When we went back outside, the neighbors were on their porches. From down the block and across the street, they watched us quietly, solemnly, like mourners, as we carried in boxes. I waved at them, but they didn't wave back.

By the time the moving van showed up with the furniture, washer and dryer, and other heavy things, they had gotten bolder, if not friendlier. They moved off their porches and were slowly edging toward our yard, but we were too busy then to stop and talk to them.

Coming back for another load, I found three adolescent boys in the rental van, rummaging through the boxes. One of them had found a plastic Wiffle Bat, which he was using as a machine gun, spraying the other two with mock bullets. They seemed a little big to be playing war games. The boy with the bat pointed it at me. I threw up my hands, stepped back, and begged him not to shoot.

I felt myself being pushed aside. The father of the boy had rushed down from his porch. He reached in and took the bat from him. "You know that's not acceptable behavior."

He shoved the bat at me, roughly. He was thin and delicate but shaking with rage, angry enough to be threatening. "We don't allow him to play with weapons," he said. He took the boy by his arm and started toward his house. His wife came across the yard to meet them, looking alarmed.

He gestured toward me. "He let Kevin use that bat as a machine gun." She looked at me, as if I were holding a lethal weapon. Then she bent down to the boy. She looked him over methodically for signs of abuse.

Several other people appeared. "That kid's the neighborhood sadist," said one man. He was squat, with a head as shiny and blunt as a missile. He wore a royal blue satin warm-up jacket with "ROY" stitched across the chest. "Whatever you did to him, he deserved it."

Then he reached into the back of the van and seized the two other boys by their arms, dragging them out. "Hey, that doesn't belong to you," he said, taking a drill that one of the boys was using as an Uzi. "You know better than that."

"That's okay," I said, "they're just naturally curious."

"No, sir, it's not," he said, pushing the boys off down the block. "We've taught them to respect other people's property."

I had picked up a box full of linens. "Let me give you a hand," he said. He reached in and got another box, which he placed on top of the one I was holding. He picked up a small box and placed it under his arm.

"You really bought this old place?" he asked, following me toward the house, still carrying my drill as well as the box.

"I guess you could say that. The bank owns about ninety percent of it."

He looked at me as if astonished. "You couldn't afford to pay what little they were asking for this old wreck?"

"It seemed like a lot to me."

"How much did you pay?"

I stopped on the sidewalk to shift my load, which was threatening to fall. He helped me rebalance the top box. "How much?" he asked.

"I think I'd rather let that be a confidential matter between me and the bank."

"Sure, I can understand that. But I sure hope you didn't pay what they were asking. They were plenty eager to sell—before it collapsed. Real drag on the market. Vacant year and a half, two years."

"Yeah, I know."

"Why do you suppose that was?" he asked.

"I don't know."

"You don't?"

"No, do you?" I was at the top of the porch steps now, and I leaned against a post to rest.

"You might have checked with the neighbors before you bought," he said, sounding irritated. "You know, to see if there was something wrong with it or something."

"Is there?"

"Not that I know of." He hit his chest with his fist then and bowed his head, contritely. "Mother of Jesus," he said, "I haven't even introduced myself. Roy Phillips."

"Scott Ryan. I'd shake your hand, but I'm a little incapacitated at the moment."

"I live right over there," he said, pointing to a two-story house with dirty aluminum siding. "The family castle. It belonged to my wife's family. Didn't cost me a penny, personally."

"Sometimes it's not easy living with in-laws."

"It is now. They're dead."

"Sorry about that."

"I'm not."

Kathy came through the front door then, on her way back to pick up more boxes. I introduced her to Roy.

"We're glad to see you move into the neighborhood," he told her.

"We're glad to be here," she said.

"There's a lot of new people moving in around here. Never thought we'd be so thankful for all these yuppies and muppies and guppies."

"It's nice to feel welcome," she said.

"We were worried about this place," he said. "It was up for sale so long we were afraid we might get some Whoomes for neighbors."

"Whoomes?" Kathy said.

"Yeah," Roy said, "you know how they're always saying to the police, 'Who me, man?' Members of the Mau Mau persuasion."

"Apparently there was some problem with this house," I told her.

"Not that I know about," Roy said. He started clicking the trigger of the drill, so rapidly I was afraid it might break.

"Seems a little flimsy," he said. "It never pays to buy cheap tools."

"I thought I was buying a good one," I said.

He aimed the drill at me, just as his son had, and pulled the trigger again. "I'll give you five bucks for it," he said.

"I think I'd better hang on to it," I said.

He laid it on the porch almost reluctantly. "Yeah," he said, "with this old place, you'll be needing it."

He took the small box from under his arm and shook it. He checked the label printed on the side. "Made in South Korea. Cheap goods."

"I think that was just an empty box we got somewhere to pack small toys."

He shook it again, more vigorously, listening to the contents rattle around inside. "Yeah, it doesn't sound fragile to me."

"There's someone in our van," Kathy said. She had noticed a woman leaning through the rear doors. From the porch, we could only see the rear half of her, round and lumpy, so that it looked as if a giant beanbag had tumbled into the street. She seemed to be sorting through our boxes.

"That's Mary Agnes," said Roy. "She's my second wife. You've got to meet her. She's a real bell ringer. No shrinking violet like Pauline."

He called and waved. She came up to the porch, jiggling and puffing. He introduced her. "We're glad to have you as neighbors," she said.

"We know."

"You have such nice things," she told Kathy. She held up a cardigan sweater that she'd taken from one of the boxes. "I really like this."

"Thank you," Kathy said. She reached over and took the sweater from Mary Agnes, who looked disappointed, even though it was at least four sizes too small for her.

"You think you'll be having a garage sale?" she inquired.

"Not this afternoon," Kathy said. "But I'll let you know in advance when we do."

"Oh, you could have a nice one. I'm going to have one myself as soon as I get enough stuff together. I hope you can come to it. Maybe we could have one together."

"What are those little bastards doing now?" Roy said. His boys had climbed back into the van and knocked over a box, spilling sheets and towels onto the wet pavement. "Hey, Darryl . . . Howard. Outta there!"

Kathy hurried out to the van, with Mary Agnes not far behind, shouting threats at the children.

"They're just trying to be helpful," Roy said. "They get a little too eager sometimes is all. We've taught them to be good neighbors. You need a hand with some of these boxes, I know they'd be glad to pitch in, earn a little spending money."

"I think I can handle things for now," I said.

"Yeah, you look like you got everything under control." He held the front door open and followed me in. "You don't mind, I'll have a look around. I might be able to give you some free advice. From the look of things, you'll be needing plenty of that."

The moving van had come late in the afternoon. We had the movers pile most of the furniture into the side parlor and another spare room downstairs, leaving the other rooms bare so we could work on them without obstruction. I carried a stepladder into the living room and began to hack at loose wallpaper.

"Shouldn't we unpack first?" Kathy asked.

"You go ahead," I said. "I just want to see what's under here."

"It's always second things first with you, isn't it?" she said. "You might as well do the job right."

Then she went off, and when she came back, a few minutes later, she had a bucket of water, a paint roller, and another scraper.

The faded gray floral wallpaper was brittle and peeling. Using the roller, I soaked the walls with water. The paper came off in wide uneven strips, which curled into wet piles on the floor.

Beneath the paper, cracks formed jagged spider legs in the dull yellowing plaster. As I stripped the paper, Kathy worked behind me, washing the walls and spackling the cracks. After a while I stopped to rest. I sat on the floor and watched Kathy. The spackle that she smoothed into the cracks made the walls look solid again.

I looked down at the week-old newspaper spread on the floor beneath me. I read an article about a family that had been terrorized and robbed by two men impersonating detectives. When I finished the article, I climbed back on the ladder and resumed scraping.

The older children paid no attention to us. They ran from room to room, shrieking and laughing, their voices echoing through the empty house. Kathy had to stop working when they woke the baby, but I kept at it until she called me for dinner.

"Hold everything," I said, "it's time for a formal christening." I dug through a box and came up with a bottle of wine.

"What's that?" Kim asked me.

I looked at the label. "Cold duck."

"Cold duck!" shouted Mark.

"Yeah, Big Bird for adults."

"Hot duck is more like it," Kathy said, feeling the bottle. "We need to put it in the freezer for a while."

"You can wait if you want to, but I'm not that particular. I'll settle for room temperature."

After we had finished the wine and dinner, I went into the living room and scattered pillows on the floor around the fireplace. Then I insisted that the children turn off the television and come into the room while I lit a fire. But the wood was too wet, and the chimney was partly blocked. The room quickly filled with smoke, and I had to throw water on the smoldering fire.

We put a mattress on the floor of one bedroom for the older children. They talked and giggled for a long time before falling asleep. Kathy and I carried another mattress into the master bedroom. Without any other furniture, the room seemed so vast and gloomy that we felt as if we were camping in a deep cavern.

We were both exhausted, but we did not go to sleep right away. Afterward, Kathy cried very quietly. I watched the cold rain as it trickled down the windowpane and turned to ice.

3

The next day was gray and wet. The dampness crept into the pores of the house and spread through the empty rooms like a debilitating mist. When I got out of bed, my bones and muscles ached. I was not used to such strenuous physical labor. Tennis hadn't prepared me for the contortions of moving, for lifting heavy boxes and assaulting old paint and wallpaper. The children were wound up at breakfast. They didn't mind the disorder and turmoil that surrounded us, the decay and sonorous gloom. They had found themselves in a giant playhouse and complained about having to leave it for school.

As soon as they were gone, we started to work. By noon I had the paper stripped from the living room walls. It lay on the floor in soggy matted piles. I did not stop to clean it up. While Kathy washed and spackled the walls and ceiling, I carried the ladder into the dining room and began to scrape. Here the paper did not come off so easily. There were at least three layers, each one sealed by paint. I gouged away with the scraper, cutting deep grooves and pockmarks into the plaster. It was slow, painful work. When I managed to clear a patch, I found that the plaster was crusted with gray calcimine.

We kept the radio tuned to the classical music station and worked to the shifting tempos of Bach and Debussy, Mahler and Xenakis. The hourly newscasts never seemed to vary. The announcer always began with a report of a motorist who had gone berserk on an interstate highway. He rammed his RV into a dozen automobiles and killed seven persons. He was evidently attempting to take his own life, but he survived.

I had taken two weeks of vacation, expecting to work on the house at a leisurely pace. We planned to quit in the middle of the afternoon, have drinks and dinner, then relax after the children went to bed, perhaps even get out to a movie. But we found that we could not stop working. We ate hurriedly, then pressed on. We worked late into the night, refusing to stop until we were too fatigued to go on. Then we collapsed on the bare mattress, often without bothering to take off our damp soiled clothes and shower.

After a few nights, the children grew tired of exploring the house. They objected because we paid no attention to them. We did not read to them. We did not play games. The older children had to run their own bathwater and put themselves to bed. The baby cried himself to sleep in his crib. We left the house only with great reluctance, when we needed groceries, work materials, or tools. We argued about who would go.

I spent most of the first week stripping the paper and paint from the dining room walls. Then Kathy helped me scrub the rough plaster with steel wool and water. The wet calcimine, mixed with tiny pieces of steel wool, splashed onto our clothes.

The radio, which had been so tranquilizing, began to wear on our nerves. The music seemed to run in cycles, like endlessly repeated selections on a jukebox. For relief, we started to listen to rock stations. The interruptions for news were even more annoying. Investigators were still trying to determine what caused the motorist to go berserk on the interstate. Police apprehended a man who had scaled the steeple of the city's tallest church. He wore nothing but climbing boots.

There were times I felt physically and emotionally depleted, too tired to go on. I would quietly put down the scraper and get off the ladder. I went upstairs to an empty room. As shabby and decaying as it was, the room was still a welcome asylum. There I could escape the drone of the radio, the smell of soggy, molding wallpaper, of calcimine and trisodium phosphate, and the sight of cracked plaster, of spreading slime and disorder.

Finally the walls were ready, patched and sanded and scrubbed, with the spackled cracks looking like faint scars against the yellowed plaster. There were still humps and rough spots, but they would barely show beneath the protective layers of paint.

It was a relief to leave the house to shop for hardware and paint. I wandered down the aisles of Toolorama with my list, lost among the augers and wrenches, the bags of mortar and insulation, all the replacement parts and domestic weaponry, the last line of defense against a buckling, crumbling, rotting, mildewing, leaking, cracking universe.

When I had filled my shopping cart with rollers, brushes, plastic tarps, and cans of primer and paint, I got in the check-out line. I paged through a copy of *Second Hand Times* while I waited, hoping I could find a used stereo for the kids, to replace the one that had been stolen the day we moved.

Looking up, I found an elderly man had dug into my cart and was holding up a gallon can of paint, checking the label. For a second I thought he was a bagger or a boxer for the store, trying to streamline the checkout process. But he wasn't dressed in a red jacket like the other employees. He wore a Dutch Boy paint cap, a Hawaiian shirt, and plaid shorts. Beneath the shorts, his bare legs looked like frail birch trees, rooted in black socks and black hightop basketball shoes.

He snorted and mumbled and grunted as he inspected the paint can. Then he put it back into the cart and looked me up and down, sourly. "Latex," he said.

I wasn't sure I heard him correctly.

"You got latex paint there," he said.

"I know."

"And these brushes," he said, picking one out of the cart. "Nylon." He tossed it back. I took a can of paint and set it on the counter in front of the cashier. She started to enter it on the register.

"Hold it, Angie," he said, then turned to me. "You done much painting?"

"A little."

He smiled. "Yeah, very little. Let me give some professional advice, sonny. You don't want latex paint."

"Latex is fine," I said, pushing the can toward the cashier. "It cleans up with soap and water."

"What business you in?" he asked.

"Marketing research."

"Yeah, I figured it was something like that."

He lifted the paint can off the counter and handed it back to me.

"Well, I spent fifty years in the paint business, and you can take my word for it. You want oil-base paint. Latex don't last."

I set the can back and nodded at the cashier. "This is okay."

"You don't want to take my word for it, is that it? If you was to give me advice on the stock market, I'd take it."

"I'm not in the stock market." I noticed that the cashier hadn't made a move to ring up my paint. She seemed to be watching me with as much impatience as he was.

"And look at this," he said, retrieving a paintbrush from my cart and holding it up as if it were a rotten sock, for everyone in the store to see. "Nylon. You shouldn't use anything but pig bristles."

"Look," I said, trying to settle him down, "I know you want to help—"

"How do you like this guy!" He was almost shouting. He had an audience now, people behind me in line, people in other lines, clerks and stockboys and customers all over the store.

"He's been to college. He thinks he knows everything. He's telling me that latex paint is better than oil-base. That nylon brushes are better than real bristle. This Junior Executive is telling me! I been painting houses for fifty years!"

Over his shouts, I could hear uneasy muttering and stirring in the line behind me. I felt a cart pressing sharply against the back of my legs. "What's it going to be, sir," the cashier asked, "latex or oil-base?"

"Latex," I said, shoving the can along the counter toward her. But the old man reached around me and pulled it away.

"He wants oil-base, Angie," he said, then turned to me.

"Latex and nylon are tools of Satan," he said, his spittle flying as if from a spray gun, the folds of his chin trembling with rage. "That house of yours has got an immortal soul. You use latex and nylon, you'll hear it screaming and crying in eternal pain. It'll burn and blister and rot in hell, and so will you. You won't never get any peace."

I tried to take the paint can from him, but he refused to let it go.

"Please, sir," said the cashier, "I can't wait all day for you to make up your mind."

He let go, unexpectedly, and the can fell to the floor and rolled along the aisle. People jumped out of the way as if it were a mutilated bowling ball.

"I've had it up to my bunghole with you, sonny. You think you can shit all over my fifty years' experience. You think you can shit all over me. They teach you everything in college these days but respect and good manners and brotherly love, Mr. Stock Market Expert. I bet you don't even know shit about that. What's the price of IBM, huh? Tell me that, Mr. Dow Jones!"

Even if I'd still wanted to pay for the paint and brushes, I knew it was hopeless. The cashier had her back to me, shouting into a phone. I tried to maneuver the cart enough so that I could squeeze past and leave the store. But it was blocked by the wall of bystanders. They refused to part until a security guard bulled his way through their midst. His hand was raised threateningly over the butt of the revolver sticking from his holster.

He glared at me, then turned to the cashier, who told him, "All I know is that this guy said something to Sammy."

"All I tried to do was buy this paint," I said.

"What's the story, Sammy?" the guard said.

"I don't know what's wrong with people these days," he said, perfectly calm now. "You try to give them a little friendly advice, and they treat you like you was asking for a handout. But I don't want to make a federal case out of this. I'm willing to forgive and forget."

"Well, I'm not," said a middle-aged man on the edge of the crowd. "He made an obscene remark to my wife."

I started to tell him it was okay, that the old man had lost his cool. But then I realized he was talking about me. I saw the guard unsnap his holster, letting his hand rest on the revolver butt. I saw him motion to the cashier. I watched her pick up the phone and dial 911.

Kathy was on the ladder in the living room when I got back, taking down a light fixture so we could paint the ceiling. She wanted to know why I had taken three hours to get the paint. Then I had to tell her I didn't have the paint.

She didn't seem sympathetic, even after I'd explained, as best I could, and showed her the ticket I'd gotten for disorderly conduct. "I know I can beat it," I said, "but it's just a pain in the ass to waste a half a day in court."

She left me to sand the woodwork while she went out to buy paint. I wasn't in any shape to work. I went upstairs to the empty bedroom. I sat on the floor in a corner. From here I could see that the floorboards sagged. My clothes were damp and cold. I hugged my knees to protect myself from the chill. I thought I heard a scratching noise in the attic, a dull persistent clawing. I listened carefully, but all I could hear was the March wind and rain battering the storm windows.

4

The rain had stopped when I woke at three the next morning. I hadn't been able to sleep any later than that since we'd moved, no matter what time I went to bed. I'd been up till almost midnight, watching a special edition of a newscast that turned out to be more special than anybody anticipated. The anchorwoman had reached the involuntary retirement age of thirty-five and was officially being replaced by a younger, blonder, thinner model. They were supposed to cheerfully pass the torch on the live broadcast, but the aging anchorwoman took out a gun and shot herself in the head. We were just thankful that the children weren't awake to see it.

Rather than stay in bed, wondering about the noises from other parts of the house, I got up to check the children, to see if the doors and windows were locked. The moon was as strong as a floodlight. Looking out a kitchen window, I could see that a garbage can was overturned, with papers, bottles, and cans scattered over the alley. The collectors came early, and unless the trash was in a can they ignored it. I put on my storm coat and went out to clean up.

As soon as I got outside, the cold air cleared the last traces of sleep from my head. I grabbed the snow shovel on my way out to the alley. My breath came out in a frosty vapor as I shoveled up chicken bones, cereal boxes, and formula cans. I nearly had the rubble picked up when the beam of a powerful flashlight hit me in the face. I raised my shovel to block out the glare and to shield myself from the blow I expected at any instant.

"Freeze." In the night air, his voice didn't sound real, more like a movie humanoid—a robocop or a roborobber.

"I'm already frozen," I said. I was terrified, but I thought that by acting casual, even flippant, I could keep him off guard. The flashlight wavered, and I heard the scrape of dead leaves and gravel as he moved toward me.

"Pretty late to be prowling around alleys, isn't it?" he said. From behind the blinding funnel of light, all I could make out was a large and menacing shape.

"I wasn't prowling," I said.

"Let's see your driver's license."

"I'm not out for a drive. I'm picking up the trash."

"Trash, huh. What do you think you're gonna find?"

"I'm not trying to find anything. I'm cleaning the alley. This is my house. We just moved in."

"Let's see an ID."

"I don't usually carry an ID to the alley. I'm wearing my sweats under this coat."

I started to say that I had plenty of identification inside, but

I didn't want him anywhere near my house, no matter whether he was a policeman or a mugger.

"What's your name?"

I was less frightened now than I was cold and anxious. I wanted to get this over with, whatever it was, and go back inside. I didn't think he meant to rob or kill me, but he might have been a policeman.

"Scott Ryan," I said.

He hesitated, then lowered the flashlight onto the clipboard he carried. "Social Security number?"

With the glare out of my eyes, I could see him a little more clearly. His face was still obscured by what looked like a riot helmet. He obviously wasn't a uniformed policeman, but he was dressed in a paramilitary outfit, a combination of *Patton* and *Star Wars*. His trousers were tucked into his boots. His parka was tightly belted, with what looked like canisters and other hardware hanging from it. He had a canvas bag slung over his shoulder.

"Social Security number?" he repeated. I was too distracted by the look of him to answer right away. Reflected off the clipboard, the flashlight threw horror movie shadows on his face. He was almost a comic monster. Even so, I gave him the number, which he then checked against a paper on his clipboard.

Next he took a walkie-talkie from the canvas bag. "Sentry Three," he said into the mouthpiece, "Captain Midnight. False alarm. Hold the backup squad. The guy checks out. Just moved into the neighborhood. Decided his alley needed beautifying. Yeah, at four in the morning."

He mumbled a few more words, put the walkie-talkie away, and turned to me with what seemed to be a friendly but patronizing smile. It was hard to tell since his face was still partly hidden beneath his helmet visor. "Well, Scott," he said, "you really set off all the bells and whistles in our defense system."

He took off a glove and held out his hand. "Jerry Klammish," he said. "Welcome to the neighborhood."

I shook his hand, but warily. "Is this some kind of a practical joke?"

"Not unless you like to make jokes about burglary, robbery, rape, and murder," he said. "If I were you, I wouldn't be out in this alley after dark. I wouldn't be out in this neighborhood after dark."

"I couldn't sleep, and I didn't see any harm in picking up the trash."

"No harm, huh? That's what Wes Gallagher thought and look what happened to him and his family."

That caused me to shudder. A year or so ago, the papers had been filled with stories about the Gallagher family. "I didn't realize that happened around here," I said.

"Three blocks west," he said. Then he reached down and picked up several stray papers, handing them to me.

"And I wouldn't put out my trash till it's time for the pickup."

"Yeah," I said, "it looks like something got into it—dogs or squirrels or raccoons."

"More likely some other kind of wild animal—human scavengers looking for papers just like this, with your credit card numbers, bank accounts, charge accounts. That's what I thought you were doing out here. You're lucky I was on duty and not one of those hotheads like Vince or Abigail. They don't bother to ask questions first."

"In that case, I am glad you were on duty," I said.

"And I'm glad I ran into you," he said. "We need volunteers for our neighborhood surveillance support group. Four hours a night, twice a week. You have your choice of two shifts.

Ten to two or two to six. If you need Mace, cuffs, flares, I can get them for you at ten percent over cost. We're not supposed to carry guns, but don't let that stop you. The police'll usually look the other way."

He checked his watch by the flashlight. "I'm way late in my rounds. We'll talk some more. See you around the neighborhood . . ."

"Yeah," I said.

". . . but not in any dark alleys," he said, finishing the sentence for me. As he faded into the night, I realized that if I did run into him again, I probably wouldn't recognize him without his uniform.

I went back inside and turned on the coffee machine. I knew I'd never get back to sleep now. While the coffee was brewing, I got my tape measure and walked through the house, taking inventory of all the extra hardware I needed. By the time Kathy and the children got up, I had finished measuring the windows and doors and had my list ready.

Instead of painting and scraping, I spent two days on a security system, installing dead bolt locks on all the doors, chain locks and bars on the windows, nailing the ones I figured we'd never really use. I put up stickers warning intruders that the house was hot-wired directly to police headquarters, even though with all the other expenses I couldn't begin to afford such a sophisticated electronic system. I was able to rig some homemade alarms using bells, bottles, wire, and tape. Then I drilled Kathy and the kids so they couldn't accidentally trigger them. No matter how primitive, the system really cut into our decorating budget.

When the house seemed secure, we started to work on the dining room floor. I pried up a layer of linoleum while Kathy worked behind me with a heat gun, scraping off the adhesive so we could get down to the bare oak. Beneath the many layers, the adhesive was as thick and gummy as melted rubber, which is how it smelled when the hot air from the gun hit it. It took an hour to clean each square foot.

We hadn't been working long one night when we heard a terrible noise on the second floor, where the two older children were supposed to be getting themselves ready for bed. It wasn't a routine shriek, the kind that usually resulted from a minor injury or a sibling territorial dispute. We both dropped everything and ran upstairs. Mark was standing in the hallway. His cries had awakened the baby, who was screaming from his crib, making a duet of tiny howler monkeys.

We were relieved to find there was nothing visibly wrong with him. No blood or broken bones, but he seemed to be screaming about a pain in his "cosaurus," which I assumed was an obscure scientific term for a body part that he'd heard about on public television. Finally Kathy got him calmed down enough so his complaint was intelligible. "She drowned my styracosaurus," he said.

"Where did she drown it?" I asked. He pointed behind him toward the bathroom, where Kim was watching us guiltily, halfway hidden behind the door. Beyond her, I could see the toilet, water still spilling over the sides onto the puddle on the floor.

I worked for an hour with a plunger, but I couldn't dislodge the plastic dinosaur. On her way to the basement, to get a plumber's snake, Kathy found that the heat gun, lying loose in the dining room, had scorched the exposed oak flooring. We would have to replace part of the floor, but at least she'd managed to discover it before the house caught fire.

I didn't have any better luck with the snake than the plunger. All I could do at that point was remove the toilet bowl from the floor. That was easy enough, according to my home repair manual, a matter of loosening a few bolts. But the bolts were so badly rusted that I had to cut them off with a hacksaw. Then, in wrestling with the toilet bowl, I broke the seal, which would also have to be replaced. Mark was happy to get his styracosaurus back, but we didn't have any water for two days while waiting for the plumber.

Toward the end of my vacation, there was a freaky warm spell. I felt as if I'd been given a brief reprieve which I had to make the most of by getting outdoors. I bought an extension ladder so I could clean out the gutters and check the damage from what had plainly been years of neglect. The gutters were clogged with decomposed leaves and other muck, which I scooped out with a garden trowel. Then I reamed the downspouts with the plumber's snake and blasts from the garden hose. Most had rust spots and peeling paint. They needed to be patched or replaced, as soon as I could get around to them.

For now, all I could manage were a quick inventory and hasty repairs. An ice storm was forecast for the next day. The temperature was already starting to drop. The ladder shook under increasingly chill blasts of wind.

Nearly hidden beneath one gutter I found a hole in an eave about three inches across that looked like the work of animals, probably squirrels. The warm weather had temporarily drawn them out of their nests. I'd seen them, fat and scruffy in their winter coats, running across the roof, along the power lines and bare tree limbs, scavenging for scraps around our back door and the trash cans in the alley. They had chewed holes into the heavy plastic cans.

I suspected that I'd discovered a squirrels' nest, that they'd picked our house for their winter home. That would explain some of the ominous noises I'd heard since we'd moved in, sounds I'd tried to dismiss as old timbers and joists creaking in the wind or the clatter of children in empty rooms.

Afraid to get too close to the nest, I poked around with a long stick, then with the plumber's snake. But the tunnel was so tightly packed with debris I could barely get past the entrance. After a while I decided that what squirrels weren't already hunting for food I'd frightened out of the house. There must have been a dozen of them in the yard and trees. They'd stopped playing and foraging and set up a threatening chorus of squalls when they saw me violating their territory.

Because they'd chewed the hole under the gutter, using it as a roof for the entrance, I couldn't get to it except from directly below. And the only way to clean it out was with my hand. I reached in and began to pull out soggy clumps of leaves, grass, shredded newspapers and plastic bags, fiberglass insulation, feathers, fur, and, I suspected, a ton of petrified squirrel guano. All of it poured down in a foul and noxious blizzard, stinging my nose and eyes.

Farther back, I came across what felt like a plastic toy. But when I managed to pull it into the light I discovered it was a skeleton. This wasn't a squirrels' nest, I realized, but a cemetery, a burial chamber, a filthy crypt that reeked of decay and death. I dragged out three more skeletons, including a baby's, before I couldn't reach any deeper. I'd also reached the limit of my endurance. I decided to let the rest of it go till summer and nailed a piece of sheet metal over the opening.

By then it was getting too late and cold to patch the other holes I saw in the eaves. The squirrels had gotten angrier and bolder. They were running frantically across the roof above me, screeching and acting as if they were about to attack. When I got off the ladder, I found that Mark and Kim were just as hysterical as the squirrels. They had stopped playing and were crying in the yard. Kathy was standing behind them, looking almost as unhappy herself and holding an old pan filled with Cheerios.

"What's this all about?" I said.

"They're upset because you destroyed their nest."

"Upset by homeless squirrels? What are you going to do with that?" I asked, pointing to the pan of cereal.

"The only way I could calm the kids down was by telling them I'd feed the squirrels."

"You're just going to make things worse," I said, brushing damp, smelly fur off my neck and shirt.

"They can be domesticated," she said.

"Oh, sure they can. Why don't you invite them inside for dinner? That'll make the kids happy. They can sleep with them too."

Then I noticed that the squirrels had started to scratch and gnaw at the eave, next to the metal patch. I threw a rock at them, and they ran off, ducking out of range behind a gable. They were back in a few minutes, chewing away even more furiously. I kept throwing rocks at them until it got too dark to see. They couldn't do much more damage than they already had, I thought, deciding that I would take care of them for good when the weather warmed up. Then I came inside and took a shower.

5

We were almost out of time. With only three days left before I had to go back to work, the walls had been primed but not painted. They had to be done before the refinisher came to sand the floor the next morning. I had taken a swipe at the floor myself with a rented sander, but it was harder to handle than an angry Doberman. I had lost control of the sander and cut a half-moon swath, which would probably leave a dip in the oak flooring when it was sanded out by a professional refinisher.

We were almost out of energy and patience too. I complained to Kathy about feeling short of breath and nauseous. She had the same complaints plus headaches that she said were caused by my complaints. She was afraid we were poisoning our systems by the unremitting exposure to the ammonia, TSP, turpentine, lacquer thinner, and other solvents. We left windows open for ventilation, but the house was constantly cold and damp and we had chills, coughs, and runny noses.

The children didn't seem to be affected by the noxious smells or the cold. The older ones spent a lot of time outdoors now, after school. We found a sitter to take the baby out in his stroller. But they still complained about the lack of attention and their steady diet of cheese sandwiches, noodle soup, and macaroni. Even though it meant working all night, we had to get away from the house ourselves. We took the children out for pizza.

The nearest pizzeria was in a shopping district that had not yet been reclaimed and rehabilitated. Half the stores were either abandoned or burned out. So we went to the Mama Mozzarella in the new mall. That meant a long and circuitous drive across town, an evasive action that took us around the areas that had been declared hostile zones and blocked off to everyday traffic. We hadn't bothered to change from our work clothes because we intended to paint as soon as we got home. The hostess said we couldn't eat in the dining room because we didn't meet the restaurant's dress code. We had to eat the pizzas in the car.

I could see something was wrong as soon as we got home and pulled into the driveway. Before Kathy and the children could get out of the car, I said, "Wait here. I'll go in first, and if I don't flick the front porch light in three minutes, drive to the nearest pay phone and call the police."

"What's this about?" Kathy said, opening her door.

I reached across her and roughly pulled it shut, pushing down the lock. "Just do what I tell you, and don't argue with me for once, okay?"

"Not until I know what you think you're doing," she said. "We're cold and we're tired, and we want to go inside." In the backseat, the children had also started to protest.

"Just keep quiet and trust me, okay? I know what I think I'm doing."

Coming into the driveway, I'd noticed a light burning in an upstairs bathroom. When we left, I had been very cautious about leaving only certain lights on, and that was not one of them. It made sense to me that if someone had broken in, he might have had to use the bathroom and then been careless about turning off the light.

I didn't tell Kathy this. I didn't want to alarm her or the children. I told them not to make any noise and watch the house. If they noticed anything suspicious, they were to get the hell out of there and call the police.

I quietly tried the front door first. Locked. Then I checked the other doors and found them locked, too. I checked all the first-floor windows, but there were no signs of a break-in. I let myself in the side door and listened, but I was so frightened that all I could hear was my heart, hammering away like a noisy water pipe. When I was breathing more normally, I could make out footsteps and whispering on the second floor.

I picked up a pry bar from my toolbox and moved up the stairs in a guerrilla crouch, hugging the wall. At the top, I could see light coming from beneath the closed bathroom door. With the pry bar raised, I crept up to the door, threw it open, and found Kurt Franklin on the seat, reading a Richard Scarry book, with a beer can on the floor beside him.

I don't know who was more frightened, Kurt at the sight of me with the upraised pry bar, or me at the sight of Kurt, with his pants around his ankles, his enormous hairy belly exposed, along with other unsightly appendages. When we'd both recovered from the shock, Kurt could at least joke about the situation. "If I were you, Scott, I'd put a lock on the bathroom door. You scared the shit out of me."

"What the fuck are you doing here?" I said.

From behind me, a woman said: "Now Scott, what the fuck kind of welcome is that? You weren't supposed to be home for another half hour."

I turned to find Joan McCrae, along with Sharon Lindsay. "Yeah," I said, acting as matter-of-factly as they were, "our evening out was cut short."

Beyond them I could see shadowy forms, whose voices I could recognize as those of friends, even if I couldn't make out their faces.

"Look at the size of this bathroom, will you?" That was Barbara Pearson, who had pushed her way in, so that it was getting as congested as the Marx Brothers' stateroom. "The tub has claws. And this wonderful old sink. It must be from the last century."

"This place is a tiny bit Gothic, isn't it?"

"A tiny bit, nothing. It's a mausoleum."

Barbara walked over and kissed me on the cheek, but she was obviously worried.

"I went down the hallway and started to go out on this enclosed porch, but it felt like it was going to collapse."

"That's going to be our conservatory," I said, "if we ever work our way up to this floor."

"It needs conserving all right," Barbara said. "It would probably qualify for federal disaster funds."

"The whole house would," Sharon said. "You're going to need a new ceiling in here—and right away. It looks like it's about ready to fall."

"Will you at least wait until I'm done before you start remodeling in here." Kurt was still on the seat, nonchalantly trying to finish his business.

"And close the door, okay?" he shouted as we moved out of the bathroom into the hallway.

"What is all this, anyway?" I asked. At this point, I knew I had to be the victim of a conspiracy, a sociable one perhaps, but it was still hard for me not to let my irritation show.

"Just a neighborly visit," said Joan.

"A neighborly break-in, is that it?" I said. "How did you get in? I had—"

Then I remembered Kathy and the children. They had probably gone off to call the police, who should have been arriving at the front door at any moment, if they didn't already have the house surrounded.

But when I started down to turn on the porch light so I could call off the police, there was Kathy, halfway up the hall stairs, holding the baby and talking to Marcia Franklin.

She was explaining to Marcia about the broken and missing spindles in the railing when I came down and said, "You were supposed to be getting the police."

"I knew there wasn't any reason to call the police."

"So you're behind this," I said.

"Behind nothing," Kathy said. "Don't make it sound like some kind of plot. It's a surprise, that's all."

"All right, I am grateful, but please, no more surprises," I said, showing them the pry bar. "I could've killed somebody. Or they could have killed me."

"There was an ulterior motive," Marcia said, with one of her coyest smiles. "We just couldn't wait to see what a mess you'd gotten yourself into now."

That was meant for me, no mistake. But Kathy either missed it or pretended to, and then Barbara Pearson appeared, saying, "It's really marvelous. So much room. Practically a mansion."

"Practically, nothing," said Jack Pearson, who came up the

stairs, handing me a can of beer. "This place is straight out of a movie."

"A horror movie maybe," Marcia said, smiling at me even more bitchily. "It needs a lot of work, but I know *you'll* do wonders with it."

She used to say that I could barely hang a picture. Noticing that Kathy was occupied with our other guests, I quietly said to Marcia, "I really am surprised to see you here."

"This isn't a social visit. Besides, you know I'm not the spiteful type."

"Oh, sure," I said, "just like you know how good I am at rehabbing houses."

"This house has so much character," said Joan McCrae, descending the stairs. "I just love that chandelier."

"Actually," Kathy said, "we were planning to get rid of that."

"It is a little old-fashioned, I guess. But this house is so wonderfully run-down. I can't wait to share my ideas with you. I'm so jealous of you having all this room."

"Yes," said Marcia, "and if you ever separate again, neither one of you will have to move out. You can live in one wing and Scott in the other, and you wouldn't see each other once a month."

"That wasn't why we bought it," Kathy said, with what I thought was admirable civility. She was much better than I at pretending not to notice indelicate sarcasm.

"You're not really going to do this all yourselves?" asked Barbara.

"Not all of it," I told her, getting anxious now, thinking about the acres of bare walls that needed to be painted before eight the next morning, when the floor refinisher was due. "Isn't that the reason for this little housebreaking?"

"Housewarming," said Kurt, coming down the stairs.

I grabbed Kurt's beer can, shook it, and sprayed him. "If we don't get started, nobody's going to be in any shape to help anybody."

By the time we got downstairs and started painting, I could tell that it was already too late. Kathy tried to take charge and impose some order and efficiency, but it wasn't even organized chaos. We were just getting in each other's way, prolonging a job that Kathy and I could have finished in half the time.

After almost two weeks of this, I was out of energy and patience. I couldn't even pretend that all this was great fun, as the others seemed to assume. Their laughter and their prattle ricocheted off the plaster walls, like atonal music in a small concert hall. I felt even more uneasy being in the same room with Marcia, trying to avoid her glances.

But after a while I was able to tune much of it out. I was absorbed by the rhythms of painting, by the rattle and hiss of the roller as it moved across the bare ceiling, back and forth, spraying me as it went, until I was soaked with white paint and sweat. I stopped to rest for a moment and found Marcia at the bottom of the ladder, looking up at me, sweetly, seductively. She held out a hand. "Time for a break," she said.

I took her hand and stepped down from the ladder. Her hand was slippery, and I noticed that she was as drenched with white paint as I was, giving her a phantom glow in the dim light. "I want that private tour you promised," she said. The others were so busy now, they didn't notice our leaving. I followed her through the entrance hall and up the stairway.

"I destroyed all the pictures of you," she said. "I couldn't bear to look at them anymore."

"I'm sorry—but relieved," I said. "You didn't have any choice. Just so long as you didn't burn them."

"What else could I do?" she said. "You looked very dashing with flames in your hair."

"That's what I'd call cruel and unusual punishment."

"You deserved it," she said, without the flicker of a smile. "Not just yet," I said.

She started to go into Kathy's and my bedroom, but that seemed unnecessarily mischievous and I pulled her off in another direction. I didn't want to desecrate the one room in the house that was halfway orderly and clean.

We went from one empty room to another, through rooms I either had forgotten about or hadn't realized existed. I was staggered by the size of the house, its shabby grandeur, as if understanding for the first time how overwhelmed we really were, how we had committed ourselves to a lifetime of interminable labor. There were dust and cobwebs everywhere. It would take us the rest of our lives just to clean all these rooms, much less make them new and livable again.

I felt so tired by then that I just wanted to sit down and rest. But Marcia kept urging me along. She refused to stop until we'd reached a cramped garret on the third floor, directly under an eave, where the ceiling and walls angled away into blackness. This seemed to please her. She smiled lasciviously.

Her smile warmed and revived me. I backed her against the wall and kissed her. Her face was flecked with paint. I stroked her cheek, smearing the paint until her face was covered with a ghostly white makeup. I brushed the paint into her long dark hair, streaking it. She began to run her sticky hands through my hair.

I unbuttoned her denim work shirt and massaged the paint into her shoulders, her chest, her ribs, her stomach, down into her pubic zone. As I rubbed and stroked, a white liquid flowed not just from her breasts but from every pore, blending with the paint. Her skin tasted as thick and sweet as cream.

My clothes were as heavy and as soaked as Marcia's. She helped me out of my sweatshirt, then undid my belt and pulled down my pants. "Look at you," she whispered. "It's pouring out of you like a faucet." She squeezed and tugged, but gently, and I could see the white fluid gushing from me, coating my thighs and legs, a pearly lubricant that made a thick puddle at our feet.

We were so hot and slippery by now, we couldn't stand. We slid down onto the floor. The slick wood creaked and splintered under our tangled bodies. I was afraid that the noise would carry downstairs. But soon we were wrapped in a white and smothering blanket of foam, and all I could hear were Marcia's pleading whispers, the desperate but muffled sound of her fingernails, digging through the milky cushion beneath us, scratching and clawing at the wooden floorboards.

We were finished by one in the morning, but it was another hour before all the equipment had been put away, the mess cleaned up, and everybody had gone home. The leave-taking took longer than necessary because sometime after midnight Kurt had taken a break for a beer and not come back. Nobody noticed until it was time to go. We found him on the floor of the butler's pantry, covered in a drop cloth. Marcia wanted to leave him there for the rest of the night, but we insisted she get him up and take him home, an ordeal that took an extra half hour.

Afterward, Kathy said she was too tired to shower and went directly to bed. When I crawled in beside her, unwashed myself, I could hardly get to sleep because of the smell of paint and turpentine.

6

Either way, I couldn't make it work. I tried parting my hair on the left, then on the right, but no matter which way I brushed and combed, swirled and patted, I couldn't disguise how wispy it was getting in front. I leaned closer to the bedroom mirror. Inspecting the damage through narrowed eyes, I could see that beneath the failing hair my scalp had the texture of a bleached lemon peel.

While my hair was disappearing, my body was spreading in various disorderly and off-center directions. The asymmetry distressed me. Though I looked almost gaunt, the skin on my face was getting loose, slipping. It seemed to be puckering forward, gathering in sour folds around my lips. Maybe a mustache would help.

But I was cheered when I put on my suit pants and found

them slack in the waist. At least I was slightly thinner from all the forced labor. If I watched what I ate and got back to the club right away, I could keep that off.

The hair was something else. It was rapidly going, and when it did, it was gone, along with much else. It had to be the chemicals, the paint and stripper, the assorted solvents. I'd been losing hair before I shut myself away like this, but not nearly so fast. I did what I could to disguise my retreating hairline, then tied my tie, put on my suit coat, and went down-stairs.

My spirits got a lift when I saw the living and dining rooms in the morning light. The walls and ceilings were a bright and impregnable white. The floors, newly sanded, stained, and varnished, seemed to reflect not only sunlight but order and solidity. Kathy was already up, rearranging furniture, hanging pictures and plants. She frequently had to stop and run into the kitchen to help the children with breakfast.

She didn't seem at all dispirited or depleted. In the year and a half since the baby had been born, she'd lost all the excess weight and more. She was slim but sturdy, a symmetrical princess with the strength and constitution of a peasant. Her hair was still luxuriant and dark. Her energy frightened me. I wondered if she had a lover.

"Can you help move the sofa?" she asked.

"I wish you would have asked before I got dressed," I said. "Can't it wait until I get home tonight?"

Mark came careening into the living room on his Big Wheel. He twisted the handlebars, causing it to slide across the polished floor, and wiped out against a baseboard. His nose was bleeding, and he was hysterical when Kathy carried him off to the bathroom.

He had left skid marks, dull and disfiguring streaks, in the impeccable finish of the floor. I picked up the Big Wheel and carried it outside, trying not to look at the black smudge and the spot of blood on the white baseboard.

Going out of the house, I felt as if I were emerging from a catacomb. I had never before been restless to get back to my office at the end of a vacation. The air was warm and had the damp, fertile smell of spring. The trees were still bare, stark against the flat gray sky, as if drawn with India ink. But here and there I could see buds, the tips of struggling leaves.

Our house was two blocks from the station. Because we'd bought it in darkest winter, I'd never had a chance to go through the neighborhood on foot. Walking along now, I was pleased by what I saw. Everywhere I looked, houses were being gutted, aluminized, vinylized, glazed, shingled, roofed, restored to life. We couldn't have moved at a better time. Our house was cheap, but the neighborhood was coming up. So were property values.

At the station, I thought I recognized a man who lived down the street. I was afraid he might recognize me. I raised the newspaper in front of my face and studied the box scores from spring-training camps. When I glanced at him a few minutes later, I saw that his face was hidden behind the newspaper, too. All around me, commuters were shielded by newspapers, as if they were trying to protect themselves from evil spirits.

I deliberately chose a seat next to a man who was deeply submerged in his newspaper. But the train had barely left the station than he had lowered the paper and was pointing out a story to me. "Did you read this?" he asked. "Jesus, there are some real nuts running around loose these days."

It was a story I had purposely not read. I found myself skipping a lot of stories like it. But it was hard for me to read anything in the paper this morning because I kept thinking about the work that had been piling up during the two weeks I was gone. Since the merger, the new management was trying to economize. The work didn't get done if you weren't there to do it yourself. Under the new rules, you went on vacation at your own risk.

The man beside me had returned to his paper. But not for long. In a few minutes, he let the paper fall and sat upright, looking so grieved I was afraid he was having a seizure. "What a day," he finally said. "Paraguay sinks one of our destroyers. Six bodies are dug up in a church basement. The Cubs blow one in the eleventh. Thank God, Dynacom is up three-eighths. I can get you some of that action, if you're interested."

I made it plain I wasn't by closing my eyes and slumping into a nap. I dozed for a minute, until I heard a whistle. Looking up, I saw a conductor moving hurriedly through the car. "Red Zone," he said, between puffs on the whistle hanging from his neck. "Red Zone, coming up."

I thought he was calling out a stop, but the train, rather than slow down, seemed to speed up. The man next to me, I noticed, had bent over in his seat, beneath window level. He had put his head between his knees and covered it with his hands and arms, the way airline travelers are told to do in preparation for a crash. All around me, I could see that the other passengers had done the same. I was the single one still upright in the car, exposed.

"Get down," my seatmate said, pulling at my sleeve. "You make a perfect target." I did as he asked. But he could tell I was puzzled, a new passenger on the line. "We're going through a

Red Zone," he said. "Snipers. They picked off three last month. We've got to take evasive action until the railroad gets an appropriation to bulletproof the cars."

My arms were starting to cramp when the conductor came back through the car, blowing a series of two short bursts on the whistle this time. My neighbor got up, straightened his suit, and went back to his newspaper. I did the same thing, assuming that the sniper alert was over.

"Dynacom is on fire now," he said, a moment later, "and getting hotter. You'd be nuts to pass it up." He smiled and handed me a business card.

As soon as I stepped off the elevator onto my floor at work, I sensed something had changed. Nothing obvious, just a faint omen. The reception area looked the same: beige tweed walls and beige tweed furniture. The pale abstract prints seemed to dissolve in the oatmeal decor.

Then there was Sandy, a bronzed sentinel at her command post, providing a distinct counterpoint to the decorous and tasteful surroundings. With her bright metallic hair, skin, and dress, she seemed more like the hostess for a health club or a tanning salon than a corporate receptionist. As nearly as I could tell from office gossip, I was the only executive on middle management level or above, female or male, who hadn't slept with her.

She looked up at me with alarm. "You're early," she said, almost accusingly.

I looked at my watch, then back at her, in mock puzzlement. "It's five *after* nine."

"No, I mean weren't you supposed to be gone *two* weeks?"

"It was two weeks."

She seemed momentarily ruffled. "I wonder what happened to that other week?"

"Check your filing drawer," I said.

"Well . . . how was it?"

"You don't really want to hear. It was two weeks on Devil's Island."

"Is that somewhere in the Bahamas?"

"No," I said, "off the coast of French Guiana."

"Oh, I hear it's gorgeous there. Did you stay at a Club Med?"

I couldn't keep it up. I felt as if I were cruelly teasing a child. "I left you a note with all the particulars."

"I never got it," she said. "You must have forgotten to give it to me."

"We didn't go anywhere," I said. "I spent the whole two weeks at home."

"Every year I say I'm going to take a vacation like that. Just stay home and do nothing."

"I don't recommend it," I said and started off to my office.

"If you'd let me know you were going to be home, I would have called and told you."

I stopped and waited. But Sandy wasn't going to give up any more information without prompting.

"Told me about what?"

"About Bill Wolner."

"What about Bill Wolner?"

"He's gone."

"Gone where?"

"He didn't tell me."

"Quit?" I asked, hesitantly.

"Terminated."

"What the hell for?"

"Nobody tells me anything. All I know is that they moved you into his office."

She was right about that much. I checked my office first, finding all my furniture, files, and papers gone, the walls stripped bare. My Barcelona chair, my *Chinatown* poster, the children's drawings—everything had been swept up and out. The room wasn't entirely empty. In place of my desk there was a large copying machine.

Except for the furniture, it had all been deposited in Bill Wolner's office. I found memos, letters, printouts, early drafts of the FurReal report boxed and stacked on the desk, cabinets, anywhere there had been a bare surface. Beneath the rubble, I found that I had evidently inherited Bill Wolner's furniture, along with his office and job. That much I couldn't complain about, since it was a grade higher than mine.

His office was not one I had ever coveted, but it did seem brighter. I counted the windows. One more than I had before. And unless I was disoriented, the room was larger. I was searching through the boxes for my tape measure when Harold Masterson came in the door, smiling wickedly.

"It's all yours, if that's what you were wondering," he said. "Your new conglomerate's way of welcoming you back from vacation. Where'd you go? Someplace peaceful, I hope."

"Club Med," I said.

"Yeah," he said, "the one in Mexico or—"

"French Guiana. I left you a memo with all the exciting details. What happened to Wolner?"

"You're not sorry to see him gone?" He idly walked over to one of my boxes, took out a paper, and began reading it.

"Under other circumstances, I'd be delighted," I said. "But this was a little sudden."

"He was a casualty of the merger, that's all. They're cutting back everywhere. Rebalancing the work force, according to the official memo."

"I thought the merger was supposed to strengthen the company."

"It did. Now we're overstaffed. Just be glad you were on vacation. They were looking around for surplus bodies. They might have asked me to rebalance you, too."

"But you would have protected me, right?"

"You're going to have to cover your own ass from now on, amigo. I'm just relieved mine is still in one piece. These boys collect 'em, stuff 'em, and hang 'em on the walls.

"And I wouldn't leave messages like this lying around," he said, holding up a paper he'd dug out of a box. "If any unfriendly types happened to see it, termination would be a merciful punishment. This could get you obliterated."

While I shredded the incriminating document by hand, Harold moved to a window, ostensibly to check out the view. But I could see him admiring his reflection, slyly, vainly smoothing his thick silvery hair. He had a bright, ruddy complexion that made it look as if he'd just come back from a Caribbean vacation himself. But broken capillaries, not tropical sunshine, were responsible. It was a permanent glow, the by-product of ninety-proof lunches and marathon happy hours. But he had the hulking physical grace and the amiable bluster of a former college football player, which naturally made him a popular and promotable executive.

"I think you're supposed to consider all this a promotion," he said, with a diabolical grin, "if you don't stop to consider that you're doing the job of two men instead of one. Anyway, as soon as you get settled into your new quarters, can you give me a memo on where we stand on FurReal? Like right after lunch, maybe?"

Harold's lunches usually stretched until late in the afternoon, so there was no immediate need for panic. There would be plenty of time for that later. I had more urgent business to attend to.

After he left, I paced off the office lengthwise, noticing that the carpet had a deeper pile than my old one. I checked the width too, then went to search for the tape measure again. Unless I'd miscalculated, I was going to have room for a full-size sofa.

7

With those first two rooms painted and decorated, we didn't feel any immediate pressure to do more. That seemed to give us a solid foundation, a place where we could be comfortable and secure, away from the creeping disorder and anarchy. The rest of the house we could finish on our own good or bad time.

For the moment, we had plenty to do just arranging our furniture through the house. We had moved from a six-room apartment, so it didn't stretch far. But there were enough pieces to give the downstairs the appearance of being adequately furnished.

Several of the upstairs rooms had to be left empty, the walls needing to be patched or replastered, painted or repapered. That pleased the children and their friends, who liked to pretend they were caves and dungeons. Amplified by the bare surfaces, their small voices boomed and rebounded down to the first floor, into the kitchen where Kathy and I obsessively planned, diagrammed, negotiated, fought over what to do next.

For several months, nothing got done. The weather turned warm, then hot, then hotter. We spent most of our time outdoors, working in the yard. The inside could wait until winter. We cut down and planted trees, weeded, mulched, repaired the fence. I planted three spreading junipers around the foundation. I put a combination fertilizer and weed killer on the lawn, but the grass turned yellowish, like straw, and died.

We sat on the porch, in the inert and humid shadows of twilight, and made more plans. Kathy talked about starting to work on another room. But I was too weary when I returned home at night, and I had begun spending Saturdays at the office. A man who worked with me was accused of exposing himself to a child in the park and I received another promotion, along with a larger office, but that left me even busier and wearier.

One morning, long before dawn, in the middle of that summer, I had a horrifying experience. I usually had no trouble falling asleep at night, but I always woke up very early, sometimes as early as two or three. I'd lie in bed, desperately trying to get back to sleep until it was time to get up for work.

This morning, however, something drew me from the bed almost immediately, as if a psychic alarm had gone off. I went down to the living room and switched on the light. I saw it right away, a thin ugly crack that cut its way erratically from the baseboard to the molding at the ceiling.

I found many smaller cracks in the other walls we had painted, along with patches where the paint had bubbled and blistered from the heat and dampness. If the cracking continued, we would have to scrape, patch, and paint these walls again, very soon. I went back to bed, debating whether to wake

Kathy and tell her what I had found. Her breathing was deep and peaceful. I decided not to say anything. I didn't want to disturb her.

If Kathy noticed how the rooms had already started to deteriorate, during the next weeks or months, she didn't mention it to me. Then the cold weather arrived, suddenly and rudely. We had only a few days of autumn before a violent storm stripped the trees overnight, turning the landscape from melancholy gold into the bleak gray and brown of premature winter.

We worked in the yard as long and as late as we could, in no hurry to retreat indoors and return to the overwhelming task that awaited us there. We raked leaves until well past dark, vainly trying to keep ahead of the children, who ran through the piles and scattered them on the chill October winds. I took down awnings, put up storm windows, caulked and mortared and puttied. I felt as if I were securing a fortress against an invasion.

The squirrels were busy, too. They chewed and rifled our garbage cans in search of winter provisions. They ran up and down the trunks of the two enormous elms in our backyard, peeling away bark and twigs, which they carried off to replenish their nests. The branches of one elm hung over the house, and the squirrels leaped from them onto the roof. They chased each other over dormers and gables, around the turret and under the eaves, like children playing tag.

I had stopped to watch them when I heard rustling and heavy breathing behind me. I turned, expecting to find a child, but there was Mary Agnes, the howitzer from down the block, panting and perspiring. I'd barely seen her since we'd moved in, though Kathy had given me long and gruesome reenactments of their encounters. Her face was a slightly darker shade of pink than her sweatsuit. Except for her hair, which was teased and sprayed and lacquered into a copper helmet, she looked as if she were ready to self-destruct right there on my clean lawn.

I was about to offer to call an ambulance when she said, between gasps, "I just love what you're doing to that old place. It's going to be wonderful. But I wish you'd hurry up and finish so you can get started on ours."

I obligingly laughed along with her and said, "At the rate we're going, I don't think we'll ever be done. We're already running out of energy and money."

Over Mary Agnes's shoulder, I was relieved to see Kathy come around the corner of the house. But when she saw Mary Agnes, she hesitated. "Oh, there's Kathy," I shouted, before she could escape.

"Your husband was just telling me how desperate you are for money," Mary Agnes said, "and I was about to give him some free financial advice. I think you should have a garage sale."

"We don't have enough furniture to fill the house as it is," she said.

"What I do is," Mary Agnes said, "I go to all the garage sales, and I buy a lot of things—furniture, dishes, TVs—even if I don't need them. Then I put them in my garage or down in the basement, and every other month or so I have a garage sale myself. I mark everything up a dollar, two dollars. . . . Sometimes I charge twice what I paid for things. I always make a nice profit. People will buy anything."

I was almost grateful to have Kim appear then, even if she was screaming hysterically. It turned out to be nothing more serious than a stolen bicycle. But that meant we had to go to the station to report the theft, because it was Sunday and there was only a skeleton crew of policemen patrolling our streets. From all the sirens I'd been hearing, they must have been occupied with more critical matters.

The station resembled an emergency room—without blood and gore, but with no shortage of confusion. Kim was calm and rational herself, even happy now that I'd told her our home-owners' insurance would take care of a newer and better bike. But it was hard to concentrate with all the pandemonium around us as we tried to give the policeman the information he needed for his report.

"What color was it?" he wanted to know.

"Red, I think."

"No, Daddy, it was yellow. Mark's Big Wheel is red."

Two desks away from us, an elderly woman was sobbing. "I couldn't see his face. He was wearing a mask. And a bright pink cape. And he kept flapping his arms and jumping on one foot and screaming that he was a flamingo."

"He wore a pink cape but no pants?"

"Yeah, yellow then," I said.

"Serial number?" he asked me.

"Kim?"

"Daddy, how would I know that?"

"Can't this wait?" pleaded the elderly woman's even more elderly husband. "She's in no condition—"

"I'm sorry, but the sooner we get a description of him, the better chance we'll have of catching him."

"Was it locked?"

"It was just a child's bike," I said. "I never thought to have her lock it. I thought they only took ten-speeds."

"Let me give you some advice," the policeman said. "In that neighborhood, you don't leave anything lying around loose. You lock it, you nail it down, you bolt it, you pour concrete around it. Because if you don't, somebody will steal it. Blacks, rednecks, yellow peril, albinos, green men with goggle eyes and lobster antennas—you got 'em by the bushel around there. Don't let your guard down for a second."

As we were leaving the squad room, two uniformed patrolmen came through the door with a prisoner, his hands cuffed behind his back, his shirt smeared with either barbecue sauce or dried blood.

I tried to pull Kim aside, but she slipped out of my grasp and approached the sullen prisoner.

"Hi, Mr. Jenkins," she said. "Did you hurt yourself?"

With that, the prisoner lurched backward and began kicking at the patrolmen. But he only succeeded in throwing himself off-balance, screaming, "These motherfuckers want to kill me," as he went down.

The patrolmen were wrestling him into submission on the floor as I dragged Kim out of there. "Did you really know him?" I asked her.

"That's Mr. Jenkins," she said. "He's a counselor at my school."

One drizzly evening, a few weeks later, I came home from the office to find Kathy distraught. I was immediately afraid that she'd discovered the damage in the rooms we'd remodeled, as I knew she eventually would. But she was upset by something else.

"The squirrels," she said, "they're inside the house. I could hear them all day. They were running around in the attic, in the walls . . ." She had two glasses of chardonnay before dinner, instead of one, and that seemed to calm her down.

After we'd eaten, I went up to the third floor, pried open the trapdoor in the ceiling, and hoisted myself up. It was the first time I'd been in the attic. I was surprised to find it so cramped, barely more than a crawl space. I couldn't stand erect. I slowly let the flashlight beam drift across the rafters and joists, past cobwebs and mounds of soot—bat droppings, for all I knew.

With the light, I burrowed into all the corners and concealed niches. I fully expected to catch the glint of tiny eyes, to hear the scrape and slither of fur and claws. I saw no squirrels, but I did turn up evidence that they'd been up there, digging through the rock-wool insulation, gnawing at the joists.

I wasn't alarmed. How much damage could squirrels do? But I didn't have to live with them; Kathy did. That weekend I got out the extension ladder. I climbed onto the roof and crawled cautiously along the edge, looking for places where they might be getting inside.

It didn't take long to discover them, two small ragged holes on either side of the house, partly obscured behind the gutters. The day was cold but sunny, and as far as I could tell, the squirrels were out of their nest, foraging for food and supplies. I secured the holes with pieces of tin and wire mesh.

I spent the rest of the afternoon watching the football game on television. Something was happening to our set. The color spectrum was disintegrating so that the players were hardly more than phosphorescent magenta blurs. We could not afford to have it fixed.

During the commercials, I ran out to see if the squirrels had returned. I did not want to miss their frenzy and bewilderment when they discovered the entrances to their nest were sealed.

I dozed off in front of the television, and the next thing I knew Kathy was shaking me. She was very agitated. I rushed outside, and in the frosty twilight I could see the squirrels. There must have been six of them. Two of the squirrels peered over the gutter at me, like sentries, looking wrathful but arrogant, as their confederates chewed away at the eaves.

I threw rocks at them, and they scurried off, ducking out of range behind a gable. As soon as I moved out of sight, they attacked the eaves again. It was no use throwing more rocks. They would only come back. The sound of their teeth grinding against the wood made my head ache. I would have climbed back on the roof, but it was almost dark and I did not want to take a chance on the ladder. A hole in the eave was not worth a broken leg or neck. I went inside and mixed a drink.

That night I did not sleep. I lay in bed with the pillow over my head, trying to shut out the noise of the squirrels and the sirens. I cursed the squirrels and promised that I would take care of them as soon as it was light. But when I got up it was sprinkling out, and by afternoon it had turned to a hard sleet.

I tried to read the Sunday paper, but it was filled with news of massacres and conflagrations, riots and political scandals. Kathy took the children to a PTA variety show, and I worked in a downstairs bathroom, stripping paint from the woodwork. I kept the volume of the stereo and the television turned high. If the squirrels were inside the house, at least I would not have to hear them.

When Monday morning came, I was grateful to be escaping the house. The sleet had stopped. The air was cold and clear. I got a window seat on the train. Looking out over the rooftops as it left the station, I could make out in the distance the back of my own house, the largest on the block. I could plainly see fire and smoke coming from a second-floor bedroom. In minutes the entire house would be in flames. I turned away and handed my ticket to the conductor.

8

The next weeks were filled with dread and apprehension.
Kathy was near collapse. I would no sooner walk through the
door at night than she would start her recitation of everything
that had gone wrong while I was at work. A cold-water pipe in
the basement froze and burst. The estimate on the kitchen
cabinets was twice what we had expected. She was called to
school when Mark's social studies teacher found a condom in
his backpack.

Worse, there were the squirrels. They made noise all day.
They played and fought in the ceilings and walls. She could
not take a nap for fear they would get inside and bite her
while she slept.

"Damn," I said, "I thought they were supposed to hibernate
during the winter."

"I think the cold weather must make them oversexed," she said. "It's nonstop fucking, all day long. We're going to have a population explosion before spring."

"Maybe it's the fiberglass insulation that's turning them on," I said. "I was afraid it wasn't environmentally kosher when I put it up in the attic. We're probably producing a brave new generation of mutant squirrels."

"A horny new generation, you mean."

There was nothing I could do but call an exterminator.

"How does it look?" I asked as he lowered himself from the attic.

He took his time about answering. He was a heavy older man, obviously not used to exerting himself, and the effort of crawling across the attic had left him cramped and breathless. "You've got lots of company up there," he said.

"We'd already figured that out," Kathy said. "How bad is it?"

He smiled at her, suggesting he was not as old and burned out as he looked. "Come on up, and you can see for yourself."

"That's okay," she said, "we'll take your word for it."

"Not afraid of a few squirrels, are you?" he said, brushing the dust and loose insulation off his uniform, which had a red ratbuster emblem on the chest pocket.

"It's not the squirrels that worry me," she said.

"Well, they worry me," I said. "What do we do about them?"

Before he could answer, our exterminator began to choke and gasp, theatrically, as if suffering a respiratory attack. I was thinking about calling an ambulance when he recovered his voice and smiled. "Pretty hot and dirty up there," he said. "My throat is so dry and parched, I can hardly talk."

"Let me get you something to drink," Kathy said. "A soda? Or a beer?"

"Yeah, a frozen daiquiri, that'd do the trick."

While Kathy was fixing his drink, he refused to discuss our squirrel situation with me. Waiting for her to come back, he roamed around the upstairs, appraising the scattered pieces of furniture, checking them for solidity and workmanship—and, I couldn't help but suspect, for possible resale value.

"Well, it looks like you've got a mama and a papa up there," he said, after consuming half the daiquiri that Kathy brought him, "plus a whole lot of little ones and maybe even a bunch of kinfolk—aunts and uncles and cousins and some in-laws too. It looks like a regular squirrel dynasty."

Kathy made a sick face, and he assured her: "Oh, as rodents go, squirrels aren't so bad. Just be glad you don't have rats. A lot of your neighbors do, I can tell you that. You can live with squirrels but not with rats."

"I don't see much difference," Kathy said, "and I'd rather not live with either."

"Don't blame you one bit. They can get pretty noisy inside those walls. They start to playing their games in there, you know. They start to breeding, and before you know it . . . well, I don't have to tell you what I mean. From all the toys I saw lying around . . . maybe it's the squirrels that ought to be complaining about the noise, huh?"

"Look," I said, "how do we get rid of them?"

"Well, that's not real easy, this time of the year. They're stubborn little bastards, and they've got themselves pretty well barricaded in up there. I could poison them, but that might just cause more problems. Against the law, for one thing. But even if you don't let that stop you, then you have a lot of dead squirrels rotting in your walls. Too bad these city squirrels are such scavengers, feeding on trash and garbage. Otherwise, you'd have plenty of fresh meat."

"We don't want to poison them or eat them," Kathy said. "So please, just tell us what we can do."

"What you need is some traps. I'll rent you a couple for the crawl space. Then when you catch one, you take it out to the woods and let it go. I don't guarantee they'll stay there, though. I've had people haul squirrels ten, fifteen miles into the country, and the next day those same squirrels were back. I'll bet I don't have to tell *you* what brings them back. It's the breeding instinct, that's what it is."

I could hear them breeding that night. I'd been asleep for only an hour or so when they woke me, panting and squealing amorously in the wall next to our bed. I could also smell them. I reached over and stroked Kathy's thigh. She groaned in her sleep and rolled away from me.

I got out of bed and slapped the wall. That only seemed to arouse their passion. I slapped the wall again, harder, hoping to startle them and disrupt their rhythm, disconnect or throw them out of sync. I could feel the fragile plaster start to bulge and buckle. I didn't dare hit it again, or they'd come tumbling out of the wall, spilling their fur and lust all over our bedroom, all over us.

Kathy was awake by now but not at her most coherent. "Be sure to dilute the ammonia with six parts water," she said, then fell back to sleep.

As long as she couldn't hear the squirrels, I decided it was best not to disturb her. But it was too late for me to do anything about it. I quietly put on my sweatpants, went downstairs, and got the slushy remains of a daiquiri from the refrigerator. I turned the TV to an ancient movie. The poor reception made the zombies seem even more horribly deformed and disfigured.

I lost interest in the movie and watched the fluttering patterns and ghostly images the faulty television threw on the wall. I was almost asleep when something caused me to sit up with a jerk, fully conscious and alarmed. I went over to the wall. It was covered with fissures and pustules, as if ravaged by disease. There was nothing in my home repair manuals to explain this. All I could do was get out the heat gun and cauterize the sick wall, frantically scraping away the ulcerating paint and plaster, filling the cracks with spackle, covering up its imperfections before Kathy and the children got up.

On my way out of the house, a few hours later, I heard Mrs. Underwood calling from her front porch. Even though she lived next door, we hadn't been close neighbors. A widow, she kept the outside of her house immaculate. She spent most of the day working on her yard, trying to make each blade of grass perfectly lean and symmetrical. She made it clear she didn't want it spoiled by weeds, crabgrass, or even trees. Other than an occasional friendly but cautious word over the fence, the only contact we'd had were the notes she'd left in our mailbox. She'd ask us to please not let our rampaging dandelions grow too near her fence. Or to please trim a marauding branch that was shading her grass.

Hunched and twisted out of shape from bending over her lawn all day, she came down the sidewalk at a feeble and painfully slow gallop. It was agonizing to watch her this morning. My eyes burned from lack of sleep, and I had already missed my regular train.

When she reached the fence, it must have taken another ten minutes before she was breathing regularly enough to speak. Waiting, I tried to avert my eyes from her drooping flesh and withered bones. "Oh, Mr. Ryan," she said, weakly but sweetly. "I was afraid that you didn't get the message I left last week."

"Let's see," I said, "which message was that? The one that said our junipers were out of control and needed to be cut back? Or was it the one about the box elder droppings?"

"Oh, then you didn't get it," she said. "This neighborhood is full of spies and thieves. . . . You know, I dearly love children, and, from what I can see, your little ones are precious, just darling, but those vehicles they ride around on all day, the girl's bicycle—"

"Her Barbie Cycle, you mean."

"Yes, and that loud plastic motorcycle your son . . ."

"That's his Fred Flintstone Mobile, Mrs. Underwood."

"Yes, well, they leave those vehicles parked right next to my fence, practically in my yard, where I have to look at them day and night, and I'm beginning to feel like I'm living next to a junkyard and . . ."

"I know just how you feel, Mrs. Underwood. It's a scandal and nuisance, that's what it is, and there's probably a law against it. But before you call the police, let me handle things. I have ways of making the little gangsters behave. You can be sure it won't happen again."

"I knew you'd understand, Mr. Ryan. I just wish you could make the Murdocks listen to reason."

"The Murdocks?"

"That's their house over there," she said, pointing across the street and three doors down. "He's French Canadian. And you can see, their hedge hasn't been trimmed in months, and that elm has yellow leaves . . . it's almost dead."

"I'll tend to them later," I said, heading down the sidewalk toward the station. "Maybe we can get it put on the agenda at the Neighborhood Solidarity Meeting."

By the time I got downtown, the section meeting had already started. Coming into the conference room, I mumbled an apology, something about unreliable commuter trains. But I could tell that nobody was in much of a forgiving mood, especially not the visibly irritated executive whose speech I'd interrupted.

Harold Masterson glanced at me sympathetically, but that kind of sympathy I didn't need. I'd seen that look too many times on the faces of witnesses to disasters. I had no problem finding a vacant seat around the conference table. Not long ago, these meetings had been standing room only. Either fewer of us were invited now, or there were fewer to invite.

This was supposed to be a summit conference with our new CEO. But the corporate fascist strutting around the table in his funereal pinstripe suit, taupe shirt, and paisley tie obviously wasn't him. He was an officious jack-in-the-box we'd acquired in the merger. I'd seen him popping in and out of offices, supply rooms, broom closets, and filing cabinets ever since. We hadn't formally met, and he didn't bother to introduce himself now. So I guessed it was too late for me to have that pleasure.

After I'd taken my seat and assumed the properly obedient pose, he resumed. He was apologizing because the new CEO, whose name was Kinkaid, had been unavoidably detained and couldn't personally be with us today. But rather than send us back to our offices frustrated and disappointed, Kinkaid had come up with an optional method of introducing himself. Then his lieutenant pushed a wireless remote on the desk, and one wall divided to reveal a giant television set.

In an instant we were watching the dynamic adventures of a corporate superman, working, socializing, competing, flying, faster than a Concorde or a beer commercial. One instant he was signing papers in an executive suite, the next he was checking blueprints at a foreign construction site. We saw him conferring with presidents, kings, sultans, maharajas, and prime ministers. We watched him jetting, jogging, sailing, swimming at a tropical resort with his styrene wife and three styrene children.

The tan and the stylish clothes and the careful grooming and the pancake makeup couldn't hide his puffy dissipation, the cross-hatching and permanent sunspots on his cheeks and forehead. If I hadn't known better, I might have thought this was a public service commercial about the perils of stress, overexertion, gluttony, and other practices associated with unhealthy living.

There was a jump cut to the tennis court, where all the artful splices and camera angles couldn't disguise the fact that he was struggling. Then there was a lyrical dissolve, the background music faded, and he came to the net, looking cool and refreshed, and began talking to the camera, to us, about the importance of pace, velocity, and a killer offense.

I thought he was conducting a tennis seminar instead of a corporate pep talk. "The dinkers and the lobbers and the spinners don't belong here," he was saying. "We want fast, aggressive players."

The music swelled, he stepped back, tossed the ball up, and smashed it directly at the camera, with so much pace and velocity that everybody at the table ducked.

On the way back to our offices, Harold broke our lunch date. "Sorry, amigo, but it's a personal emergency. Next week, okay?" I ate by myself at a stand-up hot dog stand, two blocks away. Walking back to work, I saw Harold coming out of a sporting goods store, carrying a new tennis racquet.

9

Without my being aware of it, Peter had become a real person. I understood that one Saturday afternoon when I came down off the ladder and found him on the back porch, playing in a bucket of mortar. He had awakened from his nap, climbed out of his crib, and made his way down the stairs. Kathy had taken the other children to swimming lessons. Peter was covered with mortar, so I had to stop tuck-pointing and put him under the shower, before he hardened into a garden cherub.

For the last year, I had been so involved in work that I was barely conscious of how he had emerged from the cocoon of infancy. Going on two, he had become a walking, talking, mischievous child, capable of getting into more trouble than his brother and sister.

I couldn't get back to my tuck-pointing right away. I let him run around the house, pulling him back from the edge of one disaster after another. The house may have seemed like a playground to him, but in its perpetual state of disarray and upheaval, it was a labyrinth of treacherous corners and precipices, pockets of danger.

Peter didn't seem as well coordinated as his brother and sister. He regularly stumbled and fell. Maybe I was watching him too closely. I felt overwhelmed by the need to protect him, charmed and burdened by his innocence.

His hair was lighter and curlier than the others'. He was the only one with blue eyes. He was the only one who took after me. I was fair and easily damaged, vulnerable to good weather and bad, unlike Kathy. I liked to call her the dark angel of our household, a reference she never seemed to think amusing. By the time she got back from the swimming lessons and could take care of Peter, the mortar had turned to rock in the bucket and I had to mix another batch.

That night we went to the Neighborhood Solidarity Meeting at a home across the street and down the block. Burt and Georgia's Rustic Manor, we liked to call the place, because of the yellow aluminum siding and the metal awnings. We never socialized with Burt and Georgia, but it was impossible to live on the same block and know them only casually.

In warm weather, they sat on their front porch and argued late into the night, mostly about his stinginess and her infidelities. More than once, they had to be restrained by police. Evidently this wasn't just a summer pastime. One winter night she reported him missing after a nasty flare-up. Police found him at the corner tot lot, passed out in a snowbank.

Kathy wasn't quite ready when Jennifer the baby-sitter arrived, so I introduced her to the children, took her through the house, and explained our rules and regulations.

"We don't mind if you have company," I said, "just so long as you only have one person."

"Thanks, but I brought a book," Jennifer said.

I thought that was a reassuring sign until I saw the cover. I recognized it as a notoriously lurid novel.

"Your parents know you're reading that?"

"Sure," she said, "we're reading it for English lit."

"If they'd caught me with that book in English class, I would have gotten kicked out of school."

She smiled, almost seductively, I thought, flipping her long, glossy reddish hair over her shoulder. She wore no lipstick, but her eyes were shadowed with a glittery cobalt blue. Watching her as we walked through the house, I could tell, despite her baggy blouse and skirt, that she was mature for her age.

By the time we got to Georgia and Burt's, the house was already filled with our neighbors. Most of them we knew only by sight. A woman our age came rushing over and asked if we were the Maxwells, a new family on the block. Kathy told her no, and the woman said, "Thank God. I'm so relieved. You look like such reasonable people."

She introduced herself as Marybeth Kemper, the mother of Gracia Kemper, then told us about the Maxwells. "Their daughter, Melissa, stops by for our Gracia every morning on the way to school. They're in the third grade together, and the stories Melissa tells about life in her house you just wouldn't believe.

"The other morning she mentioned that her father had moved out, and her mother's new boyfriend had moved in. She was very unemotional about it. She was almost boasting. That's why I was sure you weren't the Maxwells. You're here together. You seem so normal."

"From everything I hear and read," Kathy said, "that may be debatable."

I left Kathy to convince Marybeth about our normality, or lack of it, and made my way over to the dining room table. I helped myself to tortilla chips, guacamole, and a glass of punch, then squeezed over into a corner, trying to avoid the heavy traffic.

"You look like you've got a healthy prostate."

The man had come up beside me, but he was maybe a head shorter so I hadn't noticed him there, staring up at me with what appeared to be a bad case of prostate envy.

"I don't know," I said, "I haven't checked lately."

"Mine's twice the normal size," he said. "The doctor doesn't think it's anything serious, but I don't trust him. He's treating it with drugs, but I'm afraid he's going to want to operate. It's murder just taking a simple piss, I'll tell you. You aren't having any trouble pissing, are you, any burning or dripping or cramps?"

"I'll let you know," I said, finishing my punch and heading off for the bathroom. When I came out, I pushed my way through the crowd toward Kathy. She and Georgia, our hostess, were talking, or listening, to a man who was making a point with vigorous and practiced gestures. So far as I could tell, he was the only man at the party wearing a tie, which made him look like an appliance salesman for Sears.

As I walked up, I saw Kathy give me a warning glance, but it was too late. "Oh, Scott," Georgia said, "I want you to meet Truman Reece. Truman is our special guest of honor tonight."

"Really," I said. "What's the occasion? Not your birthday?"

"No," Truman said, "I'm a candidate for alderman."

"Oh," I said, "we're so far out of things these days, we didn't even know there was an election."

"That's why we're here tonight. I was just telling Kathy about Operation Stronghold. That's my eight-point program to revitalize our community, to increase property values and bring down crime rates—"

He raised a finger, preparing to go down the list, but I was too quick for him. I backed into the crowd, leaving him there, so focused on his finger that he hadn't noticed I'd slipped out of his reach. I was en route to the punch bowl when I heard a familiar voice calling me. "Oh, Mr. Ryan. I'm so pleased that you could come to the solidarity meeting. I wanted to speak to you about your lights. They're on so late every night. They keep me awake."

"I'm really sorry to hear that, Mrs. Underwood, since I've been leaving them on for your benefit."

"For my benefit?"

"The brighter our house, the less likely you are to get eyestrain."

I left her to ponder that remark, made a refueling stop at the punch bowl, then edged up to a group of men who were aggressively discussing the criminal deficiencies of the Bears' quarterback.

I was half listening to their complaints when I felt a firm hand on my upper arm. The hand belonged to a man whose severe, rocklike face made him look as if he might have played for the Bears himself, twenty years earlier. His graying hair was short but athletically styled. He was about my size, only heavier. And his bearing was so militarily erect that he seemed to be at least a head taller.

"I thought I'd see you long before now," he said.

"Sorry I missed you," I said, "but I've been pretty busy working on the house and everything."

"You're not pulling your weight around here, you know."

He was smiling, but his attitude was plainly hostile. "In that case," I said, "I'd better refill my glass of punch." But when I started to move away, his grip on my arm only tightened.

"Look, I think you've got the wrong man," I said. I introduced myself.

"We've met. In your alley. Jerry Klammish."

"Oh, yeah," I said. "We have met. Neighborhood surveillance, right?" I smiled in recognition, but that failed to break the icy glare on his face. "I didn't recognize you out of uniform."

"I expected to hear from you long ago. I thought I made myself clear that night. The Neighborhood Solidarity Association is a voluntary organization, and we expect all able-bodied men to volunteer. You look able-bodied to me."

"I've had some prostate trouble," I said, "but otherwise I guess I'm okay. It's just that we've been so busy."

"Too busy to patrol your own alley," he said. It was an accusation, not a question, and the bellicose indignation in his voice had started to attract spectators. He let go of me and took the arm of a man standing silently beside him, but much more gently.

"You probably don't recognize Ed Burnett either, do you."

Again, this was not a question. I studied Ed for a second, just to be sure we hadn't met. He was small, sad, almost a nebbish. Not somebody I'd be likely to remember—or even notice—if Klammish hadn't been dragging him toward me.

"Why don't you introduce yourself to Scott?" Klammish said, pulling Ed closer, as if we were two boxers, about to touch gloves and come out swinging. Ed smiled nervously, sternly, and ignored my tentatively extended hand.

"Some neighbor you are," he said. "Why didn't you help my daughter Friday night?"

"Your daughter?" I said.

"You must have heard her screaming."

"Screaming about what?"

"She was nearly raped behind your garage, and you didn't lift a finger to help her."

"I didn't hear—"

"Did you all hear Ed?" Klammish was directly addressing the crowd now. "His daughter was raped behind our neighbor here's garage, and he didn't lift a finger to help."

I started to protest that I hadn't heard a thing, that I would have helped if I'd known, that I— But it was clearly no use. I had already been accused, tried, and found guilty. As I backed away, the circle closed around Jerry and Ed, who were too intent on maligning me to notice I was making a getaway. At least now I knew who it was the neighbors were solidified against.

I went to look for Kathy. She was caught in the middle of a mob herself, the one surrounding Truman Reece. He had four fingers raised now and was loudly telling everyone what was wrong with the neighborhood and how he planned to fix it.

Kathy saw me signaling but made no effort to leave. I worked my way through the crowd, took her arm, and began to shuffle her off to the door.

"It's time to go," I said when I felt her resisting.

"But we just got here," she said. "We can't go now."

"We can, and we better," I said, figuring I would explain later.

We were almost to the door when Truman Reece caught up with us. "You're not leaving already?" he said. "I wanted you to know where I stand on—"

"I don't know how you can stand on anything," I said. "You're running too hard."

"Seriously," he said, "I hope I can count on your vote."

"It's a little too early for me to commit myself."

"Well, I'm sure when you've had time to compare my record with my opponent's you won't have any trouble deciding. He's under indictment for tax evasion."

Walking home, Kathy was so upset with me, assuming that I'd made too many trips to the punch bowl, that I couldn't make her understand the reason for our sudden departure. "Nothing justifies being that rude," she said.

"Rude is nothing compared to what might have happened if we had stayed. I think they were getting ready to lynch me."

"You could have tried to be diplomatic."

"I really resent being invited over there under false pretenses . . . to meet some petty grafter."

"He hasn't even been elected yet."

"Just the fact that he's running for office is proof of criminal tendencies."

When we got back, Kathy went directly upstairs to bed, leaving me to pay Jennifer and get her home. She had fallen asleep on a bed in a small room we had set aside for guests. She looked like a Renaissance angel, with her lustrous hair spreading around her serene and glowing face. The book was open on the floor, where it had fallen when she had gone to sleep. I picked it up and read several passages in amazement.

I started to wake her, then noticed that her skirt had slipped up around her waist. I was about to smooth it down over her legs, but I hesitated when I saw how tan and firm and smooth they were. I decided not to wake her. I unsnapped her skirt and carefully slid it off, letting it drop to the floor. I took off her blouse and underthings, removed my own clothes, and crawled into the bed beside her.

10

I had to protect Kathy. She still didn't realize how precarious our situation had become. She still hadn't noticed that the crevices reappeared in the plaster almost as soon as we patched the walls, that the paint seemed to bubble and flake as soon as it dried. No sooner did I replace a gasket than the faucet was dripping again. The newly glazed windowpanes rattled in their frames with the slightest breeze. The whole house constantly trembled and quivered.

If Kathy was aware of any of this, she didn't let on to me. But I could plainly see the effects of stress on her. It showed in the isolated gray hairs that stood out like high-tension wires, in the lines that were like porcelain cracks around her eyes and mouth. I had to protect her from the knowledge that everything we did was temporary. We needed her stability to preserve the hazardous balance, so the house wouldn't go teetering over the edge.

And so I said nothing about all these little calamities. I would quietly, secretly take care of them myself, whenever I got the chance, when she was sleeping or shopping or chauffeuring the kids around. But there were some things I couldn't protect her from, and one warm Saturday afternoon she came home in a state of indignation and disbelief. Kim was even more upset, her eyes red, her cheeks flush from tears.

Mary Agnes and Roy were having a yard sale across the street, and they had invited the neighbors to bring over their unwanted and unused and useless possessions. They would sell them, for a fifty-fifty split. That seemed high to me, a double scam, one that was typical of Mary Agnes and Roy. But Kathy wanted to get rid of some gifts that had been excess baggage since the day we were married.

"It doesn't matter how much we get for them," she said. "It's all profit."

"Okay, just so you don't leave anything to identify them as ours. I don't want our neighbors knowing too much about our private lives."

"They're not going to learn anything from three silver chafing dishes and two fondue pots."

"Whatever you do," I said, "don't bring anything else home with you, please."

"Oh, right," she said. "With all these tools everywhere, we could open our own hardware store."

"I never buy anything we don't need."

"I don't see why we need three circular saws. Or half a dozen drills. But we could use some kitchen chairs. We could use almost any kind of furniture, just to make the house seem a little more lived-in."

"Furniture, okay, but no Salvation Army rejects."

"You go yourself then," she said, annoyed, "if you don't trust me."

"I don't like house sales. It's just like picking through other people's musty closets. They make me feel like a peeper."

When she came back, Kathy was furious. She found me in the basement, where I had been using an auger to clean out the trap beneath our clogged laundry sink.

"You've got to go over there and see for yourself," she said, "right now. You just won't believe it."

I had shut off the water main before I opened the trap, so I couldn't wash my hands and arms. I used an old towel to wipe off the slimy lint and sludge as best I could.

Then I went across to Mary Agnes and Roy's with Kim. Kathy was afraid that she might lose control and make a scene if she went back with us.

Their yard looked like the parking lot of a discount store during a bankruptcy sale. From the front porch to the parkway, it was crammed with lawn mowers, rowing machines, boxes of games, books, and linens, lawn chairs, racks of clothes, stereos, sofas, tables loaded with mugs, shot glasses, plates, vases, and other carnival debris, all of it being forked and grappled over by a multitude of bargain hunters, whose parked and double-parked cars, vans, and pickups had turned our street into a bedlam of snarling horns, dueling bumpers, and shouted threats and curses.

A lot of the merchandise, like our chafing dishes and fondue pots, which I spotted on a deacon's bench with other kitchenware, was new and in boxes. Under other circumstances, I might have assumed that these were unwanted gifts that the owners had no more use for than we had. But not now.

Kim and I went straight for the bicycles. There were at least a dozen of them, side by side, of all models and sizes. "This is it, Daddy; it's got red fenders now, but I know it was mine. Look, here's my butterfly sticker."

Except for the red fenders and the missing chain guard and plastic wicker basket, it looked like her bike to me, too. Now I was sorry that we hadn't bothered to register the serial number with the police. The bike had been altered just enough so we had no way of being certain—or of proving—that it was Kim's.

"I think those are my fenders on that bike over there," she said.

"Don't say anything just yet," I told Kim. "We have to make sure it's yours."

"But I am sure, Daddy."

We found Roy on the front porch, where he had set up a cash box on a card table. He was negotiating with a large and stubborn woman, who insisted that he lower the price on a humidifier because one of the knobs was missing.

"I'll take off a quarter is all," he said. "That's what it costs at any appliance store. If you don't want it, put it back where you got it."

Roy stood up to his full height, which still brought his eyes barely level with her chin. Even though he was outweighed and undersized, he leaned toward her menacingly, as if he might bull her to the ground at any moment.

While we waited, he finally agreed to deduct fifty cents from the price, and the woman rolled the humidifier down the driveway to her car. "You got to watch people every second," he said, as we walked over to the bicycles. "They'll lie, cheat, scheme, steal, even kill to save a miserable quarter."

"This is the one," I said, patting the seat of Kim's bicycle.

"Oh, what sharp eyes you have," he said. "You know a good bike when you see one, all right. That's the best one we got."

"I know," I said, glancing at Kim. "You don't remember where you got it, do you?"

"Oh, sure, I bought that new at the bike shop for Darlene, when she was about your daughter's age. Hardly got a chance to ride it before she outgrew it. Still almost new. But she's real attached to it, and it's gonna break her heart when we sell it. But if you're interested, I could knock a couple of bucks off because that way it'd still be in the neighborhood and Darlene wouldn't take it so hard."

"Well, Kim does seem to like it, but the fenders aren't quite right." I paused, somewhat ominously I thought. "She likes the fenders on that one over there better."

He didn't shudder, flinch, or blink. "If that's all that's standing in the way of a deal, no problem at all," he said, then shouted, "Darryl! Howard!"

In a moment his sons had appeared at his side. No more than a year or an inch apart, they were teenage versions of their father, shorter than he was but squatter, not chips but solid chunks off the old block. To his Tweedledee, they looked like Tweedledum and Tweedledumber.

Roy had only to grunt a few times than they were at work, stripping the fenders off the bikes and switching them. "Those boys can do anything mechanical," he said. "You need something done around the house, they do quality work. Move furniture, rip out old plumbing, 'bout anything. Real entrepreneurs, those two. You need any tools, they can get 'em for you cheap, less than wholesale. Pick up a lot of nice things down at the Zulu market. Might not come with warranties or in new boxes, but it's first-rate merchandise, real bargains."

In less than three minutes, his sons had finished and wheeled the modified bike over to us. Now there was no mistake. It was Kim's, but I had no way of proving that. And I doubted that Roy or Darryl or Howard would take my word for it.

I counted out seventeen dollars, three less than the sticker price on the bike, and handed it to him. He recounted the money, too carefully, I thought, then nodded toward Darryl and Howard, who were hovering nearby. "Wouldn't hurt to give them a few dollars for their trouble. Odd jobs is what keeps 'em in pizza and movies—off the streets."

As we started to leave he added, "Have a look around. Your money's well spent here. We donate a percentage of everything to the Neighborhood Solidarity Association, so it's like making a contribution to the community."

I did have a look around before we left. Besides the stuff we'd donated to the sale, I saw some we hadn't: a garden hose, a weed eater, and a leaf blower that, like Kim's bike, had vanished from our yard.

One way or another, Kim seemed happy to get the bike back. Kathy was happy, too, until she found out that I'd had to pay for it. "There was no way I could prove anything," I said. "They're running a chop shop for bikes over there. It's a family fencing operation."

"No wonder they asked the neighbors for all their old stuff," she said.

"Yeah," I said, "that way nobody gets suspicious because they have more merchandise than a Wal-Mart."

"With any luck," Kathy said, "they'll make so much off their house sales they'll be able to move to a better neighborhood."

"In the meantime," I said, "we'd better make sure they don't take everything we own with them."

I let the clogged sink go. That meant I couldn't turn the water back on until the next day. But by then I'd marked almost all of our possessions with an etching pen, beginning with Kim's bicycle.

11

The traps weren't working. From all the peculiar noises we heard in the attic, it sounded as if the squirrels were using them for a jungle gym. I was ready to call the exterminator and tell him to take them away. Then one gray Saturday afternoon we had a strike.

It had rained earlier in the day. The squirrels were playing indoors, but I was outside working on the back porch, which I'd had to rebuild after the old one rotted away and collapsed, nearly killing the meter reader. I was brushing water seal on the raw wood when Kathy came out, so agitated I was afraid that some fresh disaster had struck one of the children.

"You should hear what's going on in the attic now," she said. I went inside to listen. It was difficult to hear anything for all the squealing, from the squirrels above and the children below. When I got the children quieted down, I could make out a dragging noise and a series of thumps in the hollow space overhead. There was no telling what perverted uses the squirrels were putting those traps to now.

By the time I got into the attic with a flashlight, the squirrels had run for cover. All, that is, except for the one miserably unhappy creature that was pulling a trap across the joists by its tail. That explained the noises. The gate to the trap had evidently closed on its tail, forcing the squirrel to drag it along like a shackle. The sight of me with the flashlight caused it to go running around the attic even more frantically, with the trap bouncing and bumping behind it.

The squirrel quickly exhausted itself. With the trap preventing its escape, there was nothing for it to do as I approached but huddle desperately in a corner, quivering in terror, shrieking with indignation and outrage. I wouldn't say the trap had worked the way it was supposed to, but it had done the job.

I couldn't help but feel a shudder of sympathy for the frightened and pathetic animal. Then it snapped at me as I bent over to pick it up. Leaping back, I slipped off the joist and my boot sank into the brittle lathing and plaster of the third-floor ceiling.

I managed to reach around and grab the trap. Regaining my footing, I lifted the trap high and outward so the dangling, twisting squirrel couldn't bite me, which it repeatedly tried to do as I carried it downstairs.

The children fled in panic at the sight of the squirrel. I expected them to be as elated as I was just to have trapped one. But I couldn't blame them for running off. It was obviously a mad and verminous animal. Even at arm's length I could smell its rancid, ratty fur and breath. I could tell how hungry its sharp yellow incisors were for a piece of my flesh.

"What are you going to do with it?" Kathy said, watching in alarm herself from behind a bedroom door.

"I hoped you could tell me," I said. "I don't think I can get it out to the woods like this."

"Just get it outside. I'm afraid it's going to get loose in here, and then we'll never get rid of it. It'll wreck the house."

"Right now I'm more worried about it wrecking me."

She followed at a cautious distance as I carried it downstairs and through the hallway.

"No," she said, "out the back way. It'll ruin the new rug. It's shitting and pissing everywhere."

"Everywhere is right," I said. My clothes were slippery and wet, not just from the heat and sweat of the struggle.

Coming out onto the back porch, I was afraid I was about to lose it. My arm was tired, and the squirrel seemed to be wriggling free of the trap. I couldn't afford to let it get away after I'd gotten this far. I saw the five-gallon bucket of wood preservative at the bottom of the porch stairs. I held the squirrel over the bucket and let it drop, with the trap still attached.

The cold and sticky preservative seemed to stun the squirrel. The trap served as an anchor. But by the time I'd found the lid, it was fighting to get out of the bucket. I used the lid as a shield and forced the snapping squirrel's head below the murky surface and held it closed.

The bucket shook and rattled for a few minutes. Gradually it stopped. Then I made sure the lid was tight and carried the bucket out to the car. I drove out to a desolate industrial area and parked on a bridge. There I dumped everything—squirrel, trap, and preservative—into the murky river.

I started going to the sports club again after getting a memo that said the company would pay half my dues as part of its executive fitness program. I was still working on the house half the night and worrying about all the work that needed to be done the other half, so I rarely felt the urge to exercise. I didn't need to lose any more weight either, though I doubt that I would have passed any fitness exams.

It often required great effort just to get over to the club three days a week at noon. But it seemed like a good idea if I expected to enjoy my other executive benefits, particularly my salary. Attendance was taken, and time sheets were filled out, logging the hours we spent on the tennis courts, the running track, and the exercise machines. These, I'd heard, went by computer directly to Kinkaid and were an important factor in our bimonthly performance evaluations.

Some days all I could do was go to the club and sit on a bench against the wall, while the runners circled the track, sweating aggressively and grimacing in pain. Just watching this sodden marathon, this blurred carousel of agony and suffering, gave me a physical and mental lift. I felt healthier just knowing that I wasn't afflicting needless abuse on my own body.

It was even more invigorating to watch the young women on the track. For most, the hours they'd devoted to conditioning their bodies hadn't been wasted. As their lithe and rippling figures went by, sultry from perspiration, I seemed to be witnessing the finals of a Miss Nautilus Pageant.

After a while I found even this was exhausting. I couldn't help but be overwhelmed by all the passing beauty, by the tormenting thought of all the rampant, promiscuous but elusive beauty in the world.

When the spectacle got to be too much for me, I would lay down on a slant board to rest. That was the position I was in one noon hour when I felt a jabbing pain in my hip. In my semicomatose state, I thought I was having a kidney attack.

The pain became more insistent. I opened my eyes to find the rubber toe of a running shoe doing a tap dance against my hip, a little harder than necessary. From somewhere above, I heard: "Are you okay? You're not sick or dying or anything, are you?"

Looking up, I saw that the impatient toe and the anxious voice belonged to a woman I'd frequently watched on the track and the exercise machines. I'd been afraid she was going to notice and get the idea I was leering at her. Her body was seductive enough, trim and firm and curved in all the right places, and I certainly was leering.

But it was her nose that I found so appealing. Without any help from calisthenics or isometrics, it had attained a perfect shape: thin and gently tilted upward, delicately planed and arched, a distinct object of desire. It was almost a ski nose, but not quite. It was too graceful and sensuous, too erotic.

Even upside down, it—and she—looked lovely, with her face flush and swollen from exertion, her precious nostrils distended. That's how I saw her, lying there on the slant board, her running shoe still digging against my ribs. She bent over me then and said, "You are okay, aren't you?"

I sat up, almost colliding with that voluptuous nose, and grinned with embarrassment and lust. "Just a little tired is all."

"You probably did too many laps," she said. "You have to pace yourself."

"Yeah, I do have a tendency to get carried away."

"Well, that's too bad," she said, finally allowing herself a faint smile. "I thought for a minute there that I might get to try out my CPR."

"In that case," I said, dropping back against the mat, "go right ahead. Don't let the fact that I'm a perfect physical specimen stop you."

Her smile faded. "If you're through with the board, I would like to use it. I really do need to work on my abdominals."

I scooted away until I had backed against a post. I sat there, resting, and watched as she began to do half sit-ups, with her arms folded against her chest.

"Wouldn't it be better if you came all the way up?" I asked.

"No," she huffed, more annoyed than winded, "these are better. They don't hurt my back."

"Maybe that's why I have this back pain," I said. "I should try doing sit-ups your way. But they look so . . . feminine."

"Do you mind," she said, stopping in the up position, breathing deeply, dramatically. "I really can't talk while I do these. And you're not doing your own body any good, just sitting there like that."

"That's one of my problems. I can't bear to work out by myself. I just get bored and lonely and extremely depressed . . ."

"I could tell."

"Oh," I said, "how?"

"I've seen you working out. You're always frowning."

"Yeah," I said, "but don't be deceived by surface appearances. That's not the real me. I'm normally a happy, exuberant, upbeat person."

"You really should try not to frown so much," she said. "It causes premature wrinkling. And when you let yourself go, you really do have a very nice smile."

She resumed her sit-ups. "I promise to smile a lot more if you'll run with me," I said, then smiled broadly for her as she reached the top of a sit-up.

"I'm not a therapist, okay," she said. "But it's a free track. You can run with me if you want. But I just wish you'd shut the fuck up. It screws up my rhythm."

We had been running together for no more than a minute when she began to talk. In short but random order, I learned her name was Susan, never Sue or Susie, that she had grown up in a suburb, was over thirty, worked as an assistant art director for an ad agency. She was about to get a divorce from a bond salesman. She was also getting rid of the twenty-five pounds she'd gained after they separated. She nearly had to quit the club when she fainted in the locker room and had an out-of-body experience. She wasn't pregnant, just undernourished from crash dieting. She was a Capricorn. After all her soon-to-be ex-husband's escapades, she was very down on men, but not permanently, she hoped. She was seeing a therapist about that.

Once I'd given her my name, occupation, and astrological sign, she didn't seem to want to know anything else about me. So I mostly listened and didn't volunteer any of the pertinent information about my weight, waist size, blood pressure, cholesterol level, or my wife and children.

We stopped to cool down for a minute or so, then hit the track again. If I kept up at this rate, I thought, Kinkaid might give me a vice presidency. Either that, or Susan would get a chance to try out her CPR. I was looking for a way to drop out of this marathon before I dropped over when I heard what sounded like a fire alarm, shrilly broadcast over the club intercom. Nobody seemed to panic, but the other runners slowly, obediently left the track and started straggling toward the exits.

"Shit," said Susan, who had stopped circling the track but was still running in place. "I'm not even halfway through my workout."

I had come to a dead stop beside her, winded and grateful for the interruption, for whatever reason. "Hadn't we better get the hell out of here?" I said, starting to move for the exit myself. "That sounded like a fire alarm. The place may be burning down around us."

"Nothing to worry about," she said. "The club is just testing the security system. They've had to do it regularly since the locker room attendants walked off the job. They threatened to blow up the club when the owners hired boat people to take their place. I just wish they'd hurry up and settle, but not if it means an increase in dues. They're way too high already."

"Right now," I said, "we seem to have the whole club to ourselves."

"We can't stay here," she said. "The security guards will find us, and we'll have to evacuate like everybody else. Come on."

I followed as she jogged out of the gym and up a flight of stairs, away from the entrance. "What I usually do when this happens is hide out in a tanning booth until the drill is over. But it looks like I'm stuck with you, and there's no room for two of us in there."

"I'd be willing to try," I said, but by then she had stopped in front of the sauna. She opened the door, and I followed her inside, closing it behind us.

"I don't like to come in here," she said. "It makes my hair frizzy." She removed her headband, shaking her hair and letting it fall across her shoulders. Through the steam, I could see light streaks among the dark spirals.

"Maybe I can help," I said. Cautiously, I reached over and touched her hair. She didn't try to stop me. I began to smooth it down. "It feels soft, silky."

I let my hand move across her cheek. It was slick and satiny with sweat, which made the freckles stand out like tiny bronze medals. I was sweating passionately myself. In the damp and infernal heat, I felt as if my workout suit were made of melted lead. "Aren't you supposed to strip before you go into a sauna?" I said.

She didn't resist as I slowly unzipped her sweatjacket. Her misty blue eyes were alarmingly impassive. She started to help when I lifted her camisole over her head. I kissed her shoulders, her breasts. I could taste body lotion and sweat. "Oh, baby," she said. That was all I wanted to hear. Her voice was a sensual lullaby in my ear. "Baby, baby."

I was about to kiss the tip of her nose when she turned away. I kissed her cheek, her chin, her mouth, I kissed her everywhere else, but not now, not once in the months ahead, would she ever let me kiss her directly, frontally on the nose.

12

By now I had developed a strategy for riding the train. It was a variation on the one that always seemed to work so well when walking through dangerous neighborhoods. Eyes straight ahead. Don't look left or right. Don't look anybody directly in the eye, man or woman. Don't even look at them. It's an invitation to trouble or much worse.

Coming onto the platform, I had the newspaper neatly folded in one hand, so I could read—or appear to be reading—as I walked. By developing an acute peripheral vision, I could navigate stairways, narrow walkways, and other hazardous passages with my eyes on the paper. I could slalom around waiting passengers, sidle onto a train, and find a seat without once looking up from the column of type.

I headed for the end of the platform, as far away as I could from where most of the other commuters congregated. As I dodged and weaved through the crowd, I spotted Don Nugent standing against a post and made a wide detour around him. Don was easy enough to take on the run, at a school potluck or in the aisles of the hardware store, but not on a crowded commuter train. Don was a lawyer. Whenever possible, I left him to his time sheets.

From the edge of my vision, I could see Don's eyes flicker in my direction, then fall back to his newspaper. He didn't want to share a seat with me any more than I wanted to share one with him. No offense, but it spared us both a long, painfully awkward ride downtown. He would rather leave me to my marketing reports.

In my haste to avoid Don, my trajectory took me directly into the path of Jim McFettridge, an ex–tennis partner of mine, who was leaning on a crutch while he read his newspaper. I swerved but not in time. Jim looked up. "Hi, Smash," he said with a predatory grin. "Hi, Ace," I said, smiling feebly.

Jim always called me Smash. Everybody called him Ace, not because he had a particularly good serve or because he was much of a tennis player. He was Ace because he was always wrapped in an Ace bandage, around an ankle or an elbow, an arm or a leg, sometimes all at once.

With all his bandages, he looked like a movie mummy, usually limping, dragging one leg, as a result of some injury he'd suffered on some court or playing field somewhere. Even unwrapped, he had a marked resemblance to other horror movie creatures. He was as bent and contorted as Igor, as misshapen as Quasimodo.

Ace always welcomed company on the train. He was a commodities broker. Getting stuck on a train with Ace could be not only hazardous and tortuous but expensive. Under extreme duress, I had let him talk me into buying a soy meal option, and I couldn't afford any more.

Using his crutch for support, Ace lunged toward me and drove his fist into my midsection, with just a little too much force to be entirely playful. "What happened to your inner tube?" he said. "You've been working out."

"Mostly all that hard labor at home," I said, defensively. "But I have been playing tennis and exercising at the club."

"God, do I envy you," Ace said. His own rigorous efforts to stay in shape were legendary in the neighborhood. Not that they did him any good. Besides being badly stooped, he had lost most of his hair, giving him the flush, straggly look of a hyperactive and slightly demented grandfather.

"I twisted my knee playing one-on-one with Melanie," he said. "I swear the aggressive little bugger kicked me deliberately."

I understood that Melanie was one of Ace's daughters, but I wasn't sure which. He had two from his first marriage and two from his second. He called them the first and second teams, and rightly so.

Though humiliated by his inability to produce sons, Ace made certain that his daughters excelled not as Girl Scouts but as jocks: basketball, softball, tennis, volleyball, soccer, racquetball, badminton, quoits—it didn't matter. Ace wasn't happy just being the head coach, athletic director, equipment manager, and trainer. He had to get some of the action himself. Judging from all of his tears, strains, pulls, cracks, and breaks, his daughters were using Ace to get rid of a lot of their hostilities.

When the train arrived in the station, I had no choice except to give Ace a hand as he hobbled onto a car. I'd hoped that it would be too crowded for us to sit together. No luck. After Ace got his crutch put away and settled down, I slid next to him. He reeked of mentholated sports cream.

Even before the train left the station, Ace was off and running, first with a play by play on the hoop game that had left him crippled, then with a report on the damage to his knee. Stuck on the aisle seat, I couldn't even pacify myself by staring out the window into the morning smog. All I could do was nod dumbly, as if my head were being dribbled in time to Ace's bruising soliloquy.

"Not to worry," he assured me. "The Ace won't be out of action much longer. I can't wait to get back on the court with that little fucker. I'll break both her knees."

Well, I assured myself, this is still better than having to listen to a presentation on garbanzo futures. The steady hammering of steel against steel, of the train's wheels hitting the track, made it nearly impossible for me to hear Ace anyway.

Even if he'd been telling me a gripping and scandalous story, I wouldn't have been able to concentrate for long. I was too worried about Kathy, whose behavior had become increasingly bizarre, even suspicious. For the last couple of months, she had been taking a ceramics class at night. I couldn't help being skeptical and irritated. Why now—when she already had so much to keep herself occupied around the house?

She insisted that she needed a means of self-expression and spiritual fulfillment, that for her sanity and ours she needed to get away one night a week. I gave my uneasy blessing. There wasn't much else I could do, since all she had to do—and did—was remind me that I was gone one night a week myself, playing tennis.

I didn't feel any more comfortable about it when she started bringing home the ceramics she'd done in class. I had to admire her industry. She was obsessive about working, and our house soon looked like a crafts museum or a pottery outlet.

Except the work seemed too abstract to have any practical value as either pottery or art—spiraled, calcareous objects, pearly mollusks, each one pinker and more labial than the other. Each one made with odd little clefts and recesses, chambers and declivities, but nothing that would hold any water or plants.

When Kathy pushed me for an opinion, I told her they were interesting. "Try again," she said.

"Okay, they're very interesting."

"I won't be pacified or stroked," she said. "I'm not looking for charity. Just blunt, honest, constructive criticism."

I told her I thought they were delicate and soulful but that she seemed to be hung up on a single color and motif.

"Do you think they're at all sensual?"

"Yes, that's the word I wanted: sensual."

"Do you think they're too sensual?"

I was beginning to get edgy about her line of questioning. It was veering into cross-examination. Also, I was trying to fix a broken living room window, and she kept distracting me.

"Not necessarily," I said. "It's just that I've never been wild about pink."

"Would you like them better if they were long and smooth and cylindrical?"

I was delicately trying to tap a pushpoint into the window frame, afraid I might crack the new pane. "Not if they were pink."

"You don't feel threatened by them, do you?"

I stopped tapping and tried not to show my impatience and irritation. "Look, I feel threatened by whoever it was that threw a brick through our window last night. If you keep this up, I'll break this new window too. Can't we talk about this later?"

We didn't talk about it later, but I thought a lot about it, especially the nights I couldn't sleep, when I'd lie in bed listening to the sounds in the attic. When the traps failed to work, I'd bought an ultrasonic pest repeller that emitted low-frequency beeps, supposedly inaudible to human ears but death on squirrels, not to mention rats, mice, bats, and fleas.

But I could plainly hear the beeping, night after night. And the squirrels seemed to be soothed by the noise, as if it were chamber music, an aural aphrodisiac. Between beeps, I could hear them purring and crooning, an atonal sing-along.

My problem with Kathy only made it worse. It wasn't just that the work she brought home was bewildering, even disturbing. She had started going out for coffee after class. She never said with whom, and I didn't ask. One night she came home much later than usual, smelling of wine. I knew her teacher was a man, and male ceramics teachers were notorious for not being able to keep their hands on their mugs and goblets.

For whatever reason, Kathy always seemed slightly distant and much less affectionate now. "I'm exhausted," she said. "There's too much going on. You should understand." I could understand, but that did not make it any better.

Between worrying about Kathy and listening to Ace, while the train rocked and clattered along, I quickly grew nauseous and dizzy. I felt as if I were riding a roller coaster. By the time the train came into the downtown station, I was bodily and mentally whiplashed.

"I'm late for a meeting, Ace," I said, springing from my seat and heading for the door, before the train had stopped. I had to make my escape, or else I'd end up playing paramedic to Ace. He was the jock; he was still agile despite the crutch and the bandages. He could manage for himself.

I decided not to take the shuttle bus. I wasn't nearly ready for the office, even if I was already late. I needed to decompress, limber up my body and brain. Never mind the cold drizzle. Never mind the congestion—not just the other commuters but the members of the misery brigade, the street beggars, the homeless, who were stationed along each block like hot dog or pretzel vendors, as if they had been licensed by the city, given franchises for their two square feet of sidewalk.

They were easy enough to avoid, although it required some artful and experienced dodging. Eyes forward. Don't look at them. Pretend they're parking meters or alarm boxes or lightpoles.

But that wasn't always possible. I was halfway to my building, eyes on the pavement as I stepped around the puddles and slick spots, when I found a pair of boat shoes blocking my path. Looking up, I saw they belonged to a man approximately my age. The rest of his outfit consisted of what looked like my own weekend uniform: stylish but weathered corduroy pants, a navy mountain parka, and an Irish tweed rain hat, pulled low over a gaunt but genial face.

I circled around him, mumbling an apology, but he swiveled along with me, smiling broadly now. "It is you," he said. "For a second there, I thought you were somebody else. You look different somehow. Not any older or anything, just different. Great, actually."

He did seem familiar, but I couldn't quite get a fix on him. Maybe somebody I'd met at a business lunch. Or at the club. Maybe even a refugee from my office, another casualty of the merger, one of the vocationally relocated, the corporately disenfranchised.

"Yeah, well," I said, knowing that I didn't look good, much less great. "I try to hang in there."

"Your family's okay?"

"Yeah," I said, a little startled. "Yours?"

Beneath the brim of his hat, his face turned grim. "Not so good," he said, "since the fire."

"Oh," I said, "the fire." He raised his head, momentarily

lifting it out of the shadows. I could see that his jaw was damp and grainy, as if it had been sprinkled with salt.

"That's why I'm wearing these gloves." He started to remove one. Seeing the red and corrugated scar tissue, I put my hand on his wrist to stop him.

"Then there was the accident . . . on the playground. When trouble comes, it seems like it always comes by the truckload."

"I'm really sorry . . ."

"I don't want your sympathy," he said curtly. "Sympathy won't help with the hospital bills or the damage to the house."

His friendly eyes had turned angry and unforgiving. Then I realized I was in a spot of trouble. I'd let him get inside my defenses. He was probing, manipulating, exploiting the weakness in my heart.

I sighed, loud enough so that he couldn't miss the annoyance and regret, then pushed a dollar at him. He regarded it as if it were a summons, which he summarily refused to accept.

"I don't want your charity," he said, looking genuinely offended. "I don't want your two-bit philanthropy."

"Okay," I said, impatient to end his streetcorner charade and get to work. "What do you want?"

"A loan, not a handout."

I was desperate to get to work now, even more desperate to get away from him. It was worth the five-dollar bill I handed over. "Buy yourself a meal, a bottle, anything. I can't stand around here all day."

He took the five but regarded it—and me—with even more contempt. "I'm sorry," he said, "but I won't accept less than one hundred dollars. You must make that much an hour."

The demand was too absurd to disregard. So I hesitated, waiting to hear how far he would carry his arrogant panhandling, his extortion, knowing I wasn't in any danger of being mugged on this busy streetcorner.

"Isn't it worth that much," he said, "to be sure that your wife and children are safe from harm?"

Now I was angry. "You don't know me. You don't even know if I have a wife and family."

"I know," he said.

I looked around then, hoping that I'd see a traffic cop. When I turned back, he was gone and so was my five dollars.

13

I had it all together now—but not quite under control. I had the product analyses. I had the printouts of lab tests. I had the consumer acceptance surveys. Science and technology, flesh and blood. But for now, those were just the raw materials, perilously stacked on my desk. We still had the focus groups and mall intercepts ahead, months of toil and trouble.

I'd been trying to find the strength all week to start refining and packaging these early results. I still had to digest and process everything, put it into concise and plain and logical English, with headlines and graphics and charts, then send it along to Masterson. After he got through redigesting and re-processing it, copies of the preliminary report would be distributed to the president of Inglewood Fur Company, then onward and upward to Kinkaid, CEO of Capisco Unlimited, which owned Inglewood, and finally to whatever ad agency got the account for FurReal.

That was the new product that I'd spent the last six months developing, getting ready for boutiques and shopping malls and upscale discount stores across the country. FurReal was a blend of genuine and synthetic fur that was going to expand and revolutionize the market. Like polyester woven with cotton or wool, it was cheaper to produce and a lot more durable, which put it within reach of Ms. Middle America. Stylish, affordable, wrinkle-free fur. Water-repellent. Maybe even bulletproof. And unless you put it under a microscope, it was indistinguishable from the real thing.

That made it a natural not just for inexpensive fur coats and stoles and muffs but for ski parkas, boots, vests, helmets, comforters, upholstery, hunting and combat jackets, ponchos, and endless other products.

It would also help disarm the militant environmentalists. As I passed a fur salon on my way to work, they were out in force, blocking the sidewalk, waving their bloody placards, and passing out leaflets with graphic pictures of slaughtered seals, beavers, rabbits, nutrias, minks, opossums, and raccoons.

With so many deterrents and distractions, I was having trouble psyching myself up enough to work on the FurReal report. It didn't help that I was running so late. As soon as I came into our reception area, Sandy said that Masterson had asked to see me.

"Oh? What time?"

"It must've been twenty minutes ago, at least," she said, returning to the newspaper crossword.

"Not what time he asked to see me. What time does he want to see me?"

"He didn't say."

"You didn't ask?"

"I just assumed that if he wanted me to know, he would have told me."

"Okay," I said, "I suppose it isn't urgent."

"He did say it was urgent."

I had one cup of coffee and was halfway through another when Masterson walked in, which meant that it must have been extremely urgent. Nowadays he usually saw people by appointment only, after sending them summonses to report to his office, then making them wait outside for a minimum of a half hour.

"How are we proceeding with FurReal?" he said, without any of his customary overtures.

"There's still a lot to be done. But I'll have a preliminary report for you Friday, right on target."

He seemed both appeased and contrite. "Yeah, it's just that Kinkaid is so hot about it. I can play you the morning videotape if you want."

"I don't have time for that. Not if you want it done by the end of the week."

His face seemed even more florid than usual. I couldn't tell if his sessions at the club had been doing him good or harm. Instead of leaving, he walked over and stretched out on my sofa. It looked as if he were measuring it, to be sure it wasn't longer than the one in his office.

I wasn't worried. Even if mine had the edge on his, he still had two matching easy chairs and a marble coffee table, while I had only a single, unmatched, unusable wooden chair.

"Feels luxurious," he said. "What kind of fabric is this?"

"I really don't know," I said. "Cotton and some miracle fiber, I think. The decorator handled it."

"You really ought to pay close attention to details," he said. I wasn't sure whether he meant to be officious or paternalistic. Maybe both.

While we talked, I had been taking the FurReal reports from my incoming basket and restacking them in the center of my desk, as if preparing to dig in.

Masterson gave the sofa another affectionate brush, got up, and straightened his suit jacket.

"That's quite a pile you've got there," he said, nodding toward the FurReal paperwork on my desk. "Just don't let it get to be a burial mound."

"Hey," I said, "I'm on top of things."

At the doorway, he paused. "You hear any rumors lately?"

"You kidding? That's all I hear."

"About anybody in particular?"

"About everybody in particular."

"Such as . . . ?"

"Christ," I said, really anxious now to get down to business, "you're the team captain. You must hear them before I do. Don't they need your initials before they go into general distribution?"

"No, seriously. My system crashed. I'm not getting any input at all."

"I thought you and Sandy were pretty close," I said, trying not to sound too disingenuous.

He remained sober for a moment, then smiled slyly.

"I'm still screwing her, if that's what you mean. But she's stopped talking to me about what's happening around here. Cut me off completely. That's one reason I'm so frustrated. She told you anything?"

"Nothing. But I'm not sleeping with her. What do you hear from Alicia?"

"Not a word," he said, glancing at me suspiciously. "How did you know about her?"

Everybody on our floor knew about him and Alicia. "Just a wild guess," I said.

"Well she's strictly a business arrangement. Wouldn't touch her otherwise." He was digging his toe into my carpet now, as if testing its spring and plushness, comparing. "Have you heard anything at all about me?" he asked.

"Nothing new, really. Same rumor I heard last week. You heard that one?"

"Yeah," he said. "You do hear anything else, you'll let me know?"

"You'll be the first."

I started shuffling through the FurReal papers, looking for the results of the humidity tolerance tests, when I noticed that Masterson was still loitering in the doorway, as if reluctant to reenter the combat zone.

"Look, amigo," he said, "I'm tied up for lunch today, but you want to get a drink after work?"

"Not tonight," I said. "I'll be lucky to get out of here before the scrubwoman."

I was long gone by the time the scrubwoman showed up for work. I had sent out for lunch, which was a strategic mistake, because I needed some distance from FurReal. By midafternoon the air in my office was bad, and I was tired and apprehensive—and as far as getting any more work done, practically useless. My mind was not on synthetic fur.

I had a cup of coffee, turned on the automatic pilot, and coasted along until it was safe to leave, as soon as Sandy had gone home, a little before five.

First I called Kathy. "I'm really blitzed," I said. "You wouldn't believe the ton of crap in front of me."

"I believe," she said, "but I hope you're not looking for sympathy. At least it's clean, wholesome crap. I started pulling the linoleum off the kitchen floor."

"Oh, shit," I said, knowing that I was going to be dragged into a job that would take two or three weekends, minimum. I had pleaded with her to put the kitchen off until we could afford to hire out most of the dirty work. "How bad is it?"

"There's more than one layer," she said. "And each one is stuck to the other. It's pretty messy with the heat gun. I haven't reached bare wood yet."

"Hearing this, I'm almost glad that I have to work late."

"How late?"

"Can't tell now. Don't wait up."

"If this gets any messier, I may not have a choice. I was hoping you could stop for pizza on the way home."

"Get it delivered, okay? I'll grab a sandwich from a machine in the lunchroom. Don't wait up."

At first, I was sure that the cabdriver had taken me to the wrong address. This couldn't be Susan's building. I knew she wasn't well off, but I had expected to find her living in something a little more tasteful and high-rent, not this squat, prefabricated bunker, migrant housing for yumps and gumps, as we called them around the shop—young urban mopes and greedy up-wardly mobile proles.

Her name was on the mailbox, a business card inserted in the slot. And it was unmistakably Susan who answered the door, even though she looked somehow different, alien almost. I had seen her only in her sweats—usually sweating, with her hair in damp, steaming curls—and here she was, perfectly dry, wearing a plaid shirt and jeans, her hair casually brushed and fluffed. An alien vision maybe, but hardly an alienating one. She looked so fresh and seductive that I lost whatever cool I had, kissing her there in the doorway.

She didn't help or resist, just eased me across the threshold and into the living room. "You are impulsive," she said, smiling as she reached around to close the door.

Once it was locked behind us, she was as impulsive as I was, more so because I was the one who finally had to call a short intermission. "Maybe I should take off my coat," I said, needing a few moments to get my bearings.

She took my coat, hanging it from a hook on the closet door. Looking around her living room, I was surprised by how spartanly she lived, by the meagerness of her furnishings—a generic beige sofa, a pair of canvas butterfly chairs, a portable television set resting on an unfinished louvered pine cabinet.

In one corner of the square room, aimed toward the television set, was an Exercycle. On the floor, leaning against the wall, was a stack of framed prints, evidently waiting to be hung.

The institutional orange carpeting was obviously intended more for soundproofing than for appearance. In either case, it wasn't very effective. From above and below, I could hear muffled footsteps, the hum of television sets, the cries of children.

Angling faintly through dusty windows, the light seemed artificial, denatured. But that only made Susan look more radiant, even healthier and more sensual than she had in the gym.

She must have noticed my dismay at the drabness of her apartment. "I let my ex-husband have most of the furniture when we split. I really didn't want anything to remind me of him. I haven't been here long enough to furnish this place. I'm not sure I ever will."

"Just passing through?" I asked.

"That's the idea," she said. "What about you?"

"That wasn't my idea. I hoped to stay a while."

"Stay as long as you like," she said, moving next to me, smiling up lecherously, her body hard and warm against mine. "You want a drink?"

"Later," I said.

Later, we had drinks on the futon in her bedroom, which was even more sparsely furnished than the living room. There was a single print on the wall, books stacked on the wood floor. An exercise machine took up almost a third of the room.

Shifting on the futon, I felt a sharp and ominous spasm in my lower back. I groaned slightly, not so much from pain as from the fear that I'd aggravated a tennis injury. Beside me, Susan rolled over and rubbed my shoulder.

"Are you okay?" she said, mildly alarmed. "It's not your heart?"

"No, my back. This mattress is pathetic. I feel like I'm lying on the floor."

"You shouldn't have tried all those tricky aerobics."

In the dark bedroom her face had a pinkish fluorescence, a mixture of fugitive streetlight filtering through the windows and the red glow of the digital clock, blinking next to us on the floor.

I wanted to unplug the clock. I didn't want it reminding me how little time I had, that Kathy and the children were waiting for me at home. I wanted to put off reentry. I wanted to delay that guilt trip as long as I could.

Susan's hair was damp now. With my fingertips, I tracked a loose strand across her forehead. I touched the two faint vertical ridges between her eyes, causing her to arch away from me, as if I'd discovered the source of hidden anxieties, delicate flaws in her soul.

I pulled myself upright, leaning against the cold wall. I wondered if there was a market for fur mattresses. "God, this is uncomfortable. I don't know how you can sleep on the floor like this. You're going to permanently wreck your back."

"Actually it's good for your back," she said. "And you get used to it after a while. I don't want to get too comfortable here. This is only temporary, like everything else."

"It looks temporary, all right."

"That's one thing I learned from marriage. Don't hang on to material possessions. Don't clutter up your life with objects. Your inner environment is all that matters."

From beneath the heap of clothes on the floor next to me, I retrieved a stuffed monkey, which I'd tossed aside when we tumbled onto the bed. "Here's one material possession you forgot to leave behind."

She took the monkey from me and nuzzled it against her cheek. "Curious George," she said. "I'd never abandon him."

"I recognized him," I said. "We have one at our house, but he doesn't belong to me."

"He was a gift," she said.

"Oh, a joke. For a second there, I was afraid I had a case of arrested development on my hands."

"He was supposed to be a joke," she said. "He was a gift from a skeptical friend, a disbeliever. But I take George very seriously. He's an article of faith."

"Faith . . . ," I said, realizing I had taken a step too far and that it was too late to back away, "in what?"

"The hundredth monkey theory," she said.

Then she told me about the tribe of monkeys that lived on a South Pacific island during the 1950s, along with a group of Japanese scientists who liked to feed them potatoes. "One of the monkeys started washing his potatoes, then all the others started washing their potatoes, too."

"Then they learned how to french fry them?" I asked.

Even in the darkness, I could see the childlike disillusion on her face, feel the silent reproach. I thought I'd better let her finish, as she was eager to do.

"Before long, monkeys were washing potatoes on islands hundreds of miles away. But they had no way of knowing what the other monkeys were doing. So there had to be some telepathic communication between them."

I knew for certain now that this was no Curious George story. And as close as we were, I sensed that I didn't know Susan nearly as well as I should have.

"That's phenomenal," I said.

"Yes," she said, "and it was verified by the Japanese scientists. So there's scientific proof that the paranormal does actually exist."

I was waiting for more evidence, but she must have taken my silence for skepticism. "You are convinced?" she said. "You're not a disbeliever, one of these people who like to debunk everything?"

She said it so earnestly and hopefully that I didn't want to betray her faith in me. "I always try to keep an open mind," I said, "but I don't understand one point. Why the *hundredth* monkey theory?"

"Oh, that's just an arbitrary number," she said. "When a certain number of monkeys learned how to wash potatoes—it could have been fifty, it could have been one hundred and fifty—that's when it became a paranormal experience. Suddenly all the monkeys knew how. Scientists call that critical mass."

"I'm a believer," I said, taking the stuffed monkey from her and gently putting him on the floor. "But we don't want to let this furry little idol come between us."

"I knew you were a believer," she said. "Right from the first, there at the club, I felt this dynamic imaging between us. We were on the same channel."

She moved on top of me then, voluptuously. I thought she might be about to start something kinky. But she reached across and turned on a cassette player. Music poured from the speakers, filling the bedroom. The music had a tidal rhythm, thick and lugubrious and consoling. I felt as if we had been swamped by a heavy surf, dragging us slowly out to sea. Closing my eyes, I could see a sunset the color of blood. I could hear a bloody mist collecting on the rubbery leaves of tropical plants and dripping onto the red sand.

Lying there, smothered by Susan's warm, aqueous, salty flesh, I still had the sensation of floating. I felt as good as I had in years, serene, free of anxiety. Renovated, rehabbed, renewed by music and passion and love. Driving my green years, I thought, vaguely remembering a line of high school poetry, driving my new age.

14

As I'd feared, Kathy had gotten me into a gruesome mess, not just in the kitchen but in the butler's pantry, which was bigger than the average modern kitchen. Both rooms were covered by linoleum so dulled by footsteps and time that I suspected the murky floral pattern was really spilled food. Beneath the linoleum were at least two other layers of linoleum, or some other vintage synthetic, plus sheets of crusted adhesive and plywood—all of them going back to antiquity, I figured, on the basis of how impossible they were to pry up.

I had argued with Kathy that it would cheaper, and a lot simpler, to have new wooden flooring installed over the old. But she insisted on restoring the original. "I know there's got to be a gorgeous wooden floor down there."

I conceded that there was probably maple flooring beneath

the linoleum, all right, but it wasn't gorgeous. "The only way to tell its age is by carbon dating."

I was using a heavy-duty scraper, a heat gun, and a crowbar. But I was starting to think I'd need a jackhammer before I got to bedrock. In addition to which, the floor was going to be perforated with nail and staple holes, assuming I could even dig out the staples and nails.

"You won't be able to see the holes when the floor's sanded," Kathy assured me, before taking Kim off to her Suzuki lesson.

I located a station on the radio that was playing a Handel string quartet, hoping to find peace and sedation. But the baroque strings were harsh and somber, in abrasive harmony with the sound of the linoleum being ripped loose. Then the announcer came on with a news bulletin. The mayor had formed neighborhood search-and-destroy patrols in his escalating war on home invaders and his faltering campaign for re-election. His community approval index had just dropped six points, corresponding with an even bigger dip in property values.

I turned on a New Age station, which only made me want to stretch out on the cold linoleum and go to sleep. By the time Kathy got back, I had stripped away half of the first layer. As grimy and fatigued as I was, I thought I'd made great headway, but Kathy wasn't interested in admiring my progress.

"I told you not to put tennis shoes in the dryer," she said. When I stopped to rest, I could distinctly hear the dryer in the basement, with the tennis shoes tumbling against the drum as it revolved.

"I haven't been using the dryer," I said. "Maybe it was Mark."

"I told him not to put his toys in the dryer," she said,

heading down the back stairs to the basement. "That's going to throw it all off-balance."

I was still prying at the floor when I thought I heard her scream. I hesitated, thinking it might have been a subterranean echo caused by either the New Age music or the shrieking linoleum. Then I heard it again, more a scream of panic and anger now than fright, and I went downstairs, carrying the crowbar.

Kathy had taken up a defensive position just outside the laundry room, armed with a plastic Wiffle Bat. She waved the bat toward a furnace duct that traversed the ceiling. "There he is," she said. "See him?" In the shadows, there was a barely perceptible movement, a furry quiver between the duct and the raw underside of the floor above.

I could hear its claws scratching against the slippery metal, trying to get a secure foothold. I could see its eyes, like pinpoint flares in a tunnel. But it wasn't until the tail came whipping out that I knew that we had trapped a squirrel and not a rat.

"He jumped out of the dryer when I opened the door," Kathy said. "He scared the hell out of me."

"I heard," I said. "He probably came in through the vent. He must've been using the dryer as an exercise machine."

We stood there watching from the doorway for maybe five minutes, waiting for him to make his move. When I realized he wasn't going anywhere, I advanced, the crowbar raised.

"Scott!" Kathy yelled. "The clean laundry."

The squirrel leaped just as I swung. The crowbar striking the metal duct sounded as if I had shot off a cannon in the basement. The duct split at the seam, dumping what looked like a century's worth of soot and dust into the room. The squirrel hit the floor on his feet, running past Kathy, out of the laundry room, and across the basement floor.

I came out of the laundry room in time to see him scramble up a support column and disappear into the drop ceiling, knocking aside a panel as he did so. One by one, I removed the rest of the panels, hoping I could trap him again.

But he was gone, probably up the space between the walls to join his comrades in one of their nests, under the floors or in the attic and eaves. Like guerrillas, they had tunnels and escape hatches everywhere. By now, I assumed the house was crevassed with them, not only weakening its superstructure but leaving us vulnerable to their pillaging, their contagious filth and parasites.

While I was putting the basement ceiling back together, Kathy mopped up the foul matter in the laundry room, vacuuming the fallout that had spilled out of the broken furnace duct and cleaning the fur and droppings from the dryer. "I'm afraid I'll never get rid of the smell," she said, scrubbing the drum with Lysol.

When she was finished, I reconnected the furnace duct, then went outside and covered the dryer vent with sheet metal. "They won't be able to use this as a back entrance anymore," I told Kathy.

She didn't seem happy about my patchwork. "We won't be able to use the dryer either."

"That's only temporary," I said. "First thing tomorrow, I'll go to the hardware store and get some wire mesh to put over it."

I didn't make it to the hardware store the next day. Lying in bed that night, awakened by the household tremors, I took inventory of the damage the squirrels had caused. Again and again, I had repaired the holes they'd chewed in the eaves, smearing thick tar over the tin and wire mesh to further discourage them. They still jumped onto the roof from the branches of an elm. I had the overhanging branches trimmed off. When that failed to stop them, I had the tree cut down.

They leaped from the branches of another tree onto a power cable and nimbly made their way to our house. I called an electrician and inquired about the possibility of electrocuting them as they walked along the wire, but he wasn't very encouraging. The only option was to have the cables buried. But that was an expensive remedy. The lawn had not yet healed where we'd had it dug up to replace clogged and broken sewer tiles.

All the while, the squirrels were eating away at the house, leaving pockmarks in the soffits and fascia, the crown molding and verge boards. There was nothing I could do to drive them off. I threw rocks at them. I struck at them with a bamboo pole. They always returned when I was out of sight.

I repaired the holes. They bored new ones until I hesitated to patch any more for fear they were seriously damaging the house because of my persistence, to the point where the roof and eaves leaked, so that rain and snow were soaking the inner walls and supports and hastening what I felt was its inevitable collapse.

Turning over and over in bed, I worked myself into a state of helpless, sleepless rage. I had long ago deactivated the ultrasonic squirrel device in the attic, so I wouldn't have to hear its beeping. But now the house reeked of naphthalene.

I had bought several large sacks of mothballs, on the advice of a friend, who told me squirrels were repelled by them. I scattered them around the attic and poured them down the walls. When I told my friend they hadn't worked, he said: "I didn't say mothballs. I said moth crystals. It's not the smell that gets to them but something in the crystals that irritates their feet."

The smell was getting to us. It crept through the walls and ceilings and impregnated our clothes. I could even detect it on our sheets and blankets and pillows, making sleep even more impossible. I sat up in bed, fully awake and angry.

"All right," I told Kathy. "That's it. We just can't let them run all over us any longer. There's a point where human rights take precedence over animal rights."

"Please, Scott, not now," she said, momentarily awakened. "It's 3:30. We can deal with this tomorrow."

I knew just how to deal with it. As soon as I had breakfast, I went off to the sporting goods store to buy a gun. Driving to the mall, I was sorry that I hadn't anticipated the need for one months ago. I could have put it on my Christmas wish list. Now it seemed more of a household necessity than the router that Kathy had given me to make bookshelves.

"I could use some light artillery," I told the salesgirl in the munitions department. Barely out of her teens, if that old, she looked like a weekend employee, who might have been temporarily transferred from running shoes or garden equipment. She was helpful enough until I told her I planned to hunt squirrels.

"Oh, what kind of squirrels?"

"Red, gray, brown, striped, spotted—any kind that I happen to see running across my backyard or my roof and chewing on my house."

"Domestic squirrels, you mean?"

"You could call them that," I said.

The salesgirl became as stern as a school principal. "I couldn't sell you a gun for that. It's against the law to shoot domestic squirrels."

"Look," I said, confidentially. "I was just kidding about the squirrels. I need a gun for my personal protection. I live in a bad neighborhood. A lot of scary things have been happening. I have reason to believe my wife and children are in danger."

She seemed pacified. Her disapproving frown turned into a neutral smile. "That's different. You know, for a second there, I was afraid you were serious about shooting domestic squirrels."

When I started browsing among the pistols, she informed me that I would need a permit, along with clearance from the police department, which could take a week, if I was lucky. Meantime, the gun would be held on layaway.

The .22-caliber handguns all looked pretty flimsy anyway, like Saturday night or Sunday morning specials, no more powerful or threatening than starters' pistols. I had my eye on a Crosman Diabolo .177-caliber Mauser, made in West Germany, a pellet gun that was exempt from police regulation.

"That's just a fancy BB gun," she said, "a toy. You won't take out any bandidos with that piece."

"That's all right," I said. "I don't really want to shoot anybody. I just want to scare them to death."

And the .177 would too. What really sold me was that it was a replica of a .44 Magnum, the Dirty Harry model. Though made of plastic, it had real heft and balance. From twenty paces, in a dark hallway or bedroom, it probably couldn't be distinguished from the real thing.

Besides frightening off any home invaders, it was powerful enough to take out domestic squirrels with very little fuss and muss. Neat and clean. No gaping wounds or bloody entrails.

When I got home, I tested the pistol's action, cocking it and pulling the trigger, letting the hammer strike the empty chambers. It sounded as solid as it felt. German technicians hadn't lost their touch.

Kathy was not as impressed by its precision engineering as I was. She refused to even take it in her hand. "I'm really afraid you're going to hurt yourself or somebody else."

"It's a BB gun," I said. "You really can't hurt anybody with it. When I was growing up, everybody had a Red Ryder rifle."

"That looks more like Clint Eastwood than Red Ryder to me," she said.

"Well, when you think of a better way to get rid of these squirrels, let me know."

After lunch, I took the gun outside, slipped the air cartridge into the handle, and loaded six pellets into the cylinder. It was bleak and wintry, only a degree or two above freezing. There were sooty patches of snow in the yard, all that remained of what was probably the season's last snowstorm, three weeks earlier.

I didn't see any squirrels in the trees or on the roof. The weather was probably too raw. I could hardly blame them for choosing to stay indoors, along with Kathy and the children, where they could be warm and protected.

I got a beer can from the alley and set it on a snowdrift. I sat down on the back steps and lined it up in the pistol sights. The weight of the pistol made it hard to hold steady. There was a disappointingly small report when I pulled the trigger, more a dull snap than an explosion. What looked like smoke was only a puff of mist. The gun had almost no kick. The pellet missed the can. I heard it ricochet off Mrs. Underwood's garage.

I aimed a little lower and more slowly on the next shot, taking the gun in both hands, Dirty Harry style. I held my breath and squeezed. There was a spray of slush a foot to the right of the can. At least I wasn't overshooting my target. I had to allow for windage. I fired a dozen more shots before a pellet hit the can. It made a gratifying ping, causing the can to teeter slightly.

I had my bearings now. I never succeeded in toppling the can. But before long it was so scarred by BB holes that I could hardly see any metal. I was ready for a live target, but the squirrels hadn't emerged from their nest.

I went indoors to thaw out, made a cup of coffee, and sat down on the sun porch with the Sunday papers. I was too distracted to read, watching for a break in the vault of gray.

Late in the afternoon, the sun appeared. I hurried outside and searched the trees and power lines but saw no squirrels. I found a spot in the yard where I had a clear shot at the roofline of the house and waited. As I expected, a squirrel stuck its head from one of the crude holes, drawn by the weak sunshine.

I took aim and waited for the squirrel to crawl onto the roof. But it evidently intended only to check the weather, its head swiveling, its nose and whiskers twitching in the chill. When it seemed clear that the squirrel wasn't going to come out, I fired.

A pellet hole appeared in a tin patch, a foot away. The squirrel looked at me, quizzically, balefully. I fired again. This time I was closer—the eave splintered a few inches from its head.

My hands were cold and stiff, throwing off my aim. I tucked the pistol under my arm and rubbed away the numbness. By then the sun was gone and so was the squirrel. It was almost dark anyway. I went inside, feeling good. Next weekend was Easter. The forecast was for sunshine and springlike temperatures.

15

I was out of bed early on Saturday, well before Kathy and the children. Getting up in the cold, gray bedroom, I was apprehensive. But when I opened a shutter I was warmed by the sight. The sky was already blue—a weak blue but rapidly brightening. There were patches of clouds, but they looked friendly enough, white and foamy, without any threat of rain.

I had been praying that the TV forecaster was right about the sunshine and mild temperatures. If this turned out to be one of those rare times when he was, I had most of the morning to take care of business. Kathy was planning to stay indoors and work on her ceramics; the children would watch cartoons until noon, if I let them, which I planned to do.

The squirrels had gotten up even earlier than I had. Long before I was out of bed, I could hear them scrambling out of the attic and across the roof. For once, it was a pleasing sound. By the time I had dressed, they were all over the yard. I stood at the kitchen window, drinking coffee, and watched them, playing happily in my happy hunting ground.

I put on a windbreaker and went outdoors. The air was cold, but it smelled fresh and damp, not like winter but spring. Along the edges of the yard, there were scattered patches of yellow and blue wildflowers. I took the pistol from my waistband, cocked it, and searched for a likely target.

There were so many squirrels it was hard to choose. Living indoors all winter had made them not only fat but fearless. Then I spotted one, fatter and lazier than the rest. He was thirty feet away, sitting upright, gorging on a walnut and switching his tail with obscene pleasure.

I was confident about my marksmanship now and tried a quick, one-handed shot, expecting to see the squirrel go down like a punk in a police movie. The pellet must have missed by a foot or more. The squirrel didn't flinch. I fired again. This one came closer, near enough so that he momentarily stopped chewing on the nut. He looked around, sniffing suspiciously, as if he had heard the pellet whistle by.

Using both hands, I aimed lower and more carefully. The pellet smacked the ground, well to the right of the squirrel. I still wasn't allowing for windage. But by now he apparently got the idea it would be wise to picnic elsewhere. Carrying the nut between his teeth, he ran off, with pellets kicking up a trail of divots as I emptied the pistol after him.

Reloading, I randomly began to fire at other squirrels, but I could soon see this wasn't going to be any shooting gallery. Hitting a stationary beer can was difficult. Moving squirrels were next to impossible. They refused to stay still long enough for me to get off a clean shot. I was firing hurriedly and badly, hitting nothing.

Even though it was sunny, there was still frost in the air and my fingers grew numb, making my shots even more inaccurate. I went inside, had another cup of coffee, and supervised the children's breakfast while Kathy got dressed. When they had eaten and settled in front of the television, I was warm and limber again, eager to resume the hunt.

No sooner had I come off the back porch than I heard my name being called. Mrs. Underwood was waiting for me beside her fence. I had seen almost nothing of her over the winter, and she seemed to have diminished considerably, so stooped now she could barely see over the top of the fence. She smiled up at me, sweetly but ominously.

"Oh, Mr. Ryan," she said, "I just love the color of your little girl's bedroom—hot pink, is that what it is?"

"I think it's more like shocking orange," I said, immediately relieved. I had expected her to be upset about the stray pellets that had nicked the siding of her house. "But I'm glad you like it."

"Well, whatever it is, it's certainly bright," she said. "When she has her lights on at night, it's like a neon sign, shining on my house."

"I'll tell her to be sure to keep her curtains closed from now on," I said, edging away.

"I just think everything you've done to your house is so stylish and tasteful and such an asset to the neighborhood, and I don't mean to be critical but—"

I stopped, my getaway momentarily stalled.

"—all those garments you've been hanging from the clothesline in your backyard."

From her tone, she didn't mean "garments" but dirty linen, soiled undies, stained hankies. I smiled at her. "Environmentally," I said, "it seemed like the way to go. No wasted energy, no air pollution."

"You're not a preservative!" she said, as if I had told her I planned to paint the whole house a neon pink.

"Not that I know of," I assured her. "I'm not a conservative either. We've just temporarily reverted to an old country custom. My grandparents were Abyssinian."

She didn't seem at all mollified or amused, and in the interest of neighborhood solidarity, and possibly her precarious health, I came clean.

"Actually," I said, "there was this little problem with our dryer, so we've had to hang our clothes out all week."

"Well, I'm glad to hear that. I was afraid you were making a public statement, that you really were an environmentalist."

"Nothing of the kind," I told her. "I'm going to fix the dryer as soon as I can. As soon as I get more urgent matters taken care of."

"Oh, I do hope it's soon," she said. "I don't mind having to look at your sheets and towels. But not your family's underwear. It makes the neighborhood look like a slum."

"No, it's definitely not an asset, and not very stylish, is it?" I was almost as eager as Mrs. Underwood to get our dryer working again. I did like the clean smell of the clothes after they'd been hanging outdoors for a day, but they were stiff and rough against my skin. Also, several pairs of Kathy's panty hose had disappeared from the line.

With any luck, I might be able to cover the dryer vent with wire mesh and reattach the exhaust duct later in the day. But I couldn't deal with that now. The morning was already starting to get away from me. I had yet to get a single squirrel. It was warming up, and the children would soon get tired of television cartoons and want to play outdoors.

In my haste, I was only wasting pellets. I put one through our garage window, but was relieved to see the hole was so small that I wouldn't have to replace the pane. Then I spotted a perfect target—a squirrel creeping along the power cable leading to our house.

I fired once. The pellet seemed to ruffle his tail. I wasn't allowing for his movement. I aimed slightly in front of the squirrel. The impact caused his head to jerk sharply, obviously a direct hit. He stopped and slowly rolled over on the cable, hanging upside down by his rigid claws.

I couldn't let him hang that way, where the children and the neighbors could see him. He looked like an old fur stole that was airing on the line. I got a shovel with a long handle, stood on an overturned garbage can, and pried him loose. After hitting the ground, he quivered and shook. He was stunned from the bullet and the fall, mortally wounded but stubbornly refusing to die.

I held the pistol a foot from his head and delivered the coup de grace. The pellet sent up a little puff of dust, fur, and blood. Like a slap in the face, that only seemed to revive him. He attempted to get to his feet, but his hind legs wouldn't work, his back apparently broken in the fall from the cable. Using his front paws, he dragged himself along the grass. I fired again and again until the hammer was striking empty cylinders. With each shot, the squirrel jerked, then kept crawling, crawling.

I picked up the shovel and hit him, once, twice. I had intended to strike him only with the shovel's flat side, but on the third and last stroke I evidently caught him with the edge. He split apart, as if I'd opened a seam, spilling a brown and pinkish slush into the grass.

To my rear, I heard shrieks. Turning, I half expected to find Mrs. Underwood, back at her fence, shrilly protesting this new and even more shocking indignity. But it was a necessary contribution to neighborhood solidarity, I would tell her. Except it wasn't Mrs. Underwood I heard but Kim, standing on the porch, with Mark and Peter bringing up the rear. In a moment, they were howling along with her.

I wanted to go over and comfort them. But if I moved, they would have a clear view of the squirrel's pulpy remains. Then Kathy came out onto the porch, naturally alarmed herself by all the wailing. "Get them out of here," I shouted, "I've got an awful mess on my hands."

When they were indoors, I shoveled the squirrel's corpse into a plastic bag. I planned to dispose of it after I'd helped Kathy comfort the children. By the time I got indoors, Mark and Peter had stopped crying and were back at the television set. But Kim was inconsolable.

"She saw you hitting that squirrel with a shovel," Kathy said. "I'm just grateful that's all it was. I thought you'd shot her. Or yourself."

"What else could I do?" I said.

"There's got to be a better way."

"I'll find one," I said.

"I explained to her," Kathy said. "I told her it was an accident. The squirrel was badly hurt. You were only being merciful. You had to put it out of its misery. She seems to understand."

"That's a relief."

"Scott, she wants to have a funeral."

"No," I said. "Didn't you explain that squirrels don't have funerals?"

"She's traumatized. She wants to give it a proper burial. In this case, I think it would be a good idea."

"Okay," I said. "Just tell her it's not going to be an open coffin. I'm not going to say any prayers."

I scooped the crushed body into a shoebox, and we had our funeral in the backyard. The children laid lilies and violets on the grave. Kim made a cross out of chopsticks. I told her we couldn't leave it there because it would only get run over by the lawn mower.

After they'd gone to bed, I went outside and dug up the shoebox, intending to drop it in the garbage can. I had just refilled the hole and was smoothing out the dirt when I was stopped by the beam of a flashlight, coming from the alley.

I was startled but not alarmed since I immediately recognized the voice behind the light. "Funny time to be working in the garden, isn't it?"

Klammish was stationed behind the fence, nearly hidden by the drooping branches of a pine. When he lowered the flashlight, I could just make out the warhead shape of his helmet.

"I was just trying to dispose of a body," I said.

There was a moment of tense silence. "You've been living around here long enough to know that you don't joke about things like that."

His voice had a gargly electronic quality, as if it came not from his mouth but from the squawk box in the canvas bag on his shoulder.

"I assumed it was okay to be digging in my own backyard," I said.

"Depends on what you're digging," he said.

"There's no need to worry. I'm not really burying any bodies."

He snorted. "It wouldn't be the first time that's happened around here."

"I know," I said, impatiently pushing dirt across the hole with the shovel, waiting for him to switch off his spotlight and leave so I could get rid of the shoebox and go to bed.

"You remember Dermott MacIntosh?" he said.

"Yeah," I said, not wanting to be reminded of Mac the

Knife, as newspaper reporters and television anchormen always referred to him.

"Yeah, well, if you remember Dermott—or Ed Burnett's daughter—then you know why we can use your help on the neighborhood surveillance team."

"I've got my hands full around here right now," I said. "But as soon as there's a break in my schedule, I'm planning to join. Meantime, you can be sure I'm not sleeping on the job. I'm doing my own surveillance."

"You'll come around," Klammish said.

"Maybe, but not tonight." I couldn't wait any longer. I was tired and increasingly annoyed by the disruption. In the shadows, he reminded me of a pit bull, standing on its hind legs, its forepaws resting on the fence.

I reached over and picked up the shoebox, my cardboard coffin, and started toward the house.

"What've you got there?" he said. The flashlight beam was fixed on my back now, like a paralyzing ray gun.

"Just a family heirloom," I said. "I'd buried it for safekeeping."

"I'm afraid I'll have to impound it," Klammish said.

"I wouldn't call that very neighborly," I said. I walked over and presented him with the shoebox.

"You're supposed to love your neighbor," he said. "But you'd better never trust him for a second."

He turned the light on the box and shook it.

"Careful," I said. "It's not only valuable but fragile."

He put it into his knapsack. "If it checks out, you'll get it back."

"Don't bother," I said, starting back toward the house. "Just consider it a contribution to Neighborhood Solidarity."

16

I didn't get another squirrel all spring or summer. Not because of my erratic marksmanship but because I abandoned the hunt. Once they'd come out of hibernation, spending all their days and nights outdoors, the squirrels were no immediate threat to our house or to us. Scrambling around the yard, they were a clear danger but not a present one.

I knew I would have to deal with them, decisively and permanently, in the fall when the weather turned cool, the leaves fell, and the offensive started all over again. For now, I put the pistol on the shelf in our bedroom closet, alongside the condoms, the Valium, and the other items that we wanted to keep out of sight and reach of the children.

Even with the siege temporarily lifted, we found little peace that murderously hot summer. Another sewer tile broke and had to be replaced. The plumbers promised that the job would take only a week, but we had an open trench in our side yard, smelling of sewage, until early fall.

Carpenter ants had ravaged the columns on the front porch, and these had to be replaced. I spent what spare moments I had scraping and tuck-pointing the foundation. From almost every angle, the house seemed to be off center, tilting perilously. I couldn't tell if it were from the foundation settling or the damage caused by ants, squirrels, and other invaders.

There were two housebreakings on our block. One day, as I was walking to the station, I noticed a poster stapled to an elm: BURGLAR ALERT, it said, warning residents to report all suspicious characters and seeking volunteers for the neighborhood surveillance patrol.

Making sure nobody was around, I ripped the poster off the tree and put it in my briefcase. However dangerous the neighborhood was getting, there was no need to advertise. This would only raise fears and lower property values. As soon as I got to work, I called and ordered an electronic alarm system for the house.

With the final FurReal deadline approaching, I had less time to spend at home, on the house. Masterson was irritable, pushy, unpredictable, obviously on the edge about that and other projects. I had reason to believe he was trying to degrade and devaluate me. I'd intercepted a report he sent to Kinkaid about a focus group that I'd conducted with militant animal rightists, to determine if they could be pacified by the introduction of synthetics for fur. It was the report I'd written, barely changed, but with his signature on it. I went through it twice and couldn't find a single mention of my name.

Sitting in Masterson's office one afternoon, waiting for him to show up for an appointment, I noticed a stack of micro-cassette tapes on his desk. I immediately suspected—knew—he was taping my phone calls. In anyone else's hands, that could have been compromising, possibly incriminating.

I wasn't worried about him listening to my conversations with Kathy. She called two or three times a day, usually to report some new catastrophe, whether it was the plumber accidentally rupturing the water main or Peter gashing his forehead on the sidewalk during a tantrum.

But Susan had taken to phoning me too, often as soon as I arrived, so she could tell me about her dreams the night before. I said nothing to her about my own dreams. My dream life was not one I wanted to relive during the daylight hours.

As Susan reconstructed her dreams on the phone, always in labyrinthine detail, she also taped them. This process was very therapeutic for her, she said, allowing her to get them out of her subconscious and onto a cassette for later, more careful analysis. I was dubious, but I couldn't very well object, since I did so little talking myself. If Masterson was taping my conversations, I thought about suggesting that he switch off his recorder when Susan called. By saving the company money in needless duplication, he could score bonus points with Kinkaid.

I had the idea that Masterson wasn't our only eavesdropper. One morning, as I came in late, Sandy glanced up from behind the reception desk, smiled coyly, and said, "You had a call." I waited for her to hand over the While-You-Were-Out . . . slip. After a long and deliberate pause, she said, "It was her again."

"Which her is that?"

"The her who isn't your wife," she said, in a tone that indicated that she not only was intimately familiar with my caller but strongly disapproved of her, and of me. I liked to think that Sandy's problem with me was based on my indifference to her sexual chemistry, not hers to mine. Either way, I assumed it didn't matter what or how much she learned about us from these conference calls. Or how much Masterson learned either. I knew enough about the both of them, together and apart, to guarantee their discretion.

Under any circumstances, I wasn't about to suggest that Susan stop calling. Her calls had become as necessary as morning coffee. I was tense and distracted until I heard from her, unable to think and work. As I listened to her dreams, many of them highly erotic fantasies from her past lives, as a Napoleonic courtesan or a gymnast in Hellenic Greece, I daydreamed about her, but always in the present. These fantasies were like stretching exercises, mental acrobatics that helped me loosen up for my daily workouts with Masterson and FurReal.

For the first few months, we met at odd times, whenever we could find a fugitive hour or two. I would leave work early, sign in at the health club, then slip away and go to her apartment. I stayed later and later, frequently missing dinner and the children's bedtimes. At first it was never late enough for either of us. I wanted to stay all night, stay the next day, stay forever.

Susan was no more pleased to see me go than I was. "You're like a worker bee," she said. "You're here only long enough to leave your pollen, then you hustle off to another flower."

"If you saw the condition of my house," I told her, "you wouldn't put it that way. It looks like it's been struck by an earthquake. There's a cesspool in our yard."

"I'd like to see your house anyway," she said. "Not just the outside. The inside. Where you eat. Where you sleep. Every room. I want to know how you live. I feel so shut out of your real life."

"You don't want to see any of that," I said, touching her pouty lip. "This is my real life. You're real. The rest is only a domestic fantasy."

But once I left Susan's, it was clear that I wasn't returning to any fantasy. Getting into my car, I could understand how reluctant she must have been to abandon one of her past lives for the uncertain and hazardous present. As I drove home, I felt like a descending astronaut, reentering the dense atmosphere of Earth, leaving my weightless state for the oppressive burdens of reality.

And yet no matter how hard I found it to leave Susan, I was still anxious, almost desperate to get home. I was eternally spooked by the thought of what might have happened while I was gone. I expected the street to be filled with fire engines and squad cars. I drove hurriedly, almost recklessly.

Pulling into the driveway, I was always glad to see that the house was intact, to see lights upstairs and down. It was an immense comfort to go inside, where it was warm and quiet, and find Kathy reading or watching television, the children already in their beds, asleep.

Relieved of dread but not guilt, I was still psychologically and emotionally unprepared for these homecomings, a drop-in visitor from another universe. I could barely deal with petty chores, conversation, or lovemaking. I would briefly complain to Kathy about the ordeal of having to work so long and so late, the hazards of traffic, the weariness I felt, then have dinner and go directly to bed.

I rarely had to worry, though, because Kathy was usually more exhausted than I was. Often she was asleep when I got home. If so, I would impulsively call Susan to let her know that I was safe, that I hadn't been wiped out by a drunk driver, that I hadn't been smashed and grabbed and executed. I whispered into the phone that I loved her, and I began to think I did.

Kathy's labors weren't entirely devoted to home and children. She had set aside a maid's room on the first floor as a ceramics workshop, a room that the children were strictly forbidden to enter. Kathy let me know that it was also off-limits to me, at least for the present. "You can see what I'm doing when I'm ready for you to see it. I don't want you getting any wrong impressions from unfinished work."

One evening she had her ceramics teacher over to critique the work she was doing at home. I had expected an older man, gray, paternal, stout, dressed in soiled work clothes. But Mario looked like an Hispanic gigolo. He wore jeans as tight as toreador pants, his slick black hair was drawn back in a ponytail, and he had a ring in one ear.

As Kathy took him through the house, he seemed to be inspecting it—and her—a little too carefully, his black eyes as alert and as furtive as a cat burglar's.

She led him into her studio and shut the door. It was a warm night, the windows were open, and their voices carried through the house like a vagrant breeze. In that situation, I couldn't help but overhear them. Mario was sympathetic at first, patronizing, then he became stern, almost sneering. "This is too smooth and symmetrical," he said. "Too bland and cheerful."

"It's meant to be cheerful," Kathy protested.

"Where's the anguish, the pain, the unhappiness?" he demanded, shouting now, so it would have been impossible for me not to eavesdrop. Upstairs, I could hear Peter crying, awakened by the commotion.

"I can't help it," Kathy said weakly, plainly intimidated. "I have my bad moments but I'm basically not unhappy."

"You are," he said, "you have to be. To be any kind of serious artist you've got to be hostile, angry, resentful, envious, half demented. And until you admit it, you'll never make contact with your innermost self. You've got to expose your soul, let out all the heartbreak and the misery."

"But I'm not miserable."

"That's what you think," Mario said. "You're trapped in this monstrosity of a house, with three little kids and a petit bourgeois husband. You're trapped in this middle-management existence. Don't tell me you're happy. If you are, then you're in real trouble and I can't help. Nobody can."

I couldn't ignore Peter's cries any longer. I went upstairs to tend to him. As I was coming down, Kathy was just showing Mario out the door. She seemed upset, totally demoralized, and he had his hand on her shoulder, supposedly trying to comfort her. At the same time, his eyes were shifting all over the hallway, sizing things up one last time.

Before he left, they kissed on the cheek, which was usually not Kathy's style. I decided that Mario might soon be paying us another visit, surreptitiously, in which case I would be waiting for him.

We had other visitors. Just as the weather turned violently hot, with a gray mass of air descending on us like fallout from a brushfire, Kathy's parents came for the long Fourth of July weekend. In one respect, the heat was a blessing. Our house wasn't air-conditioned so they stayed in a hotel, where they could escape the weather, the chaos, and the noise.

But that didn't relieve them of the obligation to check in with us every morning. Or the need to complain about the heat and humidity, the polluted air, the shabby condition of our house, the disreputable look of the whole neighborhood.

"I've noticed a lot of swarthy types on the streets," Kathy's mother remarked at the breakfast table. "Foreigners."

"Ethnics," Kathy corrected her.

"Looks like Calcutta around here to me," said her father.

"Please, Raymond, let's not exaggerate," said her mother. "I haven't seen a single person wearing a turban."

"Well, it looks like . . . Beirut. That's it. Sounds like Beirut too."

Outdoors, we could hear firecrackers. Or what I hoped

were firecrackers. The air was dense with smoke and ashes. "The kids all like to get an early start on the Fourth," I said.

"What do you know about Beirut?" Kathy's mother said to her father. "You've never been any farther east than Grand Cayman. It's bad enough around here without all this exaggeration."

"You don't have to actually go to Beirut to know how bad it is," he said, glancing up defiantly from the sports pages. "I've seen enough pictures on television to know."

"Well, it's still not that bad," she said. "It's probably more like the South Bronx."

"Oh," he said, "and I suppose you're an authority on the South Bronx."

I was about to excuse myself when Kathy's mother said: "Just look at Scott. The way he's dressed, you could all be living in the South Bronx."

Halfway out of my chair, I sank back self-consciously, expectantly, temporarily trapped in their cross fire. Kathy tried to come to my rescue. "Mother," she said, "he's got on his work clothes."

"His shirt and pants are full of stains and holes. It's just so pathetic that he can't afford decent work clothes."

As usual, she didn't bother to speak directly to me. Her remarks were addressed to Kathy, in a tone that was filled with artificial sweeteners, but one that suited her general appearance and disposition. Her face was as round and shiny as a lollipop, her hair was teased and dyed a lemony color, so it resembled cotton candy. I suppose it smelled like it too, but I never got close enough to find out.

From the atmosphere in our dining room, the expression "dead heat" took on an entirely new meaning. The air didn't move, and whenever somebody spoke, the temperature seemed to go up another degree or two. I got up from the table, figuring that even in this weather, tuck-pointing had to be more enjoyable.

"We like this neighborhood because of its diversity," Kathy was saying. "We want the kids to grow up with different types of people."

"There's such a thing as carrying diversity too far," her mother said. "I notice that Kim has started to talk with a funny accent."

"She's taking French in school," Kathy explained.

"And Mark is as brown as a Mexican."

"Swimming lessons," Kathy said.

"My God, did you read this?" said her father, who had returned to the newspaper. "It happened only a couple of blocks from here. It's worse than Beirut."

Goombah and Dotty, the children called them. Goombah came from the children's mispronunciation of Grampa, which they confused with a word they'd heard on a television police series they weren't supposed to be watching. Kathy's mother, Dorothy, didn't want to be a "grand" anything so she proposed that the kids call her Dotty. I was only too happy to call her that myself, at every opportunity, until Kathy suggested I try not to sound quite so sarcastic.

Ever since she found out Kathy and I had been sleeping together at college, Dotty was convinced I was a corrupting influence on her daughter. Our marriage had hardly changed her mind. If anything, I was in even worse graces with her, not just because she found me so personally non grata but because I was holding Kathy and her grandchildren captive in this old and rapidly disintegrating house.

Like the thermometer, her disapproval index had reached a new level this weekend when I failed to go to church. Though Kathy was just as negligent as I the rest of the time, she dutifully went along, taking the kids with her, at Dotty's insistence.

I couldn't be that submissive or hypocritical. Coerced by my own parents, I'd been a regular churchgoer until I got to be a teenager and found myself drifting into lewd and lascivious reveries one Sunday during a sermon on the pieties of St. Bartholomew.

It occurred to me that God would prefer that I stay out of His house until I got my adolescent head straight. Whatever spiritual comforts the world offered lay well beyond those tomblike doors. When the service was over, I swore I'd never again waste my time, or His, by going to church, a vow I broke only on my wedding day.

Before her parents arrived, Kathy had pleaded with me to relent this Sunday, if only for the sake of family harmony. I was firm. "I'd rather fix the broken shingles on the roof. I feel nearer to heaven there."

When she finally realized that I was a permanently lost cause, she did get me to agree to say I was too busy with household emergencies. She was afraid I'd tell Dotty and Goombah what I thought church would get them, which was nothing, absolutely nothing.

Using the same excuse, I begged off the Fourth of July parade. Kathy and Dotty left with the children but without Goombah. I'd encouraged him to go along, but Goombah said he'd stay home with me. It wasn't that he preferred my company so much as that of our television set.

Before settling down to watch the golf and tennis matches and the baseball games, Goombah had one ritual chore to perform. As soon as he arrived, he'd gone through, around, and over the house, taking inventory of the work that needed to be done. First he divided the jobs into major and minor, then narrowed these into three subcategories in ascending order of priority: tomorrow, today, and yesterday.

With his checklist in hand, Goombah led me on a tour of

the house, pointing out what I needed to do and exactly how it should be done. He scowled at the sight of peeling walls in one of the rooms we'd renovated, saying, "You haven't been using latex paint, have you?"

Whatever he said, I nodded, mumbled, tried not to be disagreeable. Even in this heat, wearing plaid shorts and a green golf shirt, his face flush with sweat, Goombah was a wintry figure, cold and stern, with a snowcap of hair, pale frosty eyes, an implacable expression.

He didn't like the look of the foundation where I'd tuck-pointed. "It won't last," he said, brushing loose mortar from a crevice with his thumb. "You're using too much water, trying to make the mortar go too far. That's false economizing. Save a quarter today, lose a dollar tomorrow."

He was most disturbed by the holes, in the fascia, the soffits, the eaves, everywhere he looked, holes that I'd clumsily patched or been forced to ignore, because of their height or inaccessibility. Now they resembled open sores, dripping pus and blood.

"It looks like the Green Berets have been using this place for target practice," he said.

"Worse," I said. "Squirrels."

"When I was a boy, we knew how to handle squirrels. With a .22 slug right between the eyes."

"I thought about that," I admitted, "but my aim isn't good enough."

"You don't have to be Daniel Boone," he said. "Anyplace you hit 'em, so long as it isn't the tail, they roll over dead."

Goombah and Dotty stayed into the week, and I was glad for the excuse to get away from the house and go back to work. I had no more than sat down behind my desk than the phone rang. I seized it passionately, knowing it would be Susan.

"I really missed you," she said. "These long holiday weekends are dreadful. We've got so much catching up to do."

What she meant was that she had stored up a lot of dreams over the four nights we'd been out of touch. Willing as I was to listen to them, I couldn't spend much time with her on the phone. I already had several other calls to return. And in a half hour I had to meet with Masterson to dope out a crucial mall intercept.

"I dreamed about you constantly," she said. "Do you remember being a captain in the Massachusetts militia during the Revolutionary War?"

I was willing to believe when she recalled her own past lives, but I was highly skeptical about her ability to remember mine. I told her I couldn't stay on the phone. "I'll be over to see you as soon as I can," I said.

"Tonight," she said.

"Not tonight. My in-laws are coming for dinner. Then I've got a tennis match." I was playing doubles on Wednesday nights now, in addition to my regular singles games on weekdays, hoping to score even more points with Kinkaid.

"We'll never have a better opportunity," she said. "The sun's in Cancer, and the moon's in Taurus. It's going to be a perfect night for wild and passionate lovemaking."

Her voice dropped to a sultry whisper, and that was the end of my tennis game for this Wednesday. I hung up and called Alex, my partner. "You'll have to get a sub for me tonight," I told him. "Kathy's parents are in town, and I'm chairman of the entertainment committee."

"Bring 'em along," Alex said. "Watching you play tennis is all the entertainment they need."

"They're old and can't take the excitement. I'll see you next week."

Leaving for the club, after dinner, I told Kathy I might be later than usual. "The guys who have the court after us don't always show up on time, so we keep playing till they come."

Susan didn't answer her door right away. I could hear babble coming from her television set, an electronic hysteria. I knocked again, a little harder, and the door nearly buckled under my fist.

When Susan opened the door, she seemed upset, almost unstrung. "They interrupted 'Cheers' for a news bulletin," she said, releasing the chain lock.

"I could hear it all the way out here," I told her. She kissed me, but her heart and mind weren't in it. She was too absorbed by the television. "Did you hear what happened?"

"I had the car radio on," I said. "Do they know how many victims?"

"Fifteen . . . maybe twenty. Nobody's counted up the score. The people they've got running around loose these days. Isn't it just incredible?"

"Yeah," I said, "but nothing would surprise me anymore." I put my arm around her, reaching beneath her sweatshirt, feeling bare skin, warm and taut.

She looked up at me and smiled for the first time since I'd entered. I picked up the remote and turned off the television.

"Hey," she said, "I really wanted to watch that."

"They'll show it again and again, over and over, all night, all day tomorrow, until you're sick of seeing it."

"But it won't be live. Replays aren't the same thing."

"Who can tell the difference? I really didn't come over to

watch TV. Sun in Cancer, moon in Taurus. The bull has big horns. Remember?"

"Oh, I remember," she said, forgetting all about the television.

Lying beside Susan later, sealed off from the tumult and the heat, I said, "This was the longest weekend of my life. I couldn't wait for it to end." I was thinking of not just the separation from her but the misery of Kathy's parents, the tropical weather, all the drudgery around the house—grief and work without end, amen.

"I couldn't wait either," she said, her face hovering over mine like a pallid tropical mask in the dim bedroom light. "I drove over to your house Monday night. I parked the car and sat for hours, just watching. I could see people moving around inside. I stayed until all the lights were out."

I didn't tell her, but I was disturbed by the thought of her parked outside my house or anywhere in the immediate neighborhood. It wasn't safe, for either of us.

"I closed my eyes and tried to imagine what it was like being in there with you. I actually think I had an out-of-body experience. I could feel myself float into the house, down hallways and up stairways, through all the rooms. Could you feel me there?"

"So that was you," I said. "I thought a ghost had crawled into bed with me."

"I didn't go that far," she said. "But I think I could draw a floor plan of your house."

As she talked about my house, I started to feel more and more uncomfortable, until I was seized with an anxiety that was close to panic, an urge to leave. But it was much too early. I had told Kathy I might be late. I wasn't expected back for hours.

After a while Susan seemed as restless as I was. She got out of bed and, without bothering to dress, went over and attached herself to her exercise machine, almost sensually. She stretched and heaved, arched and rolled. The movement of pulleys and gears seemed to shake the room. The floor vibrated beneath the mattress. Listening to her pant and groan, I felt as if I were getting an erotic workout myself.

The bedside light threw harsh shadows against the walls and ceiling. I could see spidery cracks, blistering paint, crumbling Sheetrock. I got up to examine the wall. I found damp and swollen patches. There was decay everywhere I looked. Everything seemed to molder under my touch.

With my index finger, I dug into one of the larger cracks, causing a small avalanche of plaster dust and paint chips. Susan had come up beside me, her workout interrupted. As she watched me dig, the fallout collected on her slippery body, like moon dust.

"What are you doing?" she said. "You're making a mess. You're tearing up my walls."

"Where's your spackle?" I said.

"Spackle," she said, distastefully, as if I were suggesting some deviant practice. "I don't keep anything like that around here."

"What do they build these places out of—eggshells? It's practically a tenement."

"It's almost brand-new," Susan said. "Do you know how much rent I pay here?"

I tapped on the wall to demonstrate its flimsiness, showering us with more powdery debris. Both nude, we resembled a pair of plaster sculptures, glowing faintly, sinfully. From the other side of the wall came a muffled knocking. It was not an echo,

I realized, but a reply from Susan's neighbor, knocking in protest.

I hammered on the wall again. Her neighbor hammered back. "That's right," I shouted, "keep it up! If it doesn't fall down on its own, you'll knock it down!"

Susan seized my hand, preventing me from striking the wall again. Her grip was strong, but when I relaxed it turned tender, gentle. She looked at me with alarm and patience and love.

"This place is in bad shape," I said, whispering now. "Do you know how dangerous it is? The whole building ought to be condemned."

"I'll call the manager tomorrow," she said. "He'll take care of everything."

"Okay," I said, letting her lead me away from the wall, "but if he doesn't fix those cracks, I'll come back with some spackle and fix them myself."

"Let me get you a beer," Susan said. "You're so hot. You feel feverish."

I hadn't realized how sweaty I was myself, as if I'd been stretching and flexing alongside her. "No, I'd better go," I said, hurriedly dressing, more anxious than ever to get home. I could explain to Kathy that I got overheated on the tennis court and had to quit early.

On the way out, Susan gave my cheek a farewell stroke. Her hand came away slick with sweat. "You haven't cooled down yet. I'm afraid I gave you too much of a workout. Tennis wouldn't have been nearly this strenuous."

She was about to close the door behind me when I put my hand against it, stopping her. I tapped on the door, not asking to be let back inside but to demonstrate what a fragile barrier it was between her and the rest of the world, how precariously she lived. "This has a hollow core, you know. It wouldn't stop a child, much less a housebreaker."

"I'll talk to the manager about that, too," she said. "First thing tomorrow."

Beneath my fist, I could feel her exerting slow but steady pressure. I didn't resist. I watched as the gap between us gradually narrowed and she disappeared behind the door. I waited in the hallway until I heard her fasten the locks, then I went home.

17

Masterson's call couldn't have come at a more inconvenient time. I was lying on my back in an upstairs bathroom, where I was fitfully trying to disinter the sink from a previous century. I had removed the trap and was in the midst of dislodging calcified hair and grease and fingernail parings, what must have been at least six generations worth of sludge and slime. Whatever its components, my hands, arms, and face were covered with it when Kim told me that Masterson was on the phone.

"Can I call him back?" I asked her. She returned in a minute, saying, "Daddy, he can't wait. He's in a big hurry."

Hurry didn't begin to describe Masterson's emotional state. Panic was more like it. I started to explain what a disaster I had in the bathroom when he ranted: "You've got a bigger disaster at the mall. You've got to get over there right away."

"I thought we had experts handling the project for us."

"The experts fucked up," he said. "The ape fucked up. And now the police are there to fuck it up worse. I'm afraid we're going to have TV too."

"I'd be surprised if we didn't have TV," I said. "We sent releases to all the channels—and all the radio stations and all the newspapers."

"I don't know why they called me about this," he said, suddenly cool and imperious. "It's your project, and it's going to be your ass if you don't get over there and put a cap on things before TV shows up."

There was no point in reminding him whose idea it was to hire the ape in the first place. The instant it turned into a fuck-up Masterson transferred all responsibility to me. I scrubbed off as much of the muck as I could. Then I drove out to the mall to check out the damage and see if I could do anything to patch it up.

As soon as I arrived, I could tell I would have been better off at home, with my head in a clogged drainpipe. The television crews had beat me there. I saw the spinning lights of the minicam trucks at the entrance, parked next to the police cars and the animal control wagon. This was going to be more of a media event than any of us wanted. I wouldn't have been surprised to see the governor descend in a helicopter to declare the mall a disaster area.

Once inside, I was nearly trampled by stampeding teen-agers. Trusting their instincts for chaos, I tracked them along a courtyard, up a ramp, down a tributary flanked by small shops. With all the skylights and neon and vegetation, the mall seemed as green and as surreal as a jungle theme park.

From half a block away, through the overhanging foliage, I

could make out what looked like the festive atmosphere that accompanies a riot. I could hear shouts, see floodlights, feel the rush and heat of delirious crowds. Fleeing, a young mother passed me with a screaming boy.

Outside the fur store, bystanders circled TV reporters and police. Working my way into their midst, I saw at the very center a man wearing a King Kong costume. Or half a costume. He had taken off the head and was holding it under his arm—half man, half ape. His hair was tangled and bushy, his face a bright pink, his eyes numb and fearful, so that the upper part of him looked even more bestial than the lower.

I located Keeler, the project coordinator for the agency that we'd hired to conduct the mall intercept. He was almost as dazed as Kong. "Everything went just super," he told me. "We were getting some terrific responses. People were going up to Kong, petting him, stroking his fur, cuddling him. They loved him. We even got a picture of some girls with big knockers kissing him. Then this one little girl came along and just looped out. She thought he was a real ape. Then her mother looped. Then everybody was looping. This whole end of the mall just went nuts. There was nothing I could do to stop them. They thought the ape had escaped from the zoo."

The next thing I knew, I was blinded by a floodlight. Through the glare and pandemonium, I discovered that I was nose to nose with the lens of a TV camera, a red light signaling urgently, while a blonde with blue eyes, bluer eyeliner, and red blazer pushed a mike at me. "I understand you're responsible for this stunt," she said, sounding more like a policewoman than an anchorwoman.

"It wasn't a stunt," I explained. "It was a mall intercept—a routine marketing research technique. We got permission from everybody: the owner of the fur store, the manager of the mall, mall security. We were getting shoppers' reactions to King

Kong's costume. It's made of FurReal, a revolutionary new product that's a blend of real and synthetic fur."

Just as quickly as they had appeared, the lights and camera shifted from my eyes to hers, and she was saying, "Whatever the monster's costume was made of, it seemed real enough to frighten more than a dozen children. Many of them, we've been informed, will need psychological counseling. In one horrifying moment, the beast may have crippled the dreams of those beautiful little children for years to come. We now switch you to the emergency room of Southwestern Hospital for an eyewitness report from Steve Blakely. This is Linda Goodman, live from Oak Creek Mall . . ."

The police insisted that both Kong and I go to the station with them. It was all I could do to keep them from taking him in the animal wagon. He had to remove the ape suit before they'd let him ride in the squad car. He was charged with disorderly conduct and inciting a riot. The police let me off with only a lecture and a warning. From the way they looked at my greasy work clothes, I was sure they were going to lock me up for vagrancy.

By the time I got home, I had less than an hour to get cleaned up and dressed for dinner. "Daddy," Mark said, as I came through the front door. "We saw you on TV. Why didn't you take us to see King Kong?"

"We all saw you on TV," Kim said.

"The station interrupted the cartoon show they were watching," Kathy said. She seemed as excited as the children. "The way the phone started ringing, everybody in the city must have been tuned to the same channel."

"Everybody?" I asked, hesitant to even speak Masterson's name. It wasn't necessary anyway. Kathy knew who I meant and nodded, looking as despondent now as I must have. "I asked if he wanted you to call him back. He said not to bother, he'd talk to you first thing Monday."

"Yeah," I said, "it'll wait till Monday. What about our dinner plans?"

"They won't wait. Kurt called after he saw you on TV. I thought he'd offer to cancel. But he said he's had these reservations for months."

"We might as well go," I said. "We can't very well call off the sitter now. My spirits have nowhere to go but up."

But I was doubtful. Social occasions with Kurt—Kurt and Marcia—were always tense and uncomfortable, almost antisocial. But they'd called us one night when our resistance was at its lowest, proposing to take us out on our anniversary, and we'd said okay.

They picked us up, and we drove to a desolate part of the city, past squat brick buildings with abandoned loading docks, grimy windows, and dead smokestacks. I couldn't be sure in the darkness, but I thought Kurt crossed the industrial canal that I'd used as a dump for the dead squirrel.

He drove over a freight track, eased the car across a pothole as big as a crater, then drew up to what appeared to be an empty warehouse, except for the bloodred neon sign that spelled out *L'Abattoir*.

"This can't be it," Kathy said. "I wouldn't get out of the car around here."

"You're a lot safer here than you are in your own neighborhood," Marcia said.

"This is only the hottest area in town right now," Kurt said. "All the artists and writers are moving in. We're thinking about buying a weekend place here, then making a permanent move after the kids leave home."

That's when I realized we were in the darkest heart of the

slaughterhouse district, which had been condemned and left for dead years ago. At one time it was supposed to have been leveled for a recycling center, but evidently the real estate mafia had gotten there first.

Kathy was still doubtful. "This looks like a deserted factory."

"It's only the most elegant fucking restaurant in town," said Kurt, stopping next to the ramp that led up to the building. A valet materialized and drove off with the car, its red taillights vanishing in the black vapor. Off in the distance, I imagined I heard the bellow of penned cattle, the frightened shuffle of hooves.

Even with reservations, the maître d' said there would be a wait and escorted us into the bar. "This is going to be an anniversary you won't forget, I promise you," Kurt said.

"It already has been," I said.

"Which one is it?" Marcia asked, as if she didn't know already.

"Eight," I said. "We've made it past the big bad one."

"I wouldn't be so sure," Marcia said suggestively. "You never lose that itch."

"Marcia speaks from experience," Kurt said.

"Your experience, not mine," Marcia said. I tried not to look directly at her.

"I hope we don't have to wait too long to eat," Kathy said. She was growing uneasier by the second, and not just from hunger.

"I've been waiting six months to get a reservation here," Kurt said. "A few more minutes is not going to make much difference."

It was nearly two hours before the maître d' came back to show us to our table. By then, our appetites were dulled by gin and champagne, and dinner had become a blurred and impossible hope.

The dining area was vast and open, all raw brick and chrome and bare wood. Smoke drifted up to the exposed ceiling trusses, where I watched it settle among spiderwebs and layers of soot. As we made our way through the packed room, the sawdust on the floor seemed as thick and heavy as wet pulp. Like all the other tables, ours was made of crude butcher block, grooved and scarred, I supposed, from the constant assault of hatchets, saws, cleavers, and carving knives.

Our waiter wore a white smock with brownish stains. The menu was simple, consisting entirely of steaks and chops and bigger steaks and chops. He refused to leave until we'd ordered. "Would you like to get your own steaks," he asked, "or shall I do it for you?"

He gestured toward the back wall. Its entire length was taken up by a walk-in cooler. Through the condensation on the windows, I could see men and women in white aprons sawing and hacking away at the hanging carcasses of cows and pigs.

We decided to wait at the table while Kurt went off to get our dinners for us. He came back wearing a paper apron himself. Though it was badly smeared, we could still read the slogan, "I made the cut at *L'Abattoir.*" Kurt had been a little careless, I noticed. There were specks of blood and tissue on his shirtsleeves.

"That's what's great about this place," he said. "They don't fuck around. It's back to the basics. You know, they butcher their own livestock here. You can go out back and watch."

So the anxious cattle noises I heard outside hadn't been imaginary. This was a microslaughterhouse.

Kurt ordered another bottle of wine, even though Kathy and I still had full glasses from the last bottle. Marcia's glass was almost empty, but she didn't need a refill either. She kept dropping in and out of the party, her eyelids fluttering dreamily.

"You know why I didn't shave?" Kurt said, rubbing his weekend stubble.

"I just assumed you were doing your vice cop impersonation," Kathy said.

"Because shaving is bullshit," he said. "I'm into total honesty. No hypocrisy, no polite bullshit. No bullshit whatsoever."

"Good-bye to civilization, is that it?" Kathy said. I was praying that she wouldn't encourage Kurt. His bluster could only go onward and downward.

"Good-bye to bullshit," he said. "From now on, I say what I think. If it offends you, if you don't like me for what I am, then I say, fuck off."

The waiter was serving our steaks. But after hours of waiting for a table, not to mention months of waiting for a reservation, Kurt was more interested in dispensing with the bullshit than eating.

"You don't offend me," Kathy said to him. "I think you're perfectly charming."

Marcia's eyelids flickered to attention. She drew herself up and leaned over, chest and elbows on the table. "You're not getting any funny ideas about my husband, are you?"

"I think he's sweet, that's all."

"He is sweet," Marcia said, "and if you want to fuck him, it's perfectly all right."

"He's not that sweet," Kathy said.

"It's just like Kurt said," Marcia told her. "We're both into total honesty. We're not uptight about anything. You want to fuck Kurt, all you have to do is ask."

"Okay," I said, "before we do anything we'll be sure and ask your permission."

"Who said anything about you fucking Marcia?" Kurt said.

"Not me," I assured him. "Tell you what. We've got a fundamental disagreement here. You're into total honesty. We're into total bullshit."

I picked up my steak knife. "There's just one way to settle this. Let's just skip the philosophical discussions and eat dinner, okay?"

Kurt relaxed, then raised his wineglass as if to offer a toast. "Okay," he said. "But if you want to fuck Marcia, it's all right. You don't even have to ask."

As soon as we finished dinner, Kathy went to call the sitter. We were already late, and it would probably take another hour before we made it home. "The line was busy," she said, looking worried.

"You know how teenage girls are," Marcia said. "Just be glad she's talking to him on your phone and not in your bed."

We were the last customers to leave the restaurant. The neon sign had been switched off. The block was so dark we might have been trapped in a power outage. There was nobody on the street, not even the parking attendant.

Kurt went inside to look for him. He was back in a few minutes, obviously distressed. "They don't have anybody who parks cars," he said.

Kurt called the police; I called a cab. "Sorry we can't stay and give you aid and comfort," I told him as we were leaving, "but a good baby-sitter is harder to find than a stolen car."

"Well at least I won't have to tip the bastard."

It was a long, silent, sobering cab ride home. We were both nervous enough about the phone, which was still busy when we'd left the restaurant. But as soon as the cab turned a corner onto our street, we were confronted with a vision out of our most morbid anxieties: police cars, fire trucks, rescue wagons, ladders, flashing lights, orange hoses that reached like tentacles across parkways and lawns, across the entire neighborhood. I was afraid the mall scene that afternoon had only been a rehearsal for what looked like a much bigger catastrophe.

Because of all the congestion, the cab couldn't get within a block of our house. In my panic, I leaped out before it stopped moving. Whatever was happening, I could tell, it was happening to our house. It was as brightly lit as a Halloween pumpkin, not by flames, I was relieved to see, but by spotlights.

I found Jennifer, the sitter, standing on the forward edge of the crowd. She was holding Peter, who was awake and trying to squirm out of her arms. Standing beside her, Kim and Mark were even more alert and delighted by the spectacle. I took Peter from Jennifer. "I fell asleep in front of the TV," she said, "and the next thing I knew, the smoke alarms were going off, the firemen came, and we had to be rescued from the house."

Kathy came up, and I passed Peter along to her. Then I located a policeman who seemed to be in charge. "Just a short in the wiring, from what we can tell," he said. "Your security system went off at the station. We sent a car over; they heard the smoke alarms going off and got the fire department out here."

A fireman in a moon suit approached us, carrying a charred scrap of bone, flesh, and fur. I didn't have to be told what it was.

"Here's your problem," he said. "Little bastard chewed into the BX and shorted out your power. Set off your security system and your smoke alarms. You'll need an electrician and your house will smell like a barbecue pit for a week or so, but no serious damage. Unless you're into blackened squirrel, I'll dispose of the remains."

On my way over to tell Kathy and the kids what had happened, I began to tremble and shiver, and not just from the autumn chill. The damage had been serious. The situation had reached critical mass. When it came to dealing with squirrels, just this once I was willing to concede that my father-in-law knew best.

18

By now, I had started to get a feeling for the currents and rhythms of the night. From my remote perspective, they seemed to correspond to the normal pattern of sleep. A little after midnight, a profound blackness settled over the neighborhood, a peace as civilizing as death. For a few hours, it was as if a main circuit had broken and I was isolated from all the evil and disruptive clamor around me: no horns, sirens, or train whistles, no cries of rage or passion or anguish, no rustling or scratching within the walls and ceilings.

I was barely sleeping myself—two or three hours, maximum, usually before midnight. At first, the situation was beyond my control, a matter of apprehension and regret. But then I gradually began to welcome, even depend on, these recurrent awakenings. I realized that I didn't require or want more sleep. I willingly turned into a creature of the dark, a night watchman, grateful for those hours of almost holy solitude, which had become more necessary than sleep.

When the nights were still warm and the mosquitoes not too fierce, I would stretch out in a lawn chair on the back porch, listening and waiting, planning. As the weather grew steadily cooler, I put on a sweater, a jacket, a blanket, until it was time to move indoors. Then I sat in the kitchen, the pistol on the table beside me. Framed within a cylinder of light, I knew I made a perfect target, but I wasn't concerned about snipers.

From an observation point outside the house, my Dirty Harry pellet pistol must have looked genuine, a lethal weapon. If there was someone watching, waiting for the opportunity to strike, the gun would surely be a deterrent. And there was someone watching. I couldn't hear or see them, but I could feel their presence out there. For all our sakes, I had to stay awake.

I had been on red alert since Christmas Eve, after a band of carolers had appeared on our front porch. At Kathy's insistence, I'd grudgingly come up from the basement to listen to them with the rest of the family. I'd been down there late the last four nights assembling a Victorian dollhouse for Kim. I wasn't nearly finished, and I still had to deal with Mark's Ninja Turtle Sewer Playset before the night was over.

Rather than put me in a cheerful mood, the carolers made me more anxious and downcast. I had assumed they were our neighbors, but none looked or sounded familiar. It was impossible to see them clearly anyway, with their faces obscured by scarves and stocking caps. They seemed to have a huge and inexhaustible repertoire, singing carols I'd never heard before.

It was intolerably cold, standing there in the hallway, with both doors open. I could hear the furnace laboring to keep the temperature inside the house above freezing.

After the carolers had finally gone, I made a drink and briefly warmed up in the living room, while Kathy put the children to bed. There were already numerous packages beneath the Christmas tree, some that had arrived in the mail from relatives, others that Kathy and I were giving each other. Then there were all the other presents Santa had to drop off that night, if he ever finished with the dollhouse and the Ninja Sewer.

The next morning, even though they were submerged in toys, ribbons, and torn wrapping paper, the children refused to believe they'd reached bottom, that nothing was left but the bucket of pistachios from Capisco. "Is that all?" Kim said.

"No," Kathy said to me. "That's not all. Where's the watch I got for you?" Only then did I realize that she hadn't opened the portable CD player I'd given her. Neither present was under the tree. Nor was the toaster oven that my sister asked about when we talked on the phone that afternoon.

It wasn't until that night that we found out what had happened to them. The details were on the ten o'clock news. Posing as carolers, a burglary ring had distracted homeowners while confederates entered their houses from the rear and helped themselves to Christmas presents and other valuables. A week or so later, we discovered that an heirloom set of silverware, which Kathy's grandmother had left her, was also missing.

I hadn't let my guard down since. I'm convinced that it was only through my vigilance that our house wasn't completely emptied by looters. Besides my midnight-to-dawn patrols, I had scrupulously policed the yard in the mornings all winter and spring. Checking the snow and mud and soft earth for signs of trespassers, I found cigarette butts, candy wrappers, and strange footprints, human and animal. I'd even stayed home while Kathy took the kids to a summer block party, suspecting it might be a ruse for more plundering.

In the course of my sentry duty, I had discovered the illuminating power of darkness. During the blackest hours of night, I was struck by an insight and clarity of purpose that were almost supernatural. Whether domestic, professional, or romantic, every problem I had could almost be reduced to an algebraic formula and resolved, without the confusion and lust, the ambition and guilt that obscured my daytime vision.

In some matters, I could clearly see how driven and reckless, how impulsive I'd become. In others, it was just as clear that I was doing exactly what had to be done. If I didn't want to be preyed upon, I had to turn into a predator myself.

Whatever I did, I knew that my ultimate responsibility was to my family. Whatever the cost, I had to shelter and protect them. If I could only focus on that, I could deal with everyone and everything else: Kinkaid and FurReal, Susan, the electricity and plumbing, the hardware bills, the mortgage payments, my diminishing hairline and tennis game, even the wild and alien creatures that perennially threatened to storm and infest our house.

That's why I hated to see the sky gradually begin to lighten. Once dawn came, it was as if a dark curtain had been lowered, not raised, over the world, bringing an end to dreams. First Kathy came down to the kitchen, tired and quarrelsome, fussing with the coffeemaker, unwilling at that uncivilized hour to listen to any talk of house or office. Then the children got up, even more sullen and cranky.

I was feeling a lot less alert and optimistic when I left the house. Riding the train to work, I dozed off, and those stray moments of sleep seemed to cloud everything, all my good intentions, my serenity, my undistorted angle of vision. By the time I got to the office, I was as confused and irresolute and agitated as ever.

Arriving on that bleak Monday after the mall debacle, I wasn't prepared for how abnormally calm it was. There was no message from Kinkaid, as I'd expected—either a notice of immediate dismissal or a summons to appear before an executive tribunal. Nor was there any word from Masterson.

At first, I was relieved and grateful. But before long the silence got to be eerie, almost alarming. After all the media notoriety, the Kong incident couldn't be allowed to pass without corporate action. Something had to be happening.

I waited as long as I could, then called Masterson. Sandy picked up, saying he had gone over to the Tower for a meeting with Kinkaid and his staff. "Oh, shit," I said, figuring that my fate was being decided in high-level secrecy, without my being permitted to testify on my own behalf. "You have any idea what's going on?"

"Nobody tells me anything," Sandy said. "But I don't know why you have to worry. After that weekend debut on TV, you can always get a job—as host of 'Wild Kingdom.' "

"Thanks, Sandy, just what I needed to boost my morale." Then, deliberately or not, she did exactly that by reminding me that Masterson had been called not to an emergency or contingency session but simply to the fall budget meeting, which had been scheduled for months.

Hanging up, I had started to sort through the pile of responses from the mall intercept, looking for some shred of salvation, some way of turning disaster into partial victory, when the phone rang. It was not Susan, as I'd hoped, but Ace, proposing lunch. I'd seen him at the station an hour earlier, but squeezed behind a pillar before he saw me. His invitation could only mean one thing, pork bellies, which I needed like another hole in my house. I said this was my busy season. He persisted. In my weak and desperate state, I agreed on a date three weeks off. That would give me plenty of time to come up with an excuse to break it.

When I hadn't heard from Susan by eleven, I called her but got a recording and left a message on her voice mail. To my amazement, the responses from the mall intercept, the ones they'd been able to collect before the riot squad arrived, were much more favorable than not.

"You fooled me," one woman reported, saying that she thought FurReal was a great improvement on real fur. "It felt so soft when I stroked it." I wondered which part of Kong she'd stroked.

Her comment was typical, however, and my tabulation showed them running more than four to one in our favor. Some were even better than if I had written them myself, with a number helpfully pointing out FurReal's potential benefits to the environment and to endangered species. I had to reluctantly discard several of the more extravagant ones because they were obviously the work of teenage mall heads, whose praise of FurReal was blatantly obscene.

With no interruptions, I was able to spend the afternoon writing a report. I naturally put the emphasis on how the product responses were all or more than we'd hoped for. The fact that FurReal had not only fooled but frightened shoppers, I pointed out, was conclusive evidence of its value, all the bad publicity notwithstanding. I left a copy on Masterson's desk and put another in the house mail for immediate dispatch to Kinkaid. He'd have it on his desk at the Tower the next morning.

Knowing that I had done all that I could humanly do, I went home in a weary but almost tranquil condition. My peace of mind vanished as soon as I walked through the front door.

I could smell burned wood, metal, and fur, lingering evidence of the squirrel's assault on our electrical system. Kim was brokenhearted because she hadn't been invited to a classmate's birthday party. The estimate for stripping the beams in the library was four times what we'd expected, which meant that Kathy and I would have to do it ourselves.

I was happy to find that the power had been restored and the squirrel damage temporarily repaired, but the attic needed to be completely rewired, Kathy informed me. There was even worse news. After the electricians left, she had continued to hear noises from the attic.

I could hear them myself that night, after everyone else had gone to bed, and every other night that week. As the weather got progressively colder, the squirrels got even noisier. I could see them up there, breeding and multiplying, shredding rafters and joists with their claws and teeth, burrowing into the insulation, stocking their nests for winter, turning our home into theirs.

Paradoxically, a deadly calm remained over the office, an oppressive silence that I would have gladly exchanged for the usual turbulence and unrest. I was under more pressure than ever, but this was different, more like a persistent and accumulating sense of dread.

There was no response from Kinkaid to the FurReal report. I hadn't seen or heard from Masterson either. He wasn't in his office all week. The report was still on his desk, where I'd left it. A reporter called me for an interview about FurReal. As eager as I was to talk to him about its unique properties, company policy required that all queries be referred to the vice president for public relations.

Everything was on hold, including Susan. She had stopped

calling me at the office in the morning. She didn't return my calls. She didn't answer the buzzer in the lobby of her building. I went up and knocked quietly at her door. I listened, expecting whispers and stealthy footsteps, but I could hear nothing.

The only response I got was her recorded voice, advising me that she'd return my call at the first opportunity. She hadn't said anything about leaving town. But there was always the possibility she'd been sent off on emergency business. Or that she'd won a vacation sweepstakes. Or maybe she was simply trying to get a message to me—via paranormal channels—that I was no longer the man of her dreams.

Whatever the reason, I had other business to distract and occupy me. That weekend the yard had to be raked, the branches and leaves bagged. The lawn furniture had to be stored in the garage. The hoses had to be drained, the storm windows reglazed, painted, washed, and installed. The doors needed weather stripping. There was a frost warning for early the next week. The first snow could fall at any time.

Before it did, I had to dispose of the squirrels. While I raked and bagged, I reviewed my options. I had almost none left. I had tried patching their holes, trapping them, counterattacking with mothballs, pellets, and various household tools. I had even tried to drive them crazy with an ultrasonic beeper. Poison wasn't a legitimate or practical option. Nor was heavier artillery. Or was it?

As I worked around the yard, so did the squirrels. It was almost as if we were allies in our rush to get everything done before moving inside, not just for the night but for the winter. The sky grew darker, and it started to drizzle. I stopped to watch the squirrels swarm over our house and disappear into their holes. The cold drizzle had caused them to knock off early, suggesting that they had more sense than I did.

I was bagging the last of the leaves when I heard Mrs.

Underwood summon me from her side of the fence. I approached slowly, grudgingly, hoping she'd realize how much of a hurry I was in. "I'm so glad to see you're raking your whole yard this year," she said. "It's not good for the grass, you know, to have it covered with leaves all winter."

"I know, and if I don't keep going, I won't get it all raked."

"You ought to spread some of those leaves around the base of your junipers. That way their roots will be protected. They like to have their winter blankets too."

"That's a very good idea," I said. "I'll take care of that right now."

I had only retreated a step or two when she said, "What I really wanted to speak to you about . . ."

I momentarily hesitated, then kept walking. Surely she was too much of a lady to strike while my back was turned.

". . . were your squirrels."

I was wrong. I turned toward her.

"Oh, really," I said. "My squirrels."

"Yes, I'm very concerned about them."

In the damp twilight, her words were like tiny cloudbursts. The cold air gave her wrinkled flesh an unhealthy pink coloring, reminding me that in barely more than a month I would be carving our Thanksgiving turkey.

"I'm a little concerned about them, too," I told her.

"I really wish you'd do something about them. They keep coming over into my yard and using it as a toilet."

"I've got those little fellows well trained, don't I?"

She looked strangely pleased, as if she'd been crafty enough to catch me in a trap. "I knew you were putting them up to it."

"It seemed like the neighborly thing to do," I said, giving her my broadest and most insincere smile. "I wouldn't want to keep all that good fertilizer to myself. That's why your grass was so green this summer."

"If you don't make them stop, I'm going to call the police."

"Well, I don't think that would do much for neighborhood solidarity."

"I tell you . . . I'll take you to court if your squirrels don't stop shitting in my yard!"

"Mrs. Underwood, please. The children will hear you."

I left her standing at the fence. I didn't bother to finish raking the yard. I didn't spread a blanket of leaves around the junipers. I went indoors where it was warm and I could enjoy the creature comforts with my wife, my children, and my squirrels.

19

Somehow I had to get out of the house. I had given Peter and Mark their baths and read them *Curious George Takes a Job*. Kathy and Kim had finished her Little Mermaid costume for Halloween. Once we had them all in bed, I had my choice of ways to spend the rest of the evening.

I could join Kathy in the library, where she was stripping the ceiling. I could wash the storm windows that were in the basement, still waiting to be installed. Or I could work on my creative accounting.

I had to figure out how I could pay the utility bills, the mortgage, and the carpenter who was building our kitchen cabinets when we had barely half the necessary amount in the bank. The birthday check that his grandparents had sent Peter might help. But I doubted that Kathy would endorse it for any destination other than his savings account, even on an emergency basis.

I went into the media room and turned the television to the Nostalgia Channel. But it was impossible to get wrapped up in the plight of the "Wolfman," who was making his annual reappearance in the station's week-long Halloween Horrorfest. The last thing I wanted to watch was an actor running amok in a fur jumpsuit. My troubles seemed worse than his, and the moon wasn't even full.

I switched to the stereo, but the classical station was playing "Danse Macabre." On the jazz showcase, Billie Holiday was mourning the loss of her man, which sent me into an even bluer funk.

Susan still wasn't answering her phone. At first, it was almost peaceful being disconnected from her, like having one flashing light go out on my overloaded switchboard. Free of the anxiety, the intrigue, the physical effort involved in seeing her, I could take some deep breaths and devote my badly divided attention to other matters. I could try to reconnect with Kathy and the children.

Until getting entangled with Susan, I'd never understood what it meant to have your affections alienated. After almost a week without seeing or hearing from her, I realized how attached, how dependent I'd become, not just physically but emotionally. Whether at work or at home, I was muddled and bewitched, in a perpetual state of wonder over where she was, what she was doing, who she was doing it with, and why she'd cut me off so rudely.

I had reached the place where I had to find out—that night. But I needed an excuse to leave the house. I wasn't due to play tennis until later in the week. I could offer to run out to get paint stripper for Kathy, but she knew we had several gallons in the basement. I checked the refrigerator. Plenty of milk and eggs. I rummaged through the kitchen cabinets. We had three loaves of bread and a huge stockpile of Captain Crunch, Count Chocula, Honey Nut Cheerios, and other cereals.

There were five cookies left in the Oreo package. Out of frustration, I had split one and was about to eat it when I had an inspiration. Retrieving an empty flour bag from the trash, I wrapped the Oreos in it and buried them at the bottom of the can. I went into the library, carrying the empty cookie package.

"Somebody ate all the Oreos," I said.

Annoyed, Kathy glared down at me from the ladder. "Why are you telling me about this? Now? I didn't eat them. I'm not in charge of the cookies around here."

"I'd hidden them away for myself. I was going to eat them before I went to bed, and now they're all gone."

"You know you can't hide cookies anywhere in this house. It's like trying to hide cheese from mice. The little creatures just follow their noses."

A glutinous blob of stripper and paint slid off her scraper, narrowly missed my head, and splattered at my feet, like a huge bird dropping. "Careful there," I said. "That stuff is really wrecking the floor."

"It all has to be refinished anyway. This way you get a head start."

"I don't know if these stains can be sanded out."

"It's not too late to spread some drop cloths."

"I was really counting on having those Oreos."

"If you're that desperate, why don't you go out and get some? The store's still open."

I was desperate. Zipping up my jacket, I asked, "Can I get you anything?"

"Yes, you can get out of my way."

* * *

Parking across from Susan's building, I could see a light in her apartment, a saffron glow through the gauzy Indian spread she'd hung over her window. She didn't answer her buzzer. I pushed the buttons on the combination lock in the lobby and went upstairs to her door.

I knocked gently, then harder. I heard whispers, footsteps, sighs, but they could have been coming from behind the cardboard doors and walls of any of the other apartments. The television sets were all tuned to the same program, a highly rated series that restaged infamous crimes and atrocities.

When I was certain Susan wasn't going to answer, I braced my shoulder against the doorframe, listening to the electronically amplified screams and shouts, waiting for the explosion that was sure to follow. As the gun went off, simultaneously reverberating from a dozen television sets, I gave Susan's door a strong kick.

It buckled and popped open, as easily, as quietly as if I'd torn the top off a cereal box. I went inside, quickly closing the door behind me. The living room was empty, the muted light from the single table lamp making it seem even emptier, vacant almost. I stood with my back against the door, anticipating a frantic patter of bare feet from the dark bedroom, a dance of fright, panicked voices.

But all I heard was television babble, not from Susan's set, which was silent, but from those of her neighbors, immediately beside, above, and below, absorbed in simulated beatings, killings, dismemberments. I went into the bedroom first to make sure that Susan wasn't dead or comatose on her futon, either from natural or unnatural causes. The bed was empty and unmade, looking about as it had when I'd left it last, more than a week ago. I checked the sheets, but it was impossible to know if the telltale spots were mine or someone else's.

The answering machine beside her bed was blinking. I pushed the button and was halfway through the first message when I realized the weak, mushy voice was mine. There were three more messages, all from me, each one more plaintive than the last. No wonder she was giving me the brush. If I was as much of a mope as I sounded over the phone, all she needed was a feather duster.

I erased my messages, then checked out the bathroom and closets. There was no evidence Susan had met with foul play. Her suitcases were on a closet shelf, which meant she hadn't left town. Everything else seemed to be in order, carefully hung, stacked, filed, neatly arranged in its proper place. I might have been impressed by her tidy habits except that she lived too spartanly, had too few possessions to require any real house-keeping.

From my hurried search, she didn't seem to have any se-crets, dark, deep, or otherwise. She hadn't left a clue as to where she'd gone. But it was apparent that she was gone only temporarily, that she was likely to be back soon, perhaps mo-mentarily. I had a picture of her entering the lobby at that very instant, taking the stairs two at a time in her athletic stride, about to come through that mangled front door.

I thought about waiting, confronting her, demanding to know why she'd cut me off without a word, without a consoling explanation or a parting kiss. But that really wasn't a practical option, considering how late it was already. In which case, I had to get the hell out of there, and pronto.

First I had to cover my tracks, otherwise Susan would know immediately that this was the work of an amateur, that it was I who had broken into her apartment. I began to empty her dresser drawers onto the floor. I dumped jars and bottles of makeup onto the pile. I threw clothes out of the closets. I went through her desk and flung papers across the room. I trashed the place so that it would look like the work of a home invader.

I put anything that might be of value into a suitcase: what little jewelry she owned, the cash she'd hidden in a running shoe, her cassette player, electronic horoscope, and synchro-energized goggles—plus several pairs of underpants and bras, a flourish that would give the job a diversionary touch of sexual perversion. I was almost enjoying myself. If Susan had in fact given me an unceremonious kiss-off, I could at least get revenge for the damage she'd done to my heart and mind, for literally fucking up my life.

Before leaving, I rummaged through the kitchen cabinets, looking for cookies. There were no Oreos, but I found a nearly full bag of vanilla wafers, an acceptable substitute that would save me having to stop on the way home. If Susan discovered them missing, that might convince the police that the burglar had a deviant fetish.

With the suitcase in one hand, I grabbed the television set and carried the loot down the back stairway, an entrance Susan never used. I wasn't worried about meeting another tenant. In a transient place like this, people were always packing up and checking out at peculiar hours, a step ahead of the landlord.

Driving away, I felt a jolt of elation, the high that must come to all thieves after accomplishing a dangerous mission. But whatever relief and joy I experienced was accompanied by a sense of loss, as if I'd vandalized a wayward and shadowy corner of my own heart.

Assuming this was the end for Susan and me, it was also a cause for sorrow—that we'd never gotten to do the things we so often talked about doing together, the movies, the concerts, the restaurants, the trips to sunny places. Sad to contemplate, our romance had been almost entirely confined to the sweaty, chambered gloom of her apartment.

I was halfway home before I realized that I was also left with a major physical burden: how to dispose of the stolen goods. I couldn't very well hang onto them until the next neighborhood garage sale. As I quickly sorted through my options, it came down to a single one. I detoured out to the industrial wasteland, parked on the bridge, and pitched the suitcase and the television set into the black and poisonous sludge of the canal.

That wasn't the end of my troubles. Back on the track at last, I still had to explain to Kathy how I'd managed to spend two hours shopping for Oreos, then come home with vanilla wafers.

20

As it turned out, I didn't have to worry about explaining anything to Kathy. Letting myself into the house as quietly as a cat
burglar, an undiscovered talent that I was hastily perfecting, I
found her upstairs, lying across the bed in her work clothes,
dead to the world. I was almost ready to take her pulse when
I noticed the gentle shudder of the blanket, heard a rhythmic
series of faint and exhausted sighs. It was plain that she had
been so bushed from working on the ceiling that she had
collapsed into bed, without enough energy left to undress.

I doubt that I could have disturbed her if I'd wanted to,
which I badly didn't. As I took off my clothes in the moonlit
bedroom, I watched her there, breathing as delicately, as se-
curely as a child. Now that Susan was apparently out of my life,
I felt as close to Kathy as I had in a long time. I wanted to crawl

in beside her, burrow next to her warm and consoling flesh. Instead, I crept around to my side of the bed, slipped my pillow from beneath her arm, and carried it off to a spare bedroom, like a lost camper looking for a dry, quiet place to sleep.

Freed of one burden, I slept as deeply as I had in weeks, but for no more than an hour or two. Then I was awakened by a clump and creak from the first floor, the unmistakable, the inevitable sound of footsteps, not animal this time but human. I got up and quietly went back to our bedroom, getting the pellet gun from the closet shelf.

Going down the stairway, I was thinking that no matter how much I'd anticipated something like this, how prepared I'd been, I could never have predicted how terrified I'd be. I was afraid I was going to panic and drop the pistol, not that it would be any use against a professional home invader anyway.

From all the clatter, I was sure he couldn't have been a professional. He had to be an amateur barbarian, which could make him even more volatile and dangerous. Whoever or whatever he was, he was busy pillaging the living room, making too much noise himself to hear me stumble on Mark's plastic gladiator helmet at the bottom of the stairs. I waited to be sure he hadn't been alerted, then moved along the hallway in a military crouch and peeked around a French door into the living room.

If I'd had to stake my life on it, I would have bet that I was about to encounter a ponytailed burglar of uncertain Hispanic extraction: a bandido posing as a ceramics teacher, who was determined to steal not just my wife but our most cherished possessions, a housebreaker as well as home-wrecker. *Que pasa, Mario?*

I would have lost that bet. Even in the darkness, I could recognize the squat silhouette, the ballistic shape of our mid-night visitor, who had taken the antique school clock off the wall and was presumably about to deposit it in his bulging rucksack, along with selected other valuables. While both his hands were occupied by our clock, I figured that I had the drop on him, that I had to make my move.

But I had no clue how to confront him, except the way I'd seen men do it in dozens of cop movies and television shows. "Freeze or you're dead," I shouted, pivoting around the doorframe into the living room, my pistol raised and pointed at his head.

He froze. In the murky light, I just hoped he couldn't tell how unfrozen I was, how shaky, even though I was gripping the pistol with both hands, like a movie vice cop.

After waiting a moment to collect myself, I backed over to a wall switch and turned on the ceiling light. Blinking and grinning foolishly, Roy Phillips looked like a man suddenly caught in the harsh and incriminating glare of a police lineup. "Out collecting merchandise for your next garage sale?" I said.

"Hey there, neighbor," he said, "no need for the weapon. This is just a friendly visit. You know your clock's running fifteen minutes slow? I was just setting the right time for you."

"You can do your explaining to the police," I said.

I can't be sure which came next, the cold tubular pressure of a steel barrel against the back of my head, just below my ear, or the equally cold, steely voice, saying, "Now you freeze, cat killer."

Under the circumstances, I froze as best I could. But the pressure of the steel barrel against my head only increased, harder and colder than an icicle, ready to go off. "Now let the gun drop." I let it drop.

I was glad to get rid of it. Without the gun, my chances of being shot down in a pathetic attempt to defend my home seemed to be considerably reduced, if not entirely eliminated.

As soon as the gun hit the rug, the pistol barrel came

away from my head, and I could hear the ratchetlike sound of the hammer being released. Only then did I start to breathe again. Turning slightly sideways, I could just barely make out Jerry Klammish, in his neighborhood surveillance uniform. "You've got some explaining to do yourself," he said, "starting with her."

He came around in front of me, clutching a .45 in one hand and Susan's wrist in the other. He swung her toward me, as though she were his partner in a slow and awkward square dance. In the brutal overhead light, she looked paler than I'd ever seen her, panicked and sick. When he let go of her wrist, she took a step and fell against my chest, trembling and moaning, soaking my shirt with her tears. "Scott, I thought he was going to kill me."

I pulled her head tightly against me, hugging her, stroking her hair, not so much to comfort her as to smother her cries. As urgently as I needed to talk to her, to find out where she'd been and what she was doing here, I had to calm her down, before she woke Kathy and the children.

"She told us she was a friend of yours," Klammish said. "I guess she was telling the truth about that anyway."

"What the fuck is going on here?" I said, attempting to keep my voice low and forceful at the same time.

"We spotted her three nights ago," Klammish said, holstering his .45. "She was sitting in a car down the block. She's been there every night since, acting very suspicious. We figured she was casing the neighborhood."

Looking up at me, like a tearful child explaining how she'd been misunderstood by an insensitive teacher, Susan said, "I was sending you messages from my car. I was just about to break the psychic barriers between us."

"She was sending messages to somebody all right," Klammish said. "We opened the car door, surprised her, she was babbling away. I figured she was point woman for a gang of burglars. But we couldn't find a phone or a walkie-talkie in her car."

"I was trying to make spiritual contact," Susan said, "without any cords or wires connecting us."

"Somebody's missing some wires around here," Klammish said.

While we'd been talking, Roy had set our clock down and come across the room. He recovered my pistol from the floor and pointed it at me, threateningly. Assuming it was as deadly as it looked, Susan gasped, tensed, and buried her head back in my chest.

"You were about to shoot me with this, weren't you, neighbor?" Roy said.

"Breaking into my house in the middle of the night—you're lucky I didn't shoot you," I told him, pushing the barrel away from my face. "But it wouldn't have done much damage. It's only a popgun."

He examined the pistol, skeptically. Opening the cylinder, he let the pellets roll onto the carpet. He still wasn't pacified. "You could've put my eye out."

Klammish held out his hand, palm up, and Roy gave him the pistol. "This is an unauthorized weapon," he said.

"I checked when I bought it," I assured him. "You don't have to register pellet guns with police."

"You're supposed to register any kind of weapon with Neighborhood Solidarity," he said. "Doesn't matter if it shoots BBs or mortar shells."

Klammish sighted down the barrel, aiming at one of Kathy's ceramic abstractions, and pulled the trigger on an empty chamber. "Is this what you've been using to shoot cats?" he asked me.

"I've never shot any cats."

"Guy's a practical joker," Klammish told Roy. "Thinks dead cats are funny. Gave me one in a shoebox."

"That was no cat," I said. "It was a squirrel."

"Cats, squirrels, dogs, possums—you just don't go around shooting helpless creatures in this neighborhood."

"Whatever it was," I said, "I ran over it with my car in the alley. I was trying to dispose of the remains."

"We're going to have to confiscate this weapon," Klammish said. "You want it back, you can come over and fill out the proper forms. You could sign up for the neighborhood surveillance team at the same time."

"I don't think I'd qualify," I said. "I can't even seem to defend my own home."

For a flickering instant, I thought I saw a smile crack that stonework face. Then he handed the pistol back to Roy, who'd kept an obviously greedy eye on it. I assumed he wanted to add it to his family arsenal, another plaything for Darryl and Howard.

From above, I could heard the sound of bare feet on bare floorboards. Then Kathy called from the head of the stairs. "What is going on down there, Scott? Is that the television? It sounds like you're having a party."

"It's okay," I said. "There's no problem. Everything's under control. It's just our friends from Neighborhood Solidarity. Making a routine check."

I wanted to go into the hallway, to stop Kathy from coming down the stairs. But Susan wasn't ready to let go. She held onto me as if I were preventing her from being pulled away by an undertow, while I felt as if she were dragging us both under.

"I thought I heard a woman's voice down there," Kathy said.

Klammish went to the foot of the stairs. From where I stood, I could see Kathy's shadow, drawing away at the sight of him approaching.

"Policewoman," he shouted up to her. "She came by to check your security system. Called us for backup. It turned out there was some kind of malfunction."

"I just explained to them that we'd had a problem with a squirrel and hadn't been able to get it fixed. It's okay, you can go back to bed."

"All right," she said. "But please try not to make so much noise. You're going to wake the kids."

As Kathy's shadow started to recede, Klammish shouted after her, "Sorry about the disturbance, Mrs. Ryan. We'll be leaving now."

We waited silently, like hostile conspirators, until we heard Kathy return to bed. I snapped off the ceiling light in the living room. I could feel Susan relax, drawing away from me slightly. Klammish moved toward the doorway, with Roy following. I was right behind them, holding Susan by the arm, just as anxious to get her out of there.

Going out the door, Roy thrust the pistol toward me. "You were about to shoot me with this, weren't you?"

"Roy, I told you. I'm scared to death of guns. I couldn't shoot a rat. I couldn't have pulled the trigger if my life depended on it."

He dropped the pistol into his jacket pocket. There was enough light from the street so that I could see a suspicious bulge in his other pocket. I wasn't about to make an issue of it. If I found anything valuable missing, I could always buy it back cheap at his next house sale.

"We didn't mean to disturb you either," Klammish said to Susan. "But you really oughtn't to be hanging around strange neighborhoods. And you," he said, turning on me, "really ought to get that security system fixed."

When they had gone off into the night, I walked Susan back to her car. We stayed in the shadows, out of the streetlight, in case Kathy happened to be watching from the window. I helped her into the car, then went around and got in on the passenger's side. I put my hand on hers so she wouldn't turn on the engine and drive off. I wasn't going anywhere myself.

She didn't seem to be in any hurry to leave. Sitting behind the steering wheel, she had her eyes closed, her head bowed slightly forward, her lips moving silently, almost as if she were praying. I waited, trying to control my impatience, assuming she'd explain everything when she got herself completely pulled together.

Finally she opened her eyes, seeming almost abnormally calm now, and said, "Scott, I don't like your friends."

"They're not my friends," I said. "They're my neighbors."

"I was afraid they were going to rape and kill me."

"I thought I warned you this wasn't a safe neighborhood."

"You should understand why I was out here. Why I couldn't talk to you on the phone. Why I couldn't see you. My horoscope said we had to strengthen the spiritual side of our relationship. I wanted to avoid any physical contact. I wanted to connect with you through psychic waves. I wanted to channel my thoughts into your head. That way our souls would merge. Whenever we were apart, we'd be together, soul mates. I was just about to make contact when they broke the connection."

"I was getting these weird vibrations," I told her. At that moment the only vibrations I felt were shivers. I hadn't thought to bring a coat. It was colder inside the car than outside. The heat from our bodies steamed the windows.

"You've really got to go," I said. "I've got to go. We can talk about this tomorrow. I'll try to come by tomorrow night. I can't miss my tennis match, but I'll try to stop over for a while, before or afterward."

"I'm not sure I want you to come over," she said. "I'm too upset now. I need time to think about this. We need time for spiritual rehabilitation."

I wasn't sure whether to buy that excuse, any more than I bought the rest of her story. Her behavior could just as easily be a weird ritual, an exorcism, Susan's paranormal way of giving me the kiss-off. Maybe she'd found a new lover, a more compatible soul mate.

My suspicion was reinforced when I leaned over to kiss her goodnight. She drew away, with what seemed like a terrified look in her frosty blue eyes.

"I'll be by," I said, knowing that it was a doubtful possibility at best. Besides playing tennis, I remembered that I had promised Kathy I'd buy Peter a birthday present while I was out. And there was one other major purchase I knew I had to make now.

"I'd follow you home," I said, opening the door to get out of her car. "But it's so late. You can get home okay."

"I'll be okay," she said. "Everything will be okay."

But as she drove away, I realized that everything wouldn't. Fright night wasn't nearly over for Susan yet. There was another severe shock in store when she got home and discovered what had happened to her apartment.

21

Masterson was gone. Not just gone off to the Tower to confer with Kinkaid about next year's budget. Not just gone off on a corporate errand, a spiritual retreat, a short vacation, or a long weekend in the country. He had permanently vanished. As near as I could tell, he'd been shredded, packed up, and shipped off to the corporate recycling center. There was not a trace left in his office, which I discovered when I finally went to see what had become of him.

His newly and luxuriously decorated quarters were not merely empty but sacked, desolated. The desk, sofa, coffee table, and chairs: gone. The walls were bare, stripped of all his photos, plaques, posters, and other artwork. They hadn't been hanging long enough to leave outlines on the off-white wallpaper.

The only visible signs of his former occupancy were the

small circular holes made in the carpeting by the furniture legs, which looked as if they had been neatly bored by a small animal. It was obviously expensive carpeting, stain- and crush-resistant, with supertwist pile, so I knew the holes would soon disappear, too.

The carpet looked so cushiony and seductive that I had to resist the impulse to surrender to it, to lie down and drift away, hoping that when I woke I'd be home in bed, emerging from a bad dream. But I can't say that I had been unprepared for this. For weeks now, movers had been pushing carts and dollies loaded with furniture and boxes past my doorway. The building was crawling with carpenters, electricians, and maintenance engineers, hammers and wire cutters dangling like pistols from their belts.

And as I'd walked down the hallways to Masterson's office, I'd seen nothing but vacant offices and work stations, as grim and portentous as church sanctums. After the merger, a memo had been issued to all employees, assuring us that necessary staff reductions would be effected only through normal attrition. From what I could determine, this was total annihilation.

Today, I thought, threatened to be even worse than yesterday, if possible. But without any sleep to disconnect the two days, this was turning into a single interminable day, not only the worst of my life but the longest, and with no end in sight. After last night's guests had left, I knew sleep was an extremely remote possibility, at best. But I did try. I took a Valium with a glass of zinfandel. When that didn't work, I tried harder, taking another Valium with two more glasses of wine. Then I switched to bourbon.

I knew it was hopeless when I heard the van stop in the street, its engine idling, and the newspaper land on the front porch. I made coffee and took up my post in the kitchen, spreading the newspaper across the table. But I didn't turn on the lights, afraid my eyes couldn't stand the shock. I sat there in the gray dawn, staring at a banner headline about a shootout in a warehouse club while daylight slowly invaded the house.

I must have faded out for a few minutes. The overhead lights went on, and I snapped awake, so sharply that I thought I'd dislocated my neck.

"What a horrible night," Kathy said, coming into the kitchen and pouring herself a cup of coffee. The sound of her cup against the tile counter was almost as jolting as the light in my eyes. "After all that commotion downstairs, I'd just gotten back to sleep when I started hearing noises in the attic and the walls."

"Yeah, it's these cold nights," I said, relieved that she was more concerned about the upstairs than the downstairs intruders, apparently accepting my explanation that their nocturnal visit really was a routine security check. "It looks like they're back for the winter."

"I don't know how much more we can take," she said, sliding into a chair across the table from me. She inhaled from the cup before drinking, letting the steam clear her nose and eyes. While the lack of sleep plainly showed on her face, her cheeks had a healthy natural color, even without makeup, and she seemed alert, almost vivacious, which depressed me. I hated to imagine how pale and dispirited I looked by comparison.

"Not much more," I said. "I'm going to take care of them this weekend. If I can't get them outside the house, I'll get them inside."

"It's starting to seem hopeless." Sipping coffee, she made a disgusted face. "You really made this industrial strength."

"I know just exactly what to do now," I said. "I've got a strategy. Tonight, when I go after Peter's birthday present, I'm going to pick up a reciprocating saw—"

"Scott," she said, impatiently. "No more tools, please."

"Don't worry," I said. "The saw's not a major expense—"

"It's not the money," she said. "I don't think there's room for another tool in this house. We could open our own hardware store. We could open a chain of hardware stores."

"I can't get rid of them with my bare hands."

"I'm just so discouraged by all these tools, gadgets, appliances, utensils . . . cluttering up our house, our lives: claw hammers, sledgehammers, socket wrenches, crescent wrenches, circulating saws and jigsaws and now a reciprocal saw—"

"Reciprocating," I said, thinking how alarmed she'd be to find out that the saw wasn't the only item of hardware on my shopping list. "We'll never get the house finished without them."

"That's all we ever talk about anymore. The house. What we're doing to it. What we've done. What needs to be done. What we need to do it with. Maybe that's all we have in common."

"At least we still have that much in common," I said.

I started to get up for more coffee, knowing that if I didn't leave the table we were destined for another head-on collision. But she reached over and took my hand, tenderly, almost desperately.

That caught me by surprise. Ever since Peter was born and we'd moved into the house, there had been almost no casual gestures of affection between us, no middle ground between passion and indifference, love and hostility.

In the last couple of months, we hadn't even had sex to bring us together, emotionally or physically. The last time, she'd seemed not reluctant so much as resigned, willing enough but clearly not overcome by ardor.

"You know," she'd said afterward, "the thing about fucking is that it's basically an act of male domination. You could almost say that at certain moments every sex act borders on rape."

Made so nonchalantly, her remark scared me, and I'd kept

a cautious distance ever since. But feeling her hand on mine now, seeing love and possibly desire in her eyes, gave me cause for hope, however small and misguided. If only we didn't always have to be so tentative, so guarded, so frightened, I wouldn't have needed Susan or Marcia or anyone else.

With my free hand, I wanted to reach across the table, stroke her cheek, her shoulder. I wanted to put my hand down the neckline of her nightgown, warm it against her breast. But I hesitated. I'd deceived myself, or let myself be deceived, too many times before, and I couldn't chance yet another rejection.

Perhaps anticipating such a move, Kathy shuddered and drew the collar of her terrycloth robe around her neck. I wanted to think that it was a need for warmth, not self-defense. No matter how much insulation I forced into the cracks, how thoroughly I'd patched, caulked, and tuck-pointed, the house was always too chilly.

"I'm worried about you," she said, which worried me. Did she know or suspect more than I thought? Had she been able to get through the barrier I'd put up to protect her and the children?

"It's not anything you've said or done," she said quickly, "but what you don't say or do. You're so distant. You're always tuned to a different channel."

"I don't think everybody has to be tuned to the same channel," I said. All along it had been my impression that she had been tuning me out, not vice versa, but I wasn't ready to debate the question at this hour.

"I can't connect with you anymore. You don't listen to me. You don't pay any attention to the children. You haven't said anything about your job in weeks. You used to complain constantly."

"I'll try to remember to complain more."

"Scott, I'm not kidding. If you'd only open up a little, you'd be better off. You've shut yourself away in this house. You've closed all the windows, locked all the doors, declared yourself a separate country. You're constantly out of touch."

That seemed like such a strange thing for her to say, with the two of us sitting there at the table, her hand touching mine. At times like this, she seemed distressingly, unforgivably beautiful and remote, as remote from me as she accused me of being from her. I was conscious then of how cold her hand was. I needed to turn up the thermostat.

I eased out of her grip and got up. "I'd better get ready for work," I said.

"Can't you call in sick? You could use a day off."

"I could," I said. "But this is not the day."

I left her there at the table and went upstairs to shower and dress for work. By the time I was ready, it was too late to sit down with her and the children for breakfast. When I kissed her good-bye, Kathy handed me a plastic bag of trash. I carried it through the sun porch and out the side door.

As I went down the stairs, heading for the alley, I could see squad cars parked in front of Mrs. Underwood's house. A uniformed policeman was standing on her back porch. He waved me over to the fence.

"You live there?" he asked.

"Yeah," I said warily. "Is something wrong?"

"Nice yard," he said.

"Thanks, but the credit has to go to my wife. I'm not responsible for any of it."

Based on our various conferences over her fence, I could only assume that Mrs. Underwood had called the police to formally complain about the appearance of our house and grounds. "Is there some kind of problem?" I said, convinced that we were about to be cited for violating the housing code.

"Somebody broke into this house last night," he said. "Did you see or hear anything?"

"Nothing unusual," I told him. "Is Mrs. Underwood okay?"

"She's been better. How close are you?"

"Close but not real close," I said.

"We'll need to talk to you," he said.

"I was about to go to work. I've got a killer agenda today, but I could stick around and—"

"That's not necessary," he said. "We'll get in touch with you."

On my way back to the alley, I noticed a round, white object lying near a juniper bush. I walked over to see what it was. Mrs. Underwood had been decapitated. Where, I wondered, were Klammish and his neighborhood surveillance brigade when she really needed them?

I picked up the head by the hair, trying not to look into Mrs. Underwood's accusing eyes, and put it in the plastic bag. I put the bag in the garbage can, closed the lid tightly so the squirrels couldn't get into it, and went to work.

Finding Masterson gone when I got to the office left me even more uptight and anxious, shaken by bad omens. Wherever he'd gone, Masterson had taken his secretary and everybody else in his section with him. I wandered into one office after another, finding them all as empty as his.

I knew just where to go next. If anybody was keeping score around here, it was Sandy. She had been occupied on the phone when I arrived, acknowledging me with only the faintest arch of a turquoise eyelid.

On the way back, I stopped in my office to check my messages and make sure my own desk, files, and other furnishings hadn't been hauled away into the corporate void while I was out. I had half expected, half dreaded a call from Susan, but there was no word from her or from anyone else. Compulsively, I called her office. She'd taken a sick day, I was told. That figured. Sick surely didn't begin to suggest her condition when she got back last night and discovered her apartment in ruins.

I called her home but got her electronic voice, recorded much earlier, still blissful and undisturbed by the evening's events. I merely confirmed my plans to come over later, before or after tennis, and hung up, glad that I could postpone a recap of her nightmare, with its shock ending. The daily playback of her past lives was complicated enough. I didn't think I could handle her present troubles, even though they were sure to catch up with me in just a few hours.

When I went out to the reception desk, I found Sandy noticeably decomposed. There were no glitches in her eyeliner. She was flawlessly moussed and shellacked. Yet I could tell she was in a state of emotional disorder, near panic, approaching meltdown.

"I didn't know," she said, anticipating my question about Masterson's disappearance. "I really didn't know. Nobody told me anything. Absolutely nothing. I'm totally in the dark."

"Well, whatever's going on," I said, "I'm afraid that no news is worse than bad news."

"Maybe," she said, "but I don't think this is going to make you feel any better."

She handed me a message slip, turning away as if to disclaim any personal responsibility for its contents. Scrawled in her nervous hand, the message was unmercifully brief: "Mr. Kinkaid will be expecting you at his office at 10:00 A.M. tomorrow."

"His private secretary called," she said, "just a few minutes ago." Judging by her mournful expression, I had a fair idea of how shaken and despondent I must have looked.

"Did she give you any clue what it's all about?" I asked.

"That's all she said. She didn't tell me anything. Nobody ever tells me anything."

I had folded the message, put it in my pocket, and was about to go back to my office when she said: "I really hated to give it to you. You were in such a good mood when you got to work. I didn't want to spoil it."

While she was telling me this, her face assumed a look of genuine concern and affection, as if I were a sick child or a lost pet, revealing a side of her I'd never expected to see. "I just feel terrible. I really do."

As if for dramatic effect, she let a single bronze tear slide over her cheekbone. I reached over to wipe it away, to show my gratitude for her unexpected display of compassion. The instant I touched her face the flesh seemed to peel away in my hand. Beneath the cosmetic mask her skin was pale and beautiful.

She clasped my hand in both of hers, holding it against her exposed cheek. It was soft and warm and inviting. I leaned over to kiss it, and she pulled me down, carried me down, moaning, into the recess beneath her desk, a snug playhouse built for two.

There was just room enough for us to wriggle and flex, to throw off our clothes. In a matter of seconds we were coiled in passion, tumbling and straining against the underside of the desk, sinking into the carpet, tunneling into the dark chamber. Far above us, I could hear the muffled ringing of phones, the distant echoes of lust in the empty corridors and offices.

22

With my resistance at its weakest, I did the very thing I swore I wouldn't do. Buying the rifle—a Marlin .22-caliber semi-automatic with crossbolt safety, 4×15-millimeter scope, 7- and 15-shot clips, camouflage case, and sling—I let the salesman talk me into an extended warranty. For half again the price of the rifle, I would be protected for the next thirty-six months against misfires, backfires, and other malfunctions, as long as they weren't due to any careless handling on my part.

Going into the discount store, I was pretty sure I didn't need the extra protection and was primed to say no, absolutely not. Holding the empty rifle, aiming it down the aisles, I thought it seemed solid and mechanically sound, engineered with such precision that the standard warranty would have been more than adequate.

But the salesman was persistent—insistent. I was under pressure. I had other shopping to do, appointments to keep, obligations to meet, so I caved in, just as I had when I bought the television, the washer and dryer, the car. I took the extended warranty just so I could get out of the store and be on my way.

The rifle felt so good, the weight and balance so right, especially with the banana clip in place, that I was reluctant to let it out of my hands. It was frustrating to have it sealed in a box, not to be able to fire it right away, to feel it recoil against my shoulder, to watch the empty shell casings come flying out of the chamber, to smell smoke and lightning, expended firepower.

I needed a weekend to test it in the field, to take it out into a forest preserve and check the accuracy of its scope using cans, bottles, or some of Kathy's reject ceramics. But there wasn't time. The weekend forecast was for cold, gloom—nearly ideal weather for what I had to do. All I could do now was pray for rain and put my faith in the pinpoint infallibility of modern ballistics.

When I finally got home that night, I stashed the rifle in the closet, then went into the media room and crashed on the sofa. Kathy had gone off to bed, but she'd left the television on. David Letterman's guest was a man wearing a bush jacket, pith helmet, and white whiskers, who called himself the world's preeminent small game hunter.

At first, I thought it was just another Letterman stunt, an actor plugging a safari movie or a comedian sending up a National Geographic special. But Dave's guest spoke with such zest and conviction about the pleasures of knocking off small game that it was quickly evident he was no imposter trying to squeeze cheap laughs out of slaughtered animals.

When Dave appeared skeptical, the guest assured him: "I've

shot elephants, wildebeests, grizzlies, rhinos, all the giants, the superstars of the animal kingdom, but nothing has given me more of a thrill than bringing down a numbat, a bandicoot, a jerboa, or a pygmy shrew. That kind of shooting requires a rock-steady hand, a deadly eye."

"You brought a film clip," Letterman said. "Let's show our viewers what you're all about." For the next ninety seconds, I watched our hunter stalk through jungle, veldt, glade, rain forest, shooting assorted species of tiny animal life, their heads suddenly sprouting tiny holes, erupting in tiny bursts of fur and blood.

"The great thing about small game is that you don't have to go to Africa or Asia or Tasmania or any other godforsaken place to find it," Dave's guest assured the audience after the film clip and a break for commercials. "There's plenty in nearby fields, woods, picnic grounds, even in your own backyard. And such variety! Possums, raccoons, badgers, groundhogs, chipmunks, beavers, weasels, ferrets, foxes, squirrels—"

"But never dogs," Dave said impishly. "Right?"

"Right, Dave, never dogs. Or cats."

"Well, I wouldn't go quite that far," Letterman said, with a mischievous frown.

"There's a bonus," the hunter said. "It's not like road kill. You can eat most of what you bag. Cooked extra crispy, those little critters are tasty. I'm especially fond of fricasseed squirrel."

"I hate to come off like a wet noodle," Letterman said, "but the FCC requires us to give equal time to the anti–small game lobby, so here goes." With that, he segued into a list of "Top Ten Reasons Why You Shouldn't Shoot Cute, Defenseless Squirrels," leading off with: "They help control the nut population."

Then Letterman waved at the camera and said: "That's all,

folks. We couldn't come up with a single other reason, and we're out of time. Until tomorrow night, happy hunting."

I faded out along with Letterman and his hunting companion. An hour or so later, I awoke with a cramp in my shoulder and the rude spectacle of Charlton Heston on the television screen, hacking his way through a studio jungle and preparing to defend Eleanor Parker against an onslaught of gluttonous marabuntu.

I had grave preparations of my own. Unpacking the reciprocating saw, I began to read the instructions. Miraculously, the instructions, written in some opaque form of Oriental English, were the very antidote I needed for insomnia. When I woke up, four hours later, having slept longer than I had in months, I felt almost refreshed and ready for whatever surprises Kinkaid had in store. Actually, I'd overslept. I had to skip breakfast and leave the house at a run, in order not to miss my train.

For commuting purposes, the chilly autumn weather proved to be a blessing. I bundled up in my trench coat, pulling the collar high around my face and the brim of my rain hat low over my forehead. I also wore sunglasses, which put me in even less danger of being recognized at the station, by Ace or anyone else who might be hunting for defenseless victims.

I made it onto the train safely. I found a pair of empty seats and slid into the one next to the window, stretching halfway across the aisle seat to discourage other passengers from sitting there. If the train wasn't crowded, I might be able to occupy both seats all the way downtown.

The tactic didn't work. A young man in a striped stocking cap and car coat came down the aisle, listing unsteadily. Even though there were still plenty of vacant seats, he stopped and nodded at me, indicating that he'd chosen the one next to mine. I moved aside grudgingly. As he sat down, he smiled, revealing cracked gums and discolored teeth. He smelled of discoloration and decay, like moldy fruit. I could see bits of apple pulp and tobacco on his lips, caught in his webby mustache.

"You probably noticed that I limp," he said. "One of my legs is shorter than the other. But that's not the reason for the limp. No, brother, I overcame that problem. I limp because one of my feet is two sizes smaller than the other. But not the foot on my short leg. Isn't that miraculous?"

I shrugged in mild amazement, charitably trying to minimize the severity of his handicap, then sought refuge in my newspaper. But I couldn't resist a glance toward the floor. He wore one white hightop without laces and a much smaller black one with Velcro straps. He seemed to be carrying the burdens of the world not on his shoulders but on his feet.

To my relief, he took a paperback book from his jacket pocket and began to read. My relief was only temporary. He didn't read silently to himself but aloud, wailing and rocking. I looked over to see what he was reading. It was the New Testament. But it was a version new to me. The cover illustration was as lurid as a Gothic romance, depicting a voluptuous Mary Magdalene, her bosom spilling from her gypsy blouse as she clung to Jesus on the cross, her head in the upper region of His thigh.

Jesus Himself was no frail and agonized martyr. His face was chiseled, His hair luxuriant and golden, falling over His crown of thorns. His muscles bulged, rippled, and glistened erotically, superheroically. He looked more like a Hollywood terminator than a savior, a steroid messiah.

I glanced up and found myself staring directly into my seatmate's eyes. He smiled, with an expression that was alarmingly beatific, and said: "I lift up my eyes to the hills. From whence does help come?"

He stared at me, waiting. The silence was dreadful. Finally he said: "You're supposed to answer, 'My help comes from the Lord who made heaven and earth.' You need to brush up on the 121st Psalm."

I lowered my eyes and turned away, looking out the sooty window. As the train hurtled along, it was silhouetted against the passing landscape by the early morning sun, and I could clearly pick out my own figure among the other passengers, projected against the sides of brick warehouses and factories, apartment houses, billboards, glass towers. I felt as if I were having an out-of-body experience. I was spooked by this distorted, disconnected image, realizing that I was watching not just a flickering shadow but a warped reflection of my real and precarious self.

The conductor blew his whistle then, announcing our entry into the Red Zone. I doubled over, burying my face in my arms. My seatmate also assumed the defensive position. When we emerged, I sat up, but he had dropped to the floor. He was on his knees, praying. As his voice trembled and rose, I realized that he was praying for my soul.

His prayers grew so loud and fervent that the other passengers turned toward us. He was out of sight between the seats, so they could only assume that I was the one warning them of the imminent apocalypse. They either glared their disapproval or looked away in embarrassment. I stood and tried to squeeze by. He continued to pray, even louder now, his knees, elbows, and hands locked, refusing to let me pass.

"A sinner has risen," he cried. "He is ready to renounce Satan and repent."

I had to force my way past, pushing him into the aisle. He rolled over onto his knees and resumed his prayers. "Confess your sinfulness to God, brother, and open your heart to Jesus

Christ as your Lord and savior. Believe God's word that the blood of His son, Jesus, cleanseth us from all sin."

After I'd stepped over his prone body, he raised his head and hands, Eastern fashion, as if praying not to God but to Allah. Blood dripped from his lacerated wrists onto the floor of the train. A rivulet followed me as I made my way up the aisle, red with shame.

I stood between the cars, trying not to listen to his shouts, his pleas for repentance. God knows, I was willing to repent. But to who? Not to Kathy. Not to Kinkaid. Certainly not to this unholy evangelist flopping and bleeding on the floor of our rolling tabernacle.

When the train stopped at the next station, I got off, even though it was well over a mile to the Tower. I had a little time to spare and I needed to decompress, hoping that the brisk walk and the cool air would do wonders for my head, body, and soul.

23

Except for the time we'd taken the children to the observation deck, I'd never been inside the Tower. Under other circumstances, I would have been eager to get a close look at its innermost corporate sanctums, which were reputed to be both bizarre and splendid. All too briefly, I'd even dreamed about occupying one of them. After the takeover, there were rumors that our firm would eventually be relocated in the Tower. But now it looked as if there wouldn't be anyone left to move, to judge by the rapidly declining work force, the disappearance of Masterson and so many other colleagues. Kinkaid's summons could only mean that I was about to join them.

For a few minutes, I was afraid I wouldn't make it into the Tower. The street was in turmoil, a riot of horns, brakes, jackhammers, power saws. It swarmed with pickets, hard hats, and flustered, angry pedestrians. Seeing the pickets, I immediately feared the worst, that they'd prematurely heard about FurReal and were protesting the further decimation of helpless animals, before our ad agency could get out the word on how much the slaughter had been downsized.

But from their placards and the leaflet that one of the pickets handed me, I learned that they were trying to block construction work on the Tower. After buying it, Capisco Unlimited immediately began to modernize the Gothic landmark, outside and in. Inside, they'd stripped it of the travertine marble, the brass and copper fixtures, the mahogany and oak paneling, selling it as upscale scrap and replacing it with Sheetrock, PVC, vinyl, aluminum, black and white Formica—high-tech, low-cost synthetics.

But it was the work on the exterior that brought out the pickets. Capisco was grafting an atrium onto the entrance to the Tower, a glass sphere that purists considered a desecration, a globular affront to its soaring arches and flying buttresses, its medieval ramparts.

As I pushed my way through their ranks, the pickets had the same fearsome look as the gargoyles that hovered on the limestone parapets above us. I had to pass over a narrow walkway made of I-beams, pipes, and planks temporarily erected across the excavation. I felt as if I were crossing a drawbridge over a moat to a besieged castle. Sawdust and pulverized concrete flew like contaminated snow from behind plywood barricades. I was briefly stopped by guards in the lobby when my keys set off an alarm in the security gate. Then I was escorted to an express elevator that took me to Kinkaid's floor, near the summit of the Tower.

He didn't keep me waiting. He rose to greet me from the center of a golden arch, formed by the sunlit peak of an enormous Gothic window, directly behind his desk. He offered me his right hand. In his left hand, he had a tennis racquet. I assumed this was a modern variation on the polo mallets favored as props by the legendary Hollywood moguls.

"I've been eager to meet you," he said. "Sorry it's taken so long." He seemed even more eager for me to meet his tennis racquet. "Have you tried one of these?" he said, passing it across his desk, without another word of greeting.

"I haven't quite reached this level," I said as I took the racquet, a sleek black widebody.

"Prince Vortex," he said. "Graphite composite. Constant taper beam, patented cushion grip. The latest technology. Hot off the computer. You notice anything unusual about the strings?"

I turned the racquet over in my hands, looking for something, anything unusual about the strings.

"The zigzag pattern," he said.

"Right," I said. I stroked it sensuously. The finish gleamed like black pearl in the muted light.

"Redistributes shock and vibration," he said. "Minimizes off-center hits. Gives you both power and accuracy. Try it out. Go ahead, take a couple of swings."

I swung the racquet, cautiously. "Sweet," I said.

"How do you like that dynamic stiffness? Take some more swings. Be aggressive. You won't break anything."

I took some big strokes, forehand and backhand. The air zigzagging through the strings made the racquet sound like a miniature jet. "Wow. I really can feel the difference."

He couldn't have seemed more pleased than if I'd complimented him on his personal appearance, which was equally sleek and tapered, but narrow-bodied. The subtle gray plaid suit was obviously tailored to his exact dimensions, just as everything else about him—shirt, tie, watch, haircut, glasses—

was customized and top of the line. Dressed to kill, I thought.

He wasn't quite immaculate. However elaborately curled and teased, his dark hair, I smugly noted, was sparser than mine. His face, while fashionably emaciated, was almost skeletal, with a vertical ridge of flesh, a taut wattle, beneath the jut of his chin. His summer tan had faded to a pale olive, a suspiciously Middle Eastern hue that suggested the rumors might be true. Even though Capisco was officially a Dutch conglomerate, headquartered in Amsterdam, there had been media speculation that this was all a sinister front for Arab interests.

"I understand you're quite a player," Kinkaid said, as I returned his racquet. He motioned me toward a chair, then sat down behind his desk. Reflected in its polished granite surface, he looked slippery and treacherous, as if he were floating on an oil slick. The air around him seemed to be scented with cardamom and patchouli.

"Well, I do play a lot, but my game could stand some improvement."

"We could all stand improvement," he said. "But there's no need to be modest. I've kept track of how well you play. Observe."

He gestured toward a wall of television sets, stacked like a pyramid—a giant projection screen serving as the base for a half-dozen smaller models, rising to a single set at the very top.

He pushed a button on his desk, and my picture appeared on the screens, each one a second or two out of sync with the others. The effect was disorienting. Adding to the confusion, the images were kaleidoscopically distorted by the foil wallcovering across the room from the electronic pyramid.

It reminded me of a painful exhibition of video art that Kathy had taken me to see, work by a Korean artist with tapes of fish swimming in rows of TV screens. Kathy laughed when I referred to the artist as a she. "How am I supposed to know he's a man?" I said. "His middle name is June."

When I was finally able to focus on one picture of myself, I had to admit that my form wasn't bad. My backswing was a little tentative, and I wasn't turning completely sideways on my ground strokes. But my preparation was good. I was getting into position, knees bent, stepping smoothly into the ball, smashing it back.

"You know who you remind me of?" Kinkaid said, tapping the remote button. My multiple selves shriveled and vanished in the middle of an overhead, the screens fading to black, just when I was starting to relax and enjoy my performance.

"You remind me of Roscoe Tanner," he said. "Remember him? Big hillbilly from Tennessee. Pear-shaped. Huge cheeks. Walked like a duck. No finesse. A real bulldozer on the court. Had a serve like a grenade launcher. A powerhouse. You look like him too. Less hair maybe, a little heavier around the middle—"

He was watching me deviously, savoring his backhanded compliments. I assumed he was leading up to the coup de grace—that he was about to tell me I'd have plenty of time to work on my game and my waistline while looking for another job—when he said, "What about a game of sudden death?"

I muttered, hawed, squirmed, not certain what he was proposing.

"You've got your agenda," he said. "I've got mine. We're both busy. So we won't waste each other's time. We play sudden death. How's that? No games. No sets. No ads. No deuces. First one to win ten points. Shouldn't take long."

"Well, I wasn't prepared for tennis," I said, showing him my empty hands. "I didn't bring my racquet—"

"Try mine," he said, sliding his racquet across the desk at me. "I've got another one."

"I don't have shoes, clothes."

"I've got everything you need." He stood up, then hesitated and smiled. "Unless you'd rather not play with me."

"I'm ready," I said, gamely picking up the racquet. It felt as if it were made of iron, not graphite, as I followed him out the rear door of his office and up a bleached oak spiral staircase.

"After you try that racquet, you'll never go back to your old one," he said. "I'm surprised that at your level you're still playing with that obsolete model."

"I've gotten attached to mine," I said, rather than point out what an extravagance his racquet would be on my salary.

He put a hand on my shoulder, guiding me up the stairway. "Never skimp on technology," he said. "You can buy clothes off the rack. Furniture in a warehouse. Dishes at a garage sale. But when it comes to technology, you can't settle for less than the newest and the best. That goes for electronics or sports equipment. You cut corners on technology, and you're a loser. You don't just lose tennis matches, you lose contracts, you lose wars."

The floor directly above Kinkaid's had been converted into a private tennis court and gym, fully equipped with the most technologically advanced exercise machines and other instruments of aerobic torture. We changed in a small locker room, did some hurried stretching exercises on the court, then began to warm up.

Even his practice shots were aggressive. I guessed that he intended this to be the ultimate humiliation. This was probably the same ritual he'd put Masterson through. Knowing Masterson, I figured he'd tanked, groveling for mercy. But I wanted to show Kinkaid that he was up against tougher stuff. I wasn't going to follow his scenario—not if I could help it. Maybe it was too late to salvage my job, but I could still leave with some pride and integrity.

We started to play. He jumped ahead, 3-0, winning his two serves and breaking mine. That was partly due to the strangeness of the wide-body racquet, which seemed clumsy and off-balance. It was partly his style of play, mixing up spin shots, drop shots, lobs, slicing and dicing the ball, like a chef with a cleaver. He wasn't ashamed to use any kind of junk shot to make a point. All the while, I kept hammering away at him from the backcourt, rushing the net only once, when I was absolutely sure I had the point.

I was down 5-1 before the racquet began to feel right and I was able to adjust to his loopy game. He had a big kick on his serve, but by taking two steps backward and moving over to the sideline, I could return it without much difficulty. He was having trouble with my serve, which was flat but had a lot of velocity, and I aced him twice.

I kept the pressure on, chipping away at the score until it was 9-9, with one of us on the verge of sudden death. If there was any way I could avoid it, it wasn't going to be me. He tried to finish me off quickly with a shallow change-of-pace serve, a cheap shot that came in low over the net, bounced crazily, and started to die. I managed to pick it up, barely, but my return was dangerously deep, and the momentum carried me to the net, where I was vulnerable to a passing shot.

Kinkaid didn't take a chance on trying to pass me. He raised his forefinger and shouted, "Out," an instant before the ball landed in the court, well inside the baseline. There was no question that my return was good. Standing just behind the net, I had seen it plainly—an inch or two of green court between the ball and the white line. Kinkaid wanted to win at any cost, even if it meant he had to cheat to do it. In his book, no doubt, poor sportsmanship was simply a sound business practice, an example of Capisco's corporate philosophy in action.

There was no use arguing his call. He hadn't humiliated me. He hadn't even beaten me, which he knew as well as I did.

"You had me worried for a minute there," he said. "I was almost sorry I let you borrow that racquet."

"It did make a difference," I said, handing the racquet back to him.

He didn't take it, just looked at me even more slyly. "It's yours. Consider it a gift from the company. There are plenty more where that one came from."

For a moment, I thought the racquet was intended to soften the blow, not so much of losing the match as losing my job, that it was part of the severance package. Then Kinkaid made it clear that this wasn't at all what he had in his cryptic mind.

"I wouldn't want one of our top employees to be seen in public with anything but the best available equipment," he said, putting a fraternal arm around my shoulder. "I like your style, off the court and on. That was an inspired report on FurReal and the King Kong mall intercept."

"I was afraid you hadn't seen it," I said.

"I not only saw it, I consider it a classic thesis on how to turn fiasco into victory, to capitalize on a situation that might defeat less imaginative men. I couldn't agree more on the value of negative publicity. I've always said that there's no such thing as a bad sound bite. Even black ink is good ink."

As he talked, he steered me back to the locker room, pausing long enough for us to shed our sweaty clothes. Then I followed him into the sauna.

"Here's another example of what I mean by going first class," he said, slapping a paneled wall. "This birch came from forests we own in Finland. Installed by carpenters brought over from our Helsinki headquarters. The rocks came from the shores of Lake Saimaa."

Stripped to nothing, our naked bodies shrouded in steam, we were momentary equals. But I was sweating furiously, almost deliriously, visibly melting in the heat, while it seemed to invigorate Kinkaid. The sweat covered him in oily beads. He glistened like a sheik, which only helped strengthen the Middle Eastern connection.

"I've been tracking you, Ryan," he said, sitting on a bench, "and I'm impressed. Your desk is not always neat and orderly. In fact, from what I've seen, it's usually a mess. But I admire that kind of distracted attitude in my upper managers. This is not a perfect world, not an orderly universe—nor should it be. Imperfection has always gotten a bad rap. There's creativity in chaos, order in disorder, genius in confusion."

Unless I was confusing his signals, the conversation had taken an unexpectedly upbeat direction. What was it about saunas? I wondered, recalling my last experience. That one, I had to admit, was somewhat more memorable, even if the sauna hadn't been built by Finnish slaves.

"Never let yourself be handicapped by neatness," Kinkaid continued. "Never be afraid of creating chaos. You can always get somebody to clean up after you. Einstein, for example. Do you suppose he dusted his own blackboard? Do you imagine Julia Child ever scrubbed a pot or a pan? Look at Howard Hughes. Do you think that when he finally got his hair and fingernails cut that he swept them up himself?"

"I don't think he ever got them cut, did he?" I said. "Not while he was still alive."

"That only underscores my point about confusion and disorder," Kinkaid said. "He was so busy creating that he couldn't be distracted by such elementary matters as fingernails and hair."

Creating what? I was tempted to ask, but didn't. Only more confusion and disorder. Weren't the untrimmed nails and hair, the hermetic withdrawal, only the more visible symptoms of an obsessively fastidious and paranoid mind, as the media had repeatedly advised us? I wondered how long Kinkaid would put up with my creativity if I showed up for work with nails a foot long and hair down to my shoetops?

I was not about to interrupt now—not with Kinkaid telling me that I had replaced Masterson as head of the marketing division of Capisco. "Now there's an example of a man who had no imagination," he said. "A drudge. An android. Always neatly manicured and combed and trimmed. Never a hair or a paper out of place. Never a creative thought or an original observation."

"Well," I said, "the last time I looked there weren't any papers at all on his desk. There wasn't even a desk. He certainly did a neat disappearing act."

Through the sweltering mist, I could see Kinkaid smile. The fierce heat was burning my throat, pressing against my chest, swelling in my lungs, and making it hard for me to breathe, but I managed to return a collusive smile. "That may have seemed a little abrupt," he said, "but once I've made a decision, I believe in acting decisively. And in Masterson's case, I had no other option. He wasn't the sort of man I want representing Capisco. In addition to his more apparent shortcomings, he was promiscuous. Secretaries, receptionists, colleagues' wives, cleaning ladies. He must've plugged every woman on the fourteenth floor. God knows what he had going for him on the other floors. I can't monitor the whole building.

"Don't misunderstand me," he said, with a grin. "A little free-fall sex is good for the heart and mind. Stimulating. Rejuvenating. Inspirational. But your predecessor was way overextended, and absolutely indiscreet. On the other hand, you, from what I've been able to discover, are the soul of discretion."

Within a week, Kinkaid informed me, I could expect to move into Masterson's office and assume his duties as chief of marketing. My replacement as assistant chief wouldn't be named immediately. "You'll find yourself a little shorthanded. But that's only temporary. As the economy grows, so will your staff. I know you can handle things in the meantime."

Before I left the Tower, Kinkaid had one other surprise for me, another bonus besides the tennis racquet. Back in his office, he produced a hooded, ankle-length coat, made of Fur-Real. "A prototype model," he said. "I thought it was only fitting that you have one of the first."

Stroking the fur, rubbing his cheek against it as if it were a beloved pet, he seemed almost reluctant to hand it over. "Just feel how soft and luxurious. Nobody would ever suspect that it isn't the real thing. But you said it best yourself. This is truly going to create a revolution."

I felt pretty high as I left the Tower, carrying my revolutionary tennis racquet and fur coat, and flagged a cab. It wasn't until I was almost back at my office that I started to have forebodings. No matter how strenuously Kinkaid had endorsed creative disorder, his own desk was even more bare and antiseptic than Masterson's. Then I opened the box to inspect the fur coat. I would have recognized it anywhere. It was an altered version of the costume that King King had worn at the mall intercept.

24

Somehow I didn't feel quite like celebrating—not yet. There were still major domestic matters that had to be settled before I could allow myself even a small measure of self-satisfaction. First I had to go back to the office. There was no work to be done, but I wanted to check my messages.

I found a foil balloon tied to my office chair. Attached to it was a card with a handwritten message: "Congratulations, Scott. I always knew you were up to the job. Just don't forget the people who gave you a boost." It was signed, "Sandy." How could I forget Sandy? If her pipeline reached all the way to Kinkaid's sauna, which she seemed to be suggesting, I could hardly afford to.

There was only one message, and it was from Kathy. Still

nothing from Susan, which made me uneasy. One way or another, I should have heard from her by now. She was always in such a hurry to recap her dreams—surely she'd want to share the final installment of her serial nightmare with me.

No word at all could only mean more trouble. She may simply have been too distraught to talk to me. She may have had to go to police headquarters to fill out a report. But it could just as easily mean that she hadn't been fooled by my unprofessional burglary. I might have left my fingerprints all over the job, in which case I could soon expect to hear not from Susan but from the police.

Maybe that was why Kathy had called, to warn me that the game was up. Apprehensively, I speed-dialed our number. Kathy sounded gloomy enough when she answered the phone. Off in the background, Peter was shrieking, but I could tell it was a routine tantrum and not a cry of genuine anguish and pain.

Before Kathy could deliver any bad news, I gave her the good, putting the happiest possible spin on things as I told her about my meeting with Kinkaid and my unexpected promotion—but none of my misgivings or forebodings.

"What did I tell you?" she said. "Nothing to worry about, right? I hope you told him you needed two weeks off to recover from all the stress he's caused you."

"No way I can do that right now," I said. "But I'll take some time off the first chance I get."

"Anyway," she said, "it's a big relief. I can't tell you how much sleep I've lost over this."

"I have a pretty good idea."

"Maybe now we can afford a competent exterminator," she said, all the cheer gone from her voice. "That's one reason why I called. They're back—in force. I can't begin to describe what they're doing up there. It must be a full-scale invasion."

"Yeah, that figures," I said. Turning in my chair, I could see streaks of rain on the window, angry clouds, a bruised and hostile cityscape. "They're looking for a warm nest for winter."

"They found one," she said. "Above the conservatory."

"We don't need an exterminator," I said. "I'll take care of that problem myself. First thing tomorrow, if the weather cooperates. I know just how to deal with them. What else?"

"It'll keep till the weekend. I don't want to spoil your day. I'd better see about Peter. He's frightened by the storm."

The stormier the better, I thought. Before hanging up, I said, "I may be late. I can't even guess what time it will be. It all depends on how long it takes me to get through this paperwork."

It all depended on Susan. I tried her office. Her voice mail informed me that she was temporarily away from her desk. I had a feeling that she was away for the weekend. I tried her at home, but all I got was her machine.

After all that had happened, I could hardly blame Susan if she didn't want to connect with me, either through fiber-optic or psychic channels. I decided to wait an hour for her to call back before I left. That would give me time to clean my desk—being careful not to make it too clean so as not to endanger my genius rating.

Sandy hadn't waited around to congratulate me in person. Nor had anybody else. My whole staff had taken Friday afternoon off, if I had any staff left. I went to find out.

I was tense and restless. It occurred to me that if I hadn't been terminated, I must've been ex-terminated, which may have been worse. From the becalmed air that had settled over the office, it was plain that Kinkaid hadn't put me in charge of just a sinking ship but one that had already sunk.

Walking down the hallways, I roughly figured that more than half the offices were unoccupied—vacated and stripped to the bare walls, floors, and ceilings. I was compulsively drawn to

Masterson's office, which was even more of a vacuum than the others. I went in and paced off the length and width. It was half again as large as mine, which meant I would need more furniture to fill it. Kinkaid hadn't said anything about a decorating allowance.

There was no message from Susan when I got back. If this was good-bye, I hated to let it happen without some kind of sweet but sorrowful parting gesture. At the very least, I figured I owed her a fur coat. That wouldn't begin to compensate her for the TV, cassette player, jewelry, and other valuables I'd dumped into the canal. But maybe it would give her spirits a momentary boost.

The sight of Susan wrapped in the coat might lift my depleted spirits as well. I tried to picture her face and hair circled by the shawl collar, the plush FurReal spilling over her shoulders, reaching down to her ankles. But the furry vision eluded me, probably because I had never seen her in anything but sweats or jeans.

I threw away Sandy's card, tied the foil balloon around the box with the coat, and took a cab to Susan's apartment. I was disappointed to see that she hadn't learned the most basic lesson from the break-in. Rather than install a new security door, she'd simply had a carpenter and a locksmith repair the damage to the old one.

Putting my ear to the door, I heard footsteps, the squeak of floorboards beneath the thin carpeting. When I knocked, the movement stopped. I knocked again. "Susan, it's me," I said. "Please open up. I need to see you."

She came to the door, leaned against it, and said, "Go away. I can't see you now. The signs are bad."

"Just for a minute. I have something for you."

She unlocked the door. Through the crack, one blue eye appeared, looking me up and down suspiciously. Then she stepped aside so I could enter. I didn't try to hug or kiss her. Even if I hadn't known about her ordeal, I could tell from her stricken eyes that she was in no mood for romance or affection.

"I just don't want to see you now," she said. "You've brought me nothing but humiliation and grief. I was shoved around, threatened with guns, scared half to death. I came home, my apartment was burglarized. And now Mars is challenging Pluto."

"You can't hold me personally responsible for all that," I said.

"I don't hold you personally responsible for anything. But you're all out of harmony with the universe. Your chart is filled with squares and quincunxes and oppositions. You attract weird people."

"I warned you that I lived in a transitional neighborhood," I said, "that it wasn't safe to hang around after dark—even when Mars and Pluto are on their best behavior. From what I can see, you don't live in such a hot neighborhood yourself."

"Just look at this," she said, her hands sweeping the pillaged living room. "They broke down the door and took everything they could carry—most of what I own."

From my perspective, the place looked a lot better than it did when I'd last seen it. "Do the police have any idea who did it?"

"Not a clue. They were here five minutes. They said they had a hundred other burglaries to investigate."

"I hope your insurance will cover it."

"That's not the point," she said. "Most of what they took were useless possessions anyway. Now that they're gone, I'm glad to be rid of them. It made me realize how cluttered up my life had gotten."

"And I'm part of the clutter?"

She looked at me sadly, guiltily. "I think I know how you

feel," I said, handing her my consolation package. "Maybe this will cheer you up."

She examined the box skeptically. The foil balloon, nearly deflated, dribbled limply against the carpet. Lifting the coat out of the box, she seemed surprised all right, but not in the way I'd anticipated. "What is this? Your idea of a practical joke?"

"No," I said. "It's supposed to be a gift."

"Gift?" she said with a look of utter horror. She held the coat at arm's length, as if trying to repel an attacker. "You must think I'm a kept woman. Are you my sugar daddy? Am I one of your possessions?"

She did seem to be possessed. Among the many weird people I'd attracted, she was becoming one of the weirder specimens. "It's only a fur coat," I said. "I thought you'd be pleased."

"I'm supposed to be pleased with a dead animal?" she said, pushing the coat at me. "I'm supposed to be pleased that helpless creatures are being destroyed and turned into coats? You're poisoning the environment, upsetting our whole ecology system."

"No," I said, "you don't understand. The coat's only partly made of fur. It's blended with synthetics."

"Synthetics!" she said. "That's even worse, ecologically. That means wasted oil and wasted energy—and slaughtered animals."

I was quickly losing my patience, trying to reason with her while grappling with the bulky coat. "No, what it means is that we're preserving the ecology by cutting the destruction in half."

"The way to preserve the ecology is not to cut the destruction of animals in half but to stop it completely," she said. "Now if you'll excuse me, I've got to run."

I followed her out the door, down the stairs, and through the foyer, dragging the coat behind me like a large and stub-

214

born pet. Outside, she inhaled deeply and lifted her face to the sky, checking for further signs of rain. The storm had passed and the sun was out, but it was fleetingly obscured by clouds.

Satisfied that the showers were over, Susan tightened the laces on her running shoes, zipped her anorak against the autumnal gusts, and began limbering up, stretching, bending, jogging in place.

She seemed to be performing a ritual dance. As clouds floated across the sky, she was haloed by sunlight one instant, darkened by shadows the next. I couldn't get a focus on her. She was like a figure in an experimental film, a blurred image that flickered from positive to negative, back and forth, over and over.

I wanted to reach out and take her by the shoulders, hold her steady, embrace her. All I could do was wave my arms uselessly, helplessly, comically. "Will you stop just for a second," I said. "There are a few things I'd like to say to you."

"Later," she said. "I can't stop now."

Then it was too late. She was gone, running along the sidewalk, running across the parkway, running down the street, running out of my life, already a fugitive memory.

She hadn't even bothered to try on the coat, which had slipped to the ground. Lying there by the curb, a lump of discarded fur, it did look like a dead animal, I had to admit, like a monstrous road kill. I picked up the coat, brushed off the dirt and leaves, and carefully folded it back into the box.

The street was dark when I got home, and so was our house. "The storm knocked out the power," Kathy said as I let myself in the door. "Right after I talked to you. I called back, but you didn't answer."

"I was in conference," I said. "But I can't say I'm unhappy about missing your call."

She had come into the front hallway carrying an antique candelabra, a gift from some Christmas or anniversary past. She made an eerily beautiful sight in the wavering glow of the candles, and I felt grateful to be home, happier and more secure than I had in a long time. I had the sense of something gained, not lost, as if a missing heirloom had unexpectedly come back into my possession.

From above, I could hear the children, running and tumbling, their shouts bouncing off bare walls and floors. "At least they're enjoying the blackout," Kathy said. "Playing ghost in the graveyard."

"It's the season for that," I said.

"I'm afraid it spoiled my celebration," she said, handing me a warm bottle of champagne. "The refrigerator went out with the lights. So there was no way I could chill this in time."

"I wish I could be sure we had something to celebrate," I said, taking the bottle and handing her the box with the fur coat. "Anyway, here's a surprise for you."

She seemed a lot more pleased by the package than Susan had. But once she'd opened the box, her expression changed from delight to puzzlement and then dismay. "This is a surprise," she said, examining the coat by candlelight.

"Kinkaid wanted you to have it," I assured her. "It's a prototype model. Made of FurReal."

Watching her turn the coat over in her hands doubtfully, I could see that it wasn't any more her style than it was Susan's—or perhaps anyone else's. Still, I had expected her to react with a little more enthusiasm than Susan had, even if she had to fake it.

For the moment, Kathy was simply speechless, and not with joy or happiness, I could tell. As I waited for her to say something, anything, there was an aboriginal scream directly behind me.

Dropping the coat, Kathy hurried around to comfort Peter, who had wandered into the hallway and begun to howl with fright. Once she got him calm enough to talk, the reason for Peter's hysterics became painfully clear. "It's that coat," she said. "He thought it was a monster, attacking me."

I retrieved the coat from the hallway floor and carried it over to him. "It's not alive," I said. "It's only a coat, something for Mommy to wear to parties. Feel how soft it is."

Peter was not convinced. He wailed even louder and hid his face against Kathy's shoulder. "Just put it away somewhere, please," she said. "He's been upset all day. By the storm, by the blackout, by all the Halloweeners in their costumes."

"He needs to know that it isn't real," I argued. "Or else he'll just get upset all over again when he sees you wearing it."

"Just put it away," Kathy said.

I hung the coat in the hall closet, stuffing it to the rear behind some jackets and camping equipment, where Peter wouldn't be likely to discover it. I couldn't take any solace in the thought that he'd found the coat so realistic. Nor was I optimistic about being able to convince Kathy that Kinkaid would expect her to wear it to the Capisco holiday party.

The power wasn't restored until sometime after midnight, way too late to chill the champagne. But once the children were in bed, we decided to open the bottle anyway. After the first glass, it didn't matter that the champagne was warm. The more I drank, the more I convinced myself that we did have reason to celebrate.

The party went on long after the bottle was empty, long after we had gone to bed. With Kathy asleep beside me, I felt closer to her than I had in months, possibly years. Exhausted but content, I finally got to sleep myself.

I was out of bed an hour later, awakened not by nocturnal dread now so much as euphoria. I was still high from the champagne, but it was more than that—the new job, the rediscovered comforts of home, the certainty that by tomorrow we would be rid of the little terrorists that had infested our house.

Taking a flashlight, I went on a reconnaissance mission to the sun porch on the second floor, what we fancifully called the conservatory. Just a few nights earlier, we had finished replastering and painting the room. I hesitated in the doorway, aiming the flashlight into all the corners, across the flat surfaces. The white enamel walls and varnished floorboards gleamed metallically.

I walked over to a window and turned the flashlight into the yard, looking for sinister movements, deviant shadows. If there were trespassers down there, the light had sent them scurrying for cover.

According to Kathy, the squirrels had chewed into the eaves and built their nest above the sunroom, which made sense. Here the ceiling was directly below a sloping section of roof, so that the inner angle formed a perfect natural cave, cozy and remote, where the squirrels could eat, sleep, and mate. I stood in the center of the room, listening for them, but all I could hear were the wind and dry leaves shaking the windowpanes.

My strategy was obvious enough. The squirrels hadn't left me with any options. Access from above the sunroom was out of the question, unless I was prepared to patch or possibly replace the entire roof after ripping a hole in it. It would cause far less damage to strike from below, through the newly plastered and painted ceiling.

Having just renovated the sunroom, I wasn't eager to tear it up again. And the squirrels were so quiet now, as peacefully settled for the night as my own children, that it seemed almost cruel to evict them. But any feelings of charity quickly passed as it occurred to me that they were asleep and I was awake. I couldn't let myself be pacified or disarmed. Peaceful coexistence was unthinkable with wild creatures that would, innocently or not, destroy our house.

The more I thought about it, the more furious I got that they were diverting me from so many other matters that needed immediate attention, inside and out—the leaks and cracks, the corroded pipes and crumbling walls, the frayed wires and buckling foundation. It was all I could do to stop myself from attacking the ceiling, launching an offensive then and there. I went downstairs to get a drink, something to carry me over till morning.

25

From somewhere deep within the cave I heard a persistent crunch, a gnawing sound that grew steadily louder as the lights came up. Raising my head, I looked directly across the table into Peter's face, milk dribbling down his chin as he chewed his cereal, possessed by the bright colors and drawings on the back of the box. Farther off in the house, Mark and Kim were squabbling over the television, shouting to be heard above the voices of cartoon characters. Peter slid off the stool to join them, leaving milk in the bottom of his bowl. My mouth was dry from sleep and champagne. Picking up the bowl with trembling hands, I drank the rest of the sugary milk and mushy flakes.

I had gotten a little of the sleep I needed—not in bed but sitting in a kitchen chair, hunched over the table. I was momentarily too stiff and cramped to get up. Awakening was even more painful because of the light that pierced the kitchen. The ceiling light was off. Looking out into the yard, I was alarmed to see sunshine, autumnal haze, warm air rising from the dead leaves—omens of a perfect Indian summer day.

I felt as if the television weatherman had personally betrayed me with his dire forecast. At least the mild weather would give me time to prepare for the inevitable gloom and cold—later in the day, I hoped. I went to the basement and gathered up the necessary tools—claw hammer, crowbar, extension cord. Plus the reciprocating saw, still in its box. I wanted to test-fire both the saw and the rifle before putting them into action, but time was short, the pressure was on.

I went up to the conservatory. I climbed the stepladder and put my ear to the ceiling. All quiet. I didn't doubt that this was where the squirrels had built their main nest. They had just stepped out for a few minutes. I got down and went over to the window. I saw squirrels in the yard, dozens of them, large and small, brown and gray, scrambling through the leaves, digging into the earth, carrying nuts and branches, scaling trees and power lines, taking advantage of the mild weather to make their hasty preparations for winter.

The newly painted surface of the ceiling looked so pristine and solid that I was almost sorry I had to disturb it. Climbing back on the ladder, I gouged into the plaster with the crowbar, ripping away at the lathing until I located a joist. Loose plaster and sawdust fell on me, spreading across the floor. Brushing the debris out of my hair and eyes, I got the reciprocating saw and began to cut a channel between the joists.

The saw bucked and shook like a jackhammer, making a jagged gash across the ceiling. The vibration caused it to slip out of my hands, but I was able to catch it by the cord, with the blade hanging inches above the varnished floor. Working more slowly, tentatively, I got the saw under control and cut something that resembled a straight furrow connecting the joists.

I moved the ladder a few feet, preparing to make a parallel cut in the ceiling when Kathy came into the room, tying the sash on her robe. Her hair was uncombed, and she looked tired, bewildered, and angry from having her sleep disrupted. "What the fuck are you doing in here? It sounds like a demolition derby."

"I'm taking care of the squirrel problem," I said defensively.

"You're destroying the ceiling," she said. "I just spackled and painted it. And look at the new floor!"

"Superficial damage," I said. "I can patch it all up as soon as I get rid of the squirrels."

"I thought you were going to call an exterminator."

"I'm the exerminator," I said, laughing diabolically and aiming the saw at the ceiling as if it were a machine gun. "The exterminating angel."

Kathy was neither amused nor pacified. "You'll never be able to patch that ceiling."

"We need a trapdoor here anyway," I said, ascending the ladder. "It's going to look neat and professional when I'm done. I'll finish the crawl space off, and we can use it for storage."

"Scott, we've got storage space all over the house. We don't need any more."

I pulled the trigger on the saw. Whatever else Kathy said was lost in its angry buzz. I ripped into the ceiling again, a foot and a half from where I'd cut the first line. When I finished, I saw that she was gone but the children were watching me from the doorway, hypnotized with terror.

I was too busy to stop and explain. I cut a crude square and squeezed through to my waist. The squirrels were not there, but in the flashlight's beam I could see, off in one corner, the nest they'd fashioned out of leaves, twigs, rags, insulation, and other scavenged material, including what looked like one of my argyle socks.

I covered the hole with a piece of heavy canvas to block out the light from below. I didn't want to alert the squirrels that they'd had an intruder. I went downstairs to wait for the warm weather to break and make my final arrangements for their homecoming. Kathy took Kim and Mark to their lessons, then went off to a ceramics fair. I was tempted to tag along, at a discreet distance, to be sure that it wasn't a ceramics affair, with a certain Hispanic tutor, but she had left Peter in my care.

I sat with him and watched cartoons, but the color on the television set had deteriorated severely. Instead of a sickly blue, the Smurfs were now magenta, and so was everything else on the screen. I promised myself that as soon as my salary increase came through, I'd invest in a new set.

I was drowsing when the doorbell rang. Mary Agnes and Darlene were standing on the porch.

"Do you have anything to donate to our neighborhood yard sale?" Mary Agnes said, smiling a little too coyly.

"Funny," I said, "but I thought we'd already contributed more than our share."

"No, you haven't, but all your neighbors have. We'll take any old thing—appliances, dishes . . ."

"Nothing," I said, unwilling to surrender even a broken waffle iron or chipped coffee mug.

"This is the last one of the season," she said as I started to shut the door. "Half the proceeds go to Neighborhood Solidarity."

"Where do the other half go?" I said.

"For overhead," she said.

"Nothing," I said and closed the door, gently, I thought, under the circumstances.

While Peter was occupied with the television, I got the rifle out of the closet. I tested its bolt action. Going to the window, I checked the scope. I aimed the rifle up and down the street, sighting on trees, cars, lampposts, the sign in front of the Phillips house that read: FALL CLOSEOUT. EVERYTHING REDUCED.

As they moved around their front yard and porch, putting price tags on the used sofas, chairs, bicycles, I took aim at each of them in turn—Roy, Mary Agnes, Darryl, Howard, Darlene—and squeezed the trigger, dropping them one by one. They sank to the lawn at odd, twisted angles, like broken and discarded furniture.

Then I loaded the clip with .22 shells, slid the clip in the rifle, and switched on the safety. I carried the rifle upstairs and put it on the closet shelf in our bedroom.

Kathy came home with the children, and we had a picnic lunch, sitting on the back porch in the sunshine. The squirrels approached us, hungrily but cautiously. For once, I didn't try to stop the children from throwing them pieces of their peanut butter and jelly sandwiches, figuring that they deserved as much for their last supper.

Dark clouds periodically blocked the sun. Kathy took the children indoors. While I had the opportunity, I started to rake, working side by side with the squirrels. I stopped to observe one. He was plump and bushy, ready for winter. He stood on his hind legs, sniffing the air, his paws together, as if praying.

I waved the rake in the squirrel's direction, and he ran off. For such agile creatures, I thought, they seemed peculiarly graceless, moving in quick, slinky leaps, like toy animals being propelled by rubber squeeze bulbs.

As I watched, the sky grew even darker. The sun disappeared. The turbulent black clouds might have been dust raised by an advancing army, the thunder and lightning its muted artillery. In just a few seconds, the warm breeze had turned into a cold violent wind, the temperature dropped by twenty degrees or more, and I ran into the house for shelter.

By the time I got indoors, rain was hammering against the siding and windows, the wind was stripping the last leaves from the maples and oaks. I went to the basement, took off my wet clothes, and put on black work pants, black shirt, black gym shoes, and black stocking cap. I went up to the kitchen for a box of wheat crackers and a bottle of Gatorade, stuffing them into a backpack with a flashlight, extra batteries, screwdriver, and pliers. It was likely to be a long afternoon, a long siege.

I stopped at the fireplace, reached up into the chimney, and came away with a handful of soot. I rubbed the soot over my neck, face, ears, all the exposed skin from my collar to my hairline, my wrists to my fingertips. Then I went upstairs and got the rifle off the closet shelf: Away we go, Roscoe.

Kathy was sweeping the floor when I walked into the conservatory. "What kind of a getup is that?" she said. "You look like a cat burglar."

"Squirrel hunter," I corrected her. "I don't want my pale face scaring them away."

She shook her head in wonder and disapproval, as if I were a child who had been playing in dirt. "Just don't leave fingerprints all over the white ceiling." Then she saw the rifle, and her smile turned to ice.

"That's not a BB gun," she said.

"You're right," I said, going up the ladder, "it's not."

"Scott, this is not the way. You're going to kill somebody with that."

"Right again," I said, "squirrels. Dirty, verminous little animals. Rats with tails. Scavengers, digging into garbage, slime, bringing depravity and filth and decay into our house."

"I don't like them either, Scott. But this is not just dangerous, it's against the law."

What law? I wanted to ask her. Whose law? But I was
already up in the crawl space, and if we kept up this useless
dialogue, the squirrels would be frightened away. I quickly
pulled the canvas over the hole behind me, shutting out the
light, and lay across the joists, listening.

Over in the corner, I could hear them rustling around their
nest, whispering and deliberating, alert, fearful, but not enough
to abandon their dry nest for the cold wind and rain. The air
smelled of diseased wood and fur. I held my breath and tried
not to move. The corners of the joists dug into my hips and
shoulders. I should have brought along a blanket, something to
cushion me from the sharp edges and the splinters.

I waited until they were calm, then slowly, quietly pointed
both the flashlight and the rifle toward their nest. I snapped on
the light. The startled squirrels chattered hysterically, which so
startled me that I fired off a shot without really aiming.

The report was so loud, the flash so bright that I thought for
an instant the house had been struck by lightning. A small hole
popped into the siding. The squirrels were in a panic now.
They were scattering in all directions, except for one large
squirrel that I assumed to be a female. She remained behind to
cover her retreating brood, standing on a joist, her back
arched, defiantly confronting me in the funnel of light.

Her teeth worked viciously as she emitted a scolding *quak-
quak-quak-a-a-a-a-a-a*. Her tail flicked back and forth like a
whip. I carefully laid the flashlight on the joist, holding the
squirrel in its beam. I raised the rifle and fired again. The hump
of her back erupted, a magenta spurt in the yellowish glare. She
gave a short bark, then flipped over on her side, her claws still
fastened to the joist. She shuddered, then was quiet.

I could not leave her there to decompose in this musty tomb. Rain pummeled the roof. My eyes and nose were scorched by smoke. The edges of the joist cut into my knees and elbows as I crawled toward the squirrel. I reached out to retrieve the bleeding clump of fur. The squirrel was not dead. Her teeth snapped down on my fingers, and I jerked back in shock and excruciating pain.

I could not pull my hand free. I could feel her teeth sinking more deeply into my fingers, scraping against the bones. I yanked and tugged, but her claws were embedded in the joist. With my other hand, I swung the rifle at the squirrel. There was a flat, mushy thump. Her teeth relaxed slightly, yet not enough so that I could work my fingers loose.

I struck at her again and again with the rifle, not certain of whether it was the squirrel's screams or my own that thundered in my ears, whether it was her blood or mine that ran down my arm. Finally her mouth sprang open, as if a trap had been released, and she stopped moving.

I lay across the joist until the pain eased, my clothes wet with perspiration and blood. I wrapped my swelling hand in a handkerchief. I still had to retrieve the squirrel's body. I grasped her around the neck and pulled. Her claws were welded to the joist in a death grip, impossible to break or pry loose.

I got my knife from the belt holster, thankful for its serrated blade. I began to saw at her front foot. She was one tough mama. It was slow, tedious work, cutting through the fur, gristle, and bone. I had to amputate all four feet before she was free, leaving the claws in the joist. I could always dig them out later.

I was reluctant to abandon the crawl space, disappointed that I had gotten only one squirrel. But this was a promising start. And my swelling hand needed attention. Before coming down the ladder, I made sure the rifle's safety was on. I didn't want another slip of the finger. Then I took off my shirt and wrapped the squirrel in it. Kathy would not be happy if she found blood on the floor.

Nobody was in the conservatory. I had expected them to be waiting, eager to see the results of the hunt. I yelled, "Kathy, everybody, come look! I got one!" There was no reply, not even the shouts of children, the sound of their footsteps rushing up the stairs. All I could hear were my own cries, sounding increasingly less exultant and more plaintive as they resonated through the house.

I checked all the upstairs rooms, stopping to wipe up the magenta drops that had leaked from the package under my arm. I wrapped it more carefully, then went downstairs. I was irritated to find that the children had left the media room without turning off the television. They still didn't respond to my shouts.

My hand was swollen and discolored. The numbness was wearing off, the pain sharpening by the second. I needed emergency care. The squirrel might have been rabid. "Kathy!" I cried. "I need you to drive me to the hospital!"

I heard what sounded like an amplified voice from outside the house, in the yard. Somebody had left the front door open. Stepping outside, I nearly slipped on the wet leaves that had blown onto the porch. The rain had turned to a cold drizzle, and the whole neighborhood seemed to have gathered outside our house, shifting restlessly, festively behind sawhorses and yellow plastic restraining ribbons, as if awaiting the grand opening of a warehouse store.

But it wasn't just my neighbors out there. I saw men and women in uniforms, blue, gray, and khaki, dressed in boots and webbed belts, helmets and gas masks, all of them armed and dangerous—and aiming their artillery at me.

I remained cool, sweeping the crowd with a serene and

imperious gaze. Most I didn't recognize. But scattered among them, I could clearly make out Jerry Klammish, Roy Phillips, and the rest of the neighborhood SWAT team, in their berets, in full combat dress, looking like cartoon warriors in the flashing red, amber, and blue lights of police cars, fire engines, ambulances.

"Just lay down your weapons and put up your hands," came the voice from a bullhorn, "and you won't get hurt." I was happy to oblige with half the request. I raised both my arms victoriously, the rifle in one hand and the bloody squirrel in the other. I flung the squirrel toward them, raising both gasps and cheers, a flurry of applause, as the pulpy body landed in the grass.

Then I saw a tiny starburst of smoke, a flash, heard a pop, and a chunk of porch column exploded next to my head. All around me the house seemed to be splintering and popping, disintegrating, with pieces of wood, plaster, and glass flying everywhere. I dropped to the floor of the porch and crawled across the threshold, back into the house, just as an incendiary device landed in the hallway, a few feet in front of my face, spraying me with smoke and sparks and gas. All I could think of, before losing consciousness, was how outrageous it was, how insane, to endanger my life, the lives of my wife and children, how wasteful it was to expend so much wrath and firepower on a single fucking squirrel.

26

"Now wait just a second," McAllister said, theatrically slapping the bundle of documents on his glass table. "I've got your complete file here, I've read everything thoroughly, and nowhere does it say that you were under fire, by either the police or your neighbors."

I had been doubtful about McAllister from the beginning. The white hair and pink complexion, the sympathetic smile, the obliging nod, the paternal shrug—that was all trickery, professional camouflage. Now I knew for certain what he was attempting to prove. Or disprove.

I had spent a lot of hours in his office. It was a condition of my release, and I was trying my best to be cooperative. But I didn't trust him. I didn't trust the red light, the infernal whine of the tape.

During our last sessions, his attention had started to wander. He'd slumped in his chair, making little or no effort to remain alert. But now he was sitting judicially erect, trying to conceal a smile, confident that I'd been checkmated.

"You know as well as I do," I said, "all that wouldn't be in my so-called file. They'd certainly look like idiots admitting they'd gone berserk and almost killed me and my family—"

"You were treated fairly, evenhandedly, diplomatically under the circumstances," he said. "And your family was never in any danger. They had already been evacuated by police."

"If you really want evidence," I said, "the last place you'll find it is in my file. Just look up the newspaper stories. Check the TV news clips."

"I have," he said, shifting in his chrome and black chair, "and there's nothing to support your version of what happened."

"I'm telling you how I remember it," I protested, knowing it was hopeless. "There was a lot of smoke and confusion. Everything got blurred and muddled."

"I expected some approximation of truth," McAllister said, "something halfway believable. Not all this dissembling. These evasive tactics. These morbid delusions and demented fantasies."

As I'd known all along, Kinkaid was behind this. If he could impeach my credibility, he could take me off salary, could terminate my benefits. Adios, Capisco.

I couldn't just sit by compliantly and let that happen. I reached across the table toward the file. "This is full of lies and evasions," I said. "The truth is that you've magnified one small, insignificant incident into this giant fabrication—"

"There was nothing small and insignificant about it," he said, slipping a paper from the file. "Let me review just a few of the offenses you committed: unlawful possession of a firearm, creating a public disturbance, resisting arrest, reckless conduct,

lechery, adultery, larceny, heresy, misanthropy, anarchy, ly-
canthropy—"

He paused, looking over his glasses at me. "It's a long list,"
he said. "I could go on and on."

"Don't go on," I said. I stood up. McAllister shrank back in
his chair, fearful.

I walked around his desk and stared directly into the lens of
the video camera, confronting the red light. "I know what your
game is, Kinkaid, and I won't play. Just keep those benefits
coming."

I was tempted to smash the recorder. But that wouldn't
have helped my case. I thrust my chin forward defiantly until
it was almost touching the lens, distorting my reflection, my
nose almost obscenely large, my forehead so distended that my
hairline vanished, making me appear totally, irrevocably bald.

27

Mrs. Underwood is playing games with me. I frequently try to catch her, slipping over to a window that looks out on her house, quickly opening the shutter, and waving to her, with a cheerful, neighborly smile. As soon as I do, her curtain drops, almost imperceptibly. I can just make out the slightest flutter. Sometimes I can see her hunched form, retreating into the darkness.

I'm also hoping to catch her on my porch when she leaves one of her notes in the mailbox. For a woman of her advanced years and unsteady bearing, she's demonstrated an astonishing agility. Either she strikes late at night, when I'm asleep, or else she waits until I've left the house on a errand, which is not often.

They're polite notes, written in a delicate hand on lavender paper, folded in lavender envelopes, scented with lavender. However courteously phrased, her messages aren't especially friendly. One suggested that I had neglected to finish raking the backyard, and she's right. Now that the thaw has finally come, I suppose I should attend to it. The latest note proposed that front windows boarded with plywood aren't becoming to a supposedly revitalized neighborhood.

If Mrs. Underwood weren't so elusive, I would show her how I've added every one of her suggestions to my checklist, with double checkmarks to indicate that I've assigned them the highest priority. I do wish she could show more patience and community spirit. She's called the building inspector a half-dozen times, gotten me cited for falling gutters, peeling paint, and other minor violations.

She's just waiting for me to make a major mistake, a punishable offense. Besides the building inspector, the zoning commissioner, and the chief of sanitation, she's called the police three times, most recently last Thursday. I had saved all her lavender notes, taken them out into the backyard, and incinerated them in the birdbath. She accused me of practicing satanism, but I got off with a ticket for violating the ordinance against leaf burning.

She doesn't need to call the police. Whenever I look out during the day, I can see a patrol car cruising past. At night, they routinely stop and turn the spotlight on my windows. Along with the stouthearted efforts on my behalf by the neighborhood surveillance team, I should feel as protected as if I were living in an impregnable fortress. But somehow I don't.

I'm sure that all my neighbors would prefer that I pack up and vacate the premises. But I could hardly leave the house now, not with so many FOR SALE signs already posted on lawns up and down the block. I get the impression that I'm a one-man degentrification squad.

Before the house is marketable, I have to repair the damage and finish rehabbing it. It's going to take a while. I am methodically going down the checklist, but the house is self-destructing faster than I can keep up with it. Even with all my free time, it's too big a job for one person.

I wish I could be more systematic, finishing one room before beginning another. But the distractions are endless, and I find it impossible to pass up a warped floorboard, a dripping faucet, a cracked patch of plaster. Last night the ceiling collapsed in one of the upstairs bedrooms. I was relieved that it wasn't housebreakers and that it hadn't fallen on me, both of which were likely possibilities.

Snow melted on the roof and seeped into the walls. The moisture softened the paint and caused the plaster and drywall to crumble and dissolve and turn into a soggy paste.

There has to be a leak or leaks up there somewhere. They could be caused by squirrels but just as easily now by raccoons or possums or mice or termites or carpenter ants or earwigs or any of the other happy campers. Or maybe it's just plain old rot—rotten wood, rotten nails, rotten asphalt. It's almost warm enough to get out on the roof. But I'm a little shaky about that prospect, not so much because I'm afraid of heights as that I'd make such an inviting target.

I don't get around much anymore. Now that the weather is improving, I should spread my wings, walk a few blocks, do some shopping, get rid of the kinks and the cobwebs and the bends. No later than next week, I've promised.

Because of all the enforced bed rest, I've put on two inches around my waist, which seems to be spreading and descending, if the mirror is giving me an undistorted reflection. I stand in front of it, practicing my smile, trying to get rid of this scowl, this look of perpetual disapproval, as I've been advised to do. The hair-restoring shampoo may be having a slight effect.

When I was released from the hospital, I came home to a nearly empty house. Kathy had taken many of our possessions when she and the children moved out. Many of the rest were disposed of in an estate sale. While the house was empty, it was regularly visited by transient forms of animal life, I discovered, most likely teenagers.

The first thing I did was clean up the discarded bottles and cans, the petrified scraps of pizza and nachos, the cigarette butts, the syringes, the condoms. Then I scrubbed the graffiti off the walls—the declarations of eternal love and lust, the obscenities, the gang slogans.

Kathy hadn't intended to leave me with so little. But a lot of things were carried off by our guests. All they left me were kitchen utensils, the defective television set, a portable radio, a few odd tables and chairs, lots of tools, stray toys, a single bed with soiled linens, a chest of drawers, and a closetful of dress shirts, suits, and ties, none of which I wear these days.

On the floor in one of the vacant rooms, I came upon the remains of an animal. But when I poked it with a broom handle, it turned out to be the FurReal coat that Kinkaid had given me. Now I could understand Peter's reaction when he'd seen it. It was so lifelike I nearly went into shock. From all the stains and smudges, it was clear that our visitors had put the coat to uses for which it was never intended. Upon leaving, they'd considered it so despoiled or worthless that they hadn't bothered to take it with them.

I was grateful they'd left it for me. As I quickly discovered, I hadn't exaggerated its fine points in my memo to Kinkaid. It was remarkably resilient material, warm and protective, with a high insulating factor. I was able to restore its rich texture and luster. I kept the thermostat in the house turned low, and on colder nights the coat made a snug comforter—more efficient than down, though slightly pricklier.

Also for efficiency's sake, I moved almost everything into the conservatory, using it as living quarters, library, office, construction center, watchtower, and listening post. The faulty television set and the radio I stationed in other rooms. I leave them turned on constantly, both for reassurance and for protection. With the sounds amplified by all the reflective surfaces, the house is as vibrant as an echo chamber, filled with a distant, dissonant music that is somehow consoling, even uplifting.

At certain times I'm momentarily fooled into believing that the house is still inhabited. What I miss most are the sight and sound of children. Kathy has a court order. Until I get my house in order, until all the breaks and fissures are repaired, until the rehabilitation is complete, I'm prevented from coming within a block of them. I cannot simply repent. I have to do penance, totally clean up my act, which I'm trying to do— starting with TSP, Zipstrip, liquid sander, mortar mix, and 20 Mule Team Borax.

Kathy communicates with me only through a lawyer now. Her messages arrive by mail, along with utility bills, threats from credit agencies, catalogs, notifications that I've won new television sets, cars, appliances, thousands of dollars in cash prizes, and free vacations in Florida, if only I'll call and make an appointment to claim them.

Kathy does appear to be yielding slightly. On Valentine's Day, I got three hearts in the mail, made by hand on red construction paper and pasted with white doilies. It breaks my heart to be reminded that there's a little love and beauty left in the world.

The phone rings and rings. Sometimes I answer it, thinking it'll be Kathy and not one of the usual callers, the solicitors and anonymous neighbors, impolitely inviting me to abandon the house and get out of town. Kathy never calls—on the advice of her lawyer, I like to imagine.

I am repairing a broken sash cord when the phone rings. On the fifteenth ring, I answer it. "I just want you to know I understand about that missed lunch," Ace says, "and I was hoping we could reschedule."

"I'm not eating lunch out these days, Ace," I say. "I'm usually too busy rehabbing to stop for lunch."

"Which makes lunch even more of a necessity," Ace says. "I know how it is. A guy gets lonely, working by himself all the time. You can use some company, a few laughs, a nutritious meal. I'll bet you haven't been getting the minimum daily requirement of vitamins, minerals, iron, niacin. No telling what's happening to your blood pressure, your cholesterol level—"

"Look, Ace, I know your time is precious, and I don't want to waste it. I can't afford any canola or oats or barley."

"You think this phone call is about commodities?" Ace says, sounding both hurt and defensive. "This isn't about business. It's about friendship, fellowship—food and drink and good company and funny stories."

"I don't feel quite up to any of those just yet," I tell him.

"I understand perfectly," he says. "I've got a few health problems of my own. A hairline fracture of the left ankle. Thank God, it's only a walking cast, but I can't go near a court and I'm dying. Minute by minute, I can feel my body disintegrating from all this inactivity."

The doorbell is ringing now. In order to get Ace off the phone, I hurriedly reschedule our lunch for three weeks from now. Time enough to send him a postcard, saying I've decided to leave town on an unscheduled getaway vacation.

Looking out the conservatory window, I have a partial view of the front porch. I can't see who's out there, only their shadows. There are three of them. They could be process servers or Jehovah's Witnesses or environmentalists seeking signatures, both on petitions and checks. Whoever they are, I'm not receiving guests.

After a while, the doorbell stops ringing. But they aren't easily discouraged. I can hear conspiratorial voices, rattling doors and windows, bushes being trampled. I can hear breaking glass, smashed locks, footsteps on bare wood floors, creaking stairways. This is not the first time I've been invaded. I'm prepared for emergencies.

I climb the rope fire ladder into the crawl space above the conservatory, drawing it up after me. I secure the new trapdoor. I crawl on my knees along the plank pathway, squeezing into the deepest, narrowest corner, where the joists meet the rafters. I huddle against the plywood pallet and cover myself with the FurReal coat.

The squirrels are no longer shy. In seconds, I can feel their claws, feel them burrowing into the fur, snuggling against me for communal warmth and security. I pull the coat around me, warm and secure now myself, shutting out the smell of ancient dust and charred wood and corroding metal, the sound of phones and doorbells, sirens and alarms, shutting out all the mournful noises of the house, all the chaos and delirium of the world, drawing the coat tighter and tighter until there is nothing but silence, blessed silence and darkness.